**When Anna lifted** spoke. **"I will call upon your guardian this morning."**

Anna took a sip and placed the cup back in its saucer. "I will accompany you."

His brows knitted. "That would not be wise. Best to leave it to me."

She shook her head. "This is about me. For me, and I will hear what is said of me."

Tossing and turning all night had not exactly helped her decide a specific course of action. She still did not know what she should do.

But deep inside her, she knew what she would not do.

Will's mother's hand shook. "The scandal will be terrible."

"Terrible for me, for certain," Anna responded.

"And for our family!" Will's mother shot back. "No respectable mother will allow her daughter anywhere near Will after this! And the ton will take great delight in the fact that he has compromised *you*."

Because they were enemies.

Anna faced the woman. "I presume your son told you the truth of what happened."

Will's mother waved her hand. "The truth. The truth does not matter. Society will much prefer the fiction."

## Author Note

When I was young, it was Zeffirelli's movie of *Romeo and Juliet* that first made Shakespeare accessible to me, and I've always loved the 1961 movie of *West Side Story*, which, of course, was a modern retelling of Shakespeare's play. The problem with both, though, is that these romantic lovers don't have happy endings. They die! (Well, in *West Side Story* only Tony dies.) I wanted to rewrite both and make the ending turn out right!

There was always a romance writer in me even before I knew it.

This book was inspired by *Romeo and Juliet*, but Anna and Will start out as enemies at first sight instead of lovers at first sight, and although they have a lot to overcome, they do reach that happily-ever-after. I insist upon that!

# COMPROMISED WITH HER FORBIDDEN VISCOUNT

## DIANE GASTON

**HISTORICAL**

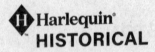

# Harlequin®
## HISTORICAL

ISBN-13: 978-1-335-53984-7

Compromised with Her Forbidden Viscount

For questions and comments about the quality of this book, please contact us at CustomerService@Harlequin.com.

TM and ® are trademarks of Harlequin Enterprises ULC.

Harlequin Enterprises ULC
22 Adelaide St. West, 41st Floor
Toronto, Ontario M5H 4E3, Canada
www.Harlequin.com

Printed in U.S.A.

Recycling programs for this product may not exist in your area.

**Diane Gaston**'s dream job was always to write romance novels. One day she dared to pursue that dream and has never looked back. Her books have won romance's highest honors: the RITA® Award, the National Readers' Choice Award, the HOLT Medallion, and the Gold Quill and Golden Heart® Awards. She lives in Virginia with her husband and three very ordinary house cats. Diane loves to hear from readers and friends. Visit her website at dianegaston.com.

### Books by Diane Gaston

#### Harlequin Historical

"The Major's Christmas Return"
in *Regency Reunions at Christmas*
*The Lord's Highland Temptation*

#### *A Family of Scandals*

*Secretly Bound to the Marquess*
*The Lady Behind the Masquerade*

#### *Captains of Waterloo*

*Her Gallant Captain at Waterloo*
*Lord Grantwell's Christmas Wish*

#### *The Governess Swap*

*A Lady Becomes a Governess*
*Shipwrecked with the Captain*

#### *The Society of Wicked Gentlemen*

*A Pregnant Courtesan for the Rake*

Visit the Author Profile page
at Harlequin.com for more titles.

To my friend Anne
just because she deserves it!

# Chapter One

Viscount Willburgh wandered through throngs of shepherdesses, harlequins, Roman gods and goddesses, kings and queens of old, clergymen and devils, and dominos of every colour, all under a blaze of a thousand lamps hung in the trees of Vauxhall Gardens. Even if the revellers of the pleasure garden had not worn masks and half masks, it still would have been impossible to tell a servant from a lord from a pickpocket. Anyone could pay a shilling to be a part of Vauxhall Gardens' masquerade.

Unfortunately his companions, lacking imagination like Will and the majority of men in attendance, had seen fit to don black dominoes with white masks. The two of them had disappeared into the throng of dancers in the Grove and Will had given up searching for them.

Why the devil had he agreed to this escapade in the first place? Attending a raucous masquerade at Vauxhall Gardens did not suit Will's nature at all. Vauxhall was all illusion and decadence, but life's reality was hard work and weighty responsibility.

Even so, there was much he could see—The Cascade. The

rope walkers. The Chinese temple. He could even seek out the hermit in the farthest corner of the Gardens. None of it held much appeal. Affairs of state were plaguing his mind, especially after the Prince Regent's message to the Lords advising the continuance of the seditious practices.

Should Parliament approve suspension of habeas corpus? There was certainly unrest throughout the kingdom, but was that not to be expected? The price of bread was high. People were starving. Should not the Lords be doing something about feeding the people instead of taking their rights away?

The festive music of the orchestra and the crowd's gaiety did not sit well with such thoughts. Will edged his way to the relatively quieter Grand Walk, but a group of drunken carousers annoyed him even more.

Maybe a visit to the hermitage would do. At least it would be quieter down the Dark Walk, darker this night, because clouds covered the moon and stars, and the air carried the scent of impending rain.

The lamps in the trees that flanked the walk grew fewer in number, as did the promenaders, couples mostly, probably looking for a secluded nook for a private tryst. A wave of envy jolted Will. He'd never had much time for dalliances and, unlike his friends, had eventually concluded that amorous affairs of the temporary kind merely left him empty.

He ought to turn back. Find a boat to take him across the river. Avoid the rain.

He was about to do that very thing when he suddenly had the Walk to himself. Until some distance ahead of him a woman jumped from the trees. A man followed and seized her from behind. The woman cried out and struggled to get free, but the man covered her mouth and pulled her back into the darkness of the wood. Vauxhall was not all merriment; danger also lurked there.

Will sprang into action, entering the woods where he saw the man and woman disappear. The man was dragging her into a shelter, a private supper room designed for assignations.

Will charged the man, wrapping an arm around the man's neck, choking him. The man, dressed in a domino and mask like himself, released his prisoner. She fell to the ground. A fist to the man's face and a kick to his groin sent the fellow fleeing for his life. Will turned to extend his hand to help the woman to her feet.

'Are you injured?' he asked.

'Shaken a bit, is all.' She looked down at herself and gasped. 'Oh, dear!' The bodice of her dress was torn, revealing her shift and stays. Her hands flew to her chest.

'Come into the shelter,' Will said. 'We can put you back to rights.'

A lamp lit the shelter enough for Will to see she wore a red hooded cape and a plain blue cotton dress covered by a pinafore. Or it had once been covered by a pinafore. The pinafore and dress were torn at one shoulder and now were held in place by the woman's hand. Her eyes were a startling light brown, lighter than her hair, a warm brown shot through with gold where the lamplight caught it. She wore it down, as if she were a girl, not a woman. How old was she? Still masked she could be anything. A maid, a shopgirl, or even a harlot—although a harlot typically would not be struggling to free herself.

The shelter held a chaise-longue and a table upon which sat the lamp and a bottle of wine with two glasses, apparently arranged ahead of time.

The woman—girl?—turned away. 'I—I am remiss in not thanking you right away, sir. I cannot imagine what I would have done had you not assisted me.'

Will could well imagine what the man had planned for her.

But he focused on the practical. 'Do you have pins with you? To pin up your dress?'

'I do.' Still with her back to him she let go of the torn dress and lifted her skirt slightly to retrieve pins concealed in her petticoat. She set to pinning the bodice in place. 'If only I could see...'

'Turn this way,' Will said. 'I'll help you.'

She'd managed to cover herself. Will needed only to straighten the fabric to make it appear as if it had been stitched. He stood close to her, close enough to feel the warmth of her body and the scent of her—lavender and mint and sunny summer days. Of one thing he was certain—she was a woman, not a young girl. He had not been so close to a woman in a long time, certainly not in such an intimate situation.

'How do you know how to pin a dress?' Her words were breathless.

His breath accelerated, heating up the inside of his mask.

'I have a younger sister.'

The confounded mask. It made it difficult to breathe and even to see.

With an annoyed grunt, he pulled it off.

The woman jumped back. 'You!'

Will was puzzled. 'You know me?'

Her voice trembled. 'Oh, yes. I know you, Lord Willburgh.' She removed her own mask.

'The devil...' Will glared at her. No. Not the devil. 'A Dorman.' The name was poison on his lips. 'The Dorman whose father killed my father.'

She bristled. '*Your* father killed *my* father! It was your father who challenged my father to a duel!'

He countered. 'It was *your* father who seduced my mother!'

She lifted a brow. 'Was it?'

This animosity had not begun with Will's father's death. The Dormans had feuded with the Willburghs for generations, purportedly over ownership of disputed land. It had really started three generations ago, when Will's great-great-grandfather and that generation's Lord Dorman fought over a woman, the woman who became Will's great-great-grandmother. After that event the discord over the disputed land heated to a fever pitch. The fire was further fuelled by more romantic rivalry—Will's great-grandfather's affair with that generation's Lady Dorman, and most tragically for Will, the seduction of Will's mother by the current Baron Dorman's ne'er-do-well brother, who knew precisely what he was about. Will's father challenged that younger Dorman to the ill-fated duel.

They killed each other in that duel, a duel that changed everything for Will. At seventeen, he suddenly inherited a title, all its responsibility, and all the scandal that engulfed the family as a result. From then on—ten years now—Will's carefree life as a young man had ceased. Life became nothing more than Duty. Duty. Duty.

Staring at this Dorman woman brought it all back. All his grief. All his anger.

Her eyes lit with fear and she backed farther away.

He did not usually allow that part of him to show. 'Do not worry. I'm not going to kill you.'

Her voice turned low. 'What are you going to do?'

Will took a deep breath and slowly released it. 'I am going to finish pinning your dress and escort you back to wherever you should be.'

Will damped down his emotions and finished pinning the pinafore. She leaned as far away as possible as he did so. Even in his anger he experienced the allure of being so close to her.

He stepped back. 'That should pass, if no one looks too closely.'

Without another word he walked to the door and put his hand on the latch. She followed. As he opened the door, a bolt of lightning lit up the sky, followed by a crack of thunder.

And pouring rain.

Damnation.

He closed the door. 'We'll wait out the storm. With any luck it will pass quickly.' He inclined his head to the chaise-longue. 'You may as well sit.'

She hesitated, looking wary, but she had nothing to fear, even if she was undisputedly lovely. He wanted nothing but to be rid of her.

She perched on the edge of the chaise as if ready to escape at any moment.

He walked over to the table and poured himself a glass of wine. 'Would you like wine?'

Again she hesitated, but finally responded by holding out her hand.

He placed the glass in it and retreated to a corner to lean against the wall.

Will's emotions waged a war within him. Again he remembered galloping across the land to try to stop the duel, arriving just in time to hear the loud report of their shots and see the smoke from their pistol barrels before both men fell. He rushed to his father. Blood poured from his father's chest which heaved with every struggled breath.

'Your duty now,' his father gasped before his eyes turned sightless and his body went limp.

Will gulped down the whole glass of wine and poured himself another. His father had often warned Will he'd be

Viscount one day and his father must train him for it. But his father never had the time.

Never took the time.

Instead his father died foolishly and Will had to learn everything on his own at seventeen.

Rain battered the roof of the shelter and thunder continued to rumble. Will concentrated on the sound until the wine and the weather lulled him back to a semblance of calm.

He glanced at the Dorman woman, sipping her wine and patting her hair.

'Your hair stayed in place,' he said, breaking their silence and remembering how he'd admired it.

Her hand returned to her lap.

'Who are you supposed to be, anyway?' He gestured to her costume.

She glared at him. 'Red Riding Hood.'

He laughed. 'And you were almost caught by the wolf.'

She straightened. 'Or perhaps you are the wolf in disguise.'

'Not the wolf. Not your grandmother either.' He poured himself the last of the wine.

She pursed her lips, disapproving.

Disapproving his drink and accusing him of being the wolf? *Who does she think she is?*

Oh. Right. She was a *Dorman*.

He tossed back a defiant look. 'So what the devil were you doing alone at Vauxhall? That was flirting with danger surely.'

'I was not alone,' she countered. 'I was with my cousin and she met with—with—gentlemen of her acquaintance. Then we became separated.'

It was his turn to be disapproving. 'Two young ladies unchaperoned, then?'

She glanced away. 'I was the chaperone.'

Will laughed. 'That was a hare-brained plan, was it not? Like two sheep to the slaughter. I daresay there is more than one wolf prowling around Vauxhall.'

She gave him a direct look. 'I undoubtedly failed, did I not?'

'Undoubtedly,' he agreed, taking a sip of wine. 'Do you and your cousin often come to Vauxhall alone?'

'We were not alone. Lord and Lady Dorman and Lucius came, as well. They will wonder where I am. And I really must find Violet.'

He scoffed. 'Cannot the *gentlemen of her acquaintance* be trusted to keep her safe?'

Anna took another sip of wine.

She certainly was not going to tell *him* that Violet had tricked her into a meeting with Mr Raskin, the Season's most notorious rake, and his vile friend, the man who'd tried to carry her off.

Where was Violet? Was she in a shelter like this with Raskin? If so, Anna feared Violet needed no force to go with the man.

It had been Anna's responsibility to keep Violet from doing anything foolish. Lord and Lady Dorman counted on her for that and would blame her for Violet's behaviour.

Willburgh broke into her thoughts, his voice scathing. 'And where was your cousin Lucius while you two young ladies met gentlemen of your acquaintance at a Vauxhall masquerade?'

Lucius and Willburgh had been schoolmates at Eton, Anna knew, and briefly at Oxford. Until the duel. Lucius returned to Oxford then. Willburgh had not.

'I was not meeting any gentlemen!' she snapped. 'Lucius…' Wait. Why should she tell *him* what happened?

He made a derisive sound. 'Let me guess. Lucius abandoned you as soon as he was able.'

'He didn't *abandon* us,' Although Lucius had pretty much disappeared into the crowd as soon as they were out of sight of Lord and Lady Dorman.

Anna ought to have insisted they all stay together as Lord and Lady Dorman expected, but would Violet and Lucius have listened to her? They'd probably planned to abandon her all along without a thought about leaving her unprotected.

A familiar ache returned, the ache of being alone in the world, belonging nowhere to no one. She could almost hear the words of her father, Bertram Dorman, her beloved papa, after her mother died—'*It is just you and me now. And I'll never leave you.*'

Thanks to Willburgh's father, that was a promise her papa could not keep.

Anna's eyes stung with sudden tears. She'd loved him so.

And he was not even really her father, merely the only father she'd ever known. Her mother, on her deathbed, had confided that her real father had been an officer in the East India Company army, killed when she was a baby. Her mother married Bertram Dorman not even a year after and he was the only father Anna could remember. She'd adored him and he doted on her as if the sun rose and set upon her.

Anna blinked her tears away. She was lucky the Dormans became her guardians and allowed her to live with them. Otherwise she'd have been sent to an orphanage.

As they often reminded her.

She glanced at the man who was her rescuer. He leaned casually against the wall, his long legs crossed at the ankles, his arms across his chest. He was taller and more muscular than she'd thought, but then, she'd never before seen him up close. She caught the scent of bergamot and sandalwood that clung to him as she had done when he pinned up her dress. He'd been so gentle pinning her torn dress, although there was no doubt of his strength. He'd displayed it by easily dispatching her assailant. He'd frightened her only briefly when his anger flared.

The Dormans hated him and the other Willburghs because of that silly family feud, so Anna had never been this close to him. She'd spied him occasionally in the village and glimpsed him at some of the Season's society balls, but she'd given him a wide berth. Lucius had gone to school with him and perhaps something there made him particularly detest Willburgh, but Anna hated him because *his* father had killed her beloved papa.

This man was not responsible for that, of course. He'd been little more than a youth at the time. But his was the face her anger settled on.

At the moment Willburgh's head was bowed, as if he were pretending she was not even there. That certainly did not help appease her anger. To be thought of as being of no consequence to anybody only angered her more.

She'd make him see her. 'Where were you bound when my—my problem—detained you? Did I interrupt some important plans? Or were you merely wandering the Dark Walk in search of damsels in distress?' Or was he planning to meet some woman in a shelter like this?

He raised his head as if he had indeed forgotten her presence. 'I was on my way to see the hermit.'

'Alone?' She raised her brows.

He gave her a direct look. 'Like the hermit, I was seeking escape from the crowds and the noise.'

Anna hated the crowds and the noise, as well. Indeed,

she was not overly fond of London and all the delights of the Season. Ordinarily being caught inside during a rainstorm would have been a pleasantness.

'You—you do not like Vauxhall?' she asked him.

'I do not,' he responded.

'Then why come?'

He shrugged. 'I was talked into it.'

'Oh, really?' She let her voice drip with scepticism. As if a man like him truly could be talked into anything he did not wish to do.

Perhaps he'd been spurned by a lady companion—although somehow that idea did not fit him.

He shifted his position and took a step towards her. 'I was separated from my companions, as were you.'

She doubted he'd been left on purpose as she had been.

He laughed dryly. 'Perhaps it was fate. So I could rescue you and be stranded here.'

She lowered her lashes. 'I am grateful to you.'

When she raised her head again their eyes met and their gazes held.

Until he took a breath and walked over to the window and looked out. 'I think the rain has stopped. I'll escort you back.'

She rose and gathered her red cape around her. Neither of them bothered to put on their masks. They reached the door together, brushing against each other as Willburgh turned the latch and opened the door.

Only to see Lucius and Lord Dorman, also unmasked, standing right outside.

'Willburgh!' Lucius reeled back as if struck in the chest. He recovered, leaning forwards again to glare at Anna. 'You are with *him*? *Him?* How shameless can you be? With *him*!'

# Chapter Two

Lucius's words slashed into Anna like knives.

'See here, Lucius—' Willburgh responded.

But Lord Dorman cut him off. 'Do you mock us, Anna? Disrespect all we have done for you? Of all men, you behave the trollop with this one?'

'She did not—' Willburgh began, only to be cut off again.

'Come, Lucius,' Lord Dorman demanded. 'Let us go back. I wash my hands of her.'

Anna stared in disbelief as they turned their backs on her and strode off.

'Make haste,' Willburgh said, but she was too stunned to move.

He seized her arm and pulled her through the door.

'It is not what it seems,' he called after Lucius and his father. 'You must hear me.'

Anna could hardly keep pace with Willburgh as he charged after Lucius and his father, their dominos billowing behind them in their haste. They did not even bother to turn around. She and Willburgh caught up with them at the Centre Cross Walk.

Willburgh released Anna and seized Lucius's arm. 'You will hear me!'

Lucius shrugged him off 'Hear you? We caught you in a

compromising position. What else is there to hear? Do you think we do not know what you were doing?' He laughed. 'Here I thought you were stiff-necked like your father. Obviously you take after your mother—'

'How horrid—' Anna broke in, appalled that Lucius would say such a thing out loud.

Other costumed people were in earshot and several stopped to observe the spectacle. They were easily recognised, having forgotten their masks.

Willburgh glanced at the observers and back to Lucius and his father. 'Have a care. Let us discuss this privately.'

'You may follow us to the supper box,' Lord Dorman said.

The way to the Dormans' supper box led them through the first Triumphal Arch and directly across from the Turkish Tent.

Lady Dorman, dressed in powdered wig and fashion from a century earlier, stood as they approached. 'You've found her, I see.' She sounded as outraged as her son and husband. Evidently the news has already reached her, even in those few minutes. She glared at Anna. 'An assignation with the enemy. How could you, Anna? After all we've done for you.'

'There was no—' Willburgh tried, only to be cut off again.

Lucius faced him. 'We will hear no excuses from you! Reprobate.'

Lucius wore a red domino, lined in black. Somehow the red of his cape was unlike hers. Instead he resembled an image of the devil she'd once seen in the window of Humphrey's Print Shop. Lord Dorman wore white powder and a colourful silk coat and breeches, matching the era of his wife.

At that moment Violet walked up, Mr Raskin in tow. 'We have just this moment heard.' She, too, turned to Anna. 'Is that why you ran off, Anna, and left me all alone?'

Anna gaped at her. 'Violet!'

Violet turned her gaze to Raskin. 'I don't know what I would have done if dear Raskin had not found me!'

Raskin bowed. 'It was my honour, I assure you.'

No one asked where he and Violet had been.

Anna looked at them all in turn. She knew she was of no real importance to them, except in the ways they found her useful. As companion to Lady Dorman and Violet, for example. Someone to fetch for them or carry parcels. But she thought they would at least *listen* to her. She thought they knew her well enough to know she would not indulge in assignations.

Lord Dorman's voice rose. 'We cannot tolerate your cavorting with this—this—sworn enemy, of all people! It is unforgivable, after all we have done for you.' He rubbed his hands together. 'I wash my hands of you!'

Willburgh's voice was even higher. 'I demand that you listen to me. You are mistaken—'

Lord Dorman's face turned red with anger. 'I heed no demands of yours, sir. Out of my way.' He pushed past Willburgh and gestured to the others. 'We are leaving! Now.'

They filed by Anna, each pointedly refusing to look at her.

Even though she remained rooted in place, Lord Dorman turned back to her. 'You may not follow. You are no longer welcome in our home.'

Only Mr Raskin looked back, a smirk on his face. The others walked away without a backward glance.

Anna finally found her voice. 'Well, this is famous. What am I to do now?'

'Damn them,' a voice next to her said. 'Damn them all. *Dormans.*'

Willburgh. She'd forgotten he was there. He was the reason the family had so roundly rejected her. Had she been caught with Raskin's friend and truly compromised, they would not have been so outraged.

He returned her glance. 'Forgive my language,' he murmured. 'And I forgot you were a Dorman.'

She used her stepfather's name, she thought, but she was definitely not a Dorman.

She glanced away, her predicament becoming more real. 'What am I to do?'

He moved so he was in front of her and he caught her gaze. 'Is—is there not a friend I can deliver you to? Someone who would assist you?'

A friend? She'd had no opportunity to make friends. She knew Violet's and Lucius's friends, but she would not dream of asking any of them to take her in.

'There is no one,' she told him with a helpless laugh. 'And I have no money. What I own is in the possession of Lord Dorman.'

'Well, I can give you money,' he responded.

A masked gentleman dressed as a harlequin strolled by, a grin on his face. 'You are in a fine pickle, are you not? Better you than me!'

'Get lost,' Willburgh snarled.

'Someone you know?' she asked.

He shrugged. 'I suppose. Good thing for him he wore a mask.'

People strolling by were slowing as they passed them and obviously talking about them. She'd always worried that Violet would someday be such an object of gossip and scorn. She never dreamed she'd be one.

'We should go,' Willburgh said. 'I've had enough of this place.'

They left the supper box and walked towards the Pro-

prietor's House entrance, passing the orchestra, which had
started playing again. Soon a tenor's voice rang out:

> *The lord said to the lady,*
> *Before he went out:*
> *Beware of false Lamkin,*
> *He's a-walking about...*

Willburgh said, 'We'll hire a hackney coach to take us over
Vauxhall Bridge.' Vauxhall Bridge had opened the previous
year. Otherwise they'd be crossing the Thames by boat. At
the entrance he sent a servant to have a coach brought around.

Anna did not know his plan. Was he intending to drop
her somewhere in Mayfair and leave her to fend for herself?
She was afraid to ask.

As if reading her mind, he said, 'I suppose I could take
you to a hotel.'

'A hotel. Yes,' she responded without enthusiasm. At least
she'd have a place to sleep for one night.

The hackney coach pulled up.

'Take us to the Pulteney,' Will called to the jarvey.

The jarvey's brows rose knowingly and he answered with
a smirk. 'Yes, m'lord. The Pulteney.'

What was this man thinking? The Pulteney was a very
respectable hotel. It had been fine enough to house the Tsar
of Russia and his sister a few years ago; it should be respectable enough for a Dorman.

Miss Dorman's cheeks flamed red at the driver's comment. She'd obviously understood the driver's reaction.

Will helped her into the coach. He sat in the backward-
facing seat, his spirits sinking even further than before. He
could not take her to a hotel, he realised. With the specta-

cle the Dormans created at Vauxhall, there was certain to be plenty of gossip already. If he took her to a hotel at this hour of the night, in the costume she wore, would that not make the situation look worse? Confirm what the Dormans believe happened? What everyone would believe happened?

'Miss Dorman, I do not think it advisable to take you to a hotel. I will tell the driver to take us to my townhouse.'

Her eyes widened in alarm. 'To your townhouse!'

'My mother is in residence. No one can make of it what it is not.' Certainly his mother would not jump to that erroneous conclusion. She knew a Dorman was the last woman he would be caught alone with.

Although that was precisely what happened. They were caught alone, unchaperoned, in one of the shelters at Vauxhall created for 'private parties.'

He stole a glance at Miss Dorman who was absently gazing out the window into the darkness. He admired that she did not go into hysterics, although she certainly had every right to do so. She'd said very few words since they were discovered, but he felt the terrible blow the Dormans inflicted on her. Accusing her. Rejecting her. Abandoning her. He sensed the aloneness they'd created in her. When his father died, Will had felt very alone, even though he'd had family and friends around him. He was alone in becoming the viscount, though. No one else shared that burden.

Will opened the window to call to the jarvey to take them to Park Street instead.

Will and Miss Dorman rode in silence until the hackney coach pulled up to Will's townhouse. He helped her out of the coach and paid the jarvey. As the hackney coach rumbled away, Will hoped no curious eyes were awakened to see him escort her into the house.

Bailey, his butler, roused himself from a chair in the hall.

'M'lord, forgive me. I must have dozed off.' He stumbled in surprise at spying Miss Dorman, who was a sight in her Red Riding Hood costume.

'You needn't have stayed up, Bailey,' Will said. 'But I am glad you did. This is Miss Dorman.'

'Miss Dorman?' The butler sounded even more puzzled.

Bailey was aware, as were all the servants, that the Dormans and Willburghs were sworn enemies. He was, though, an excellent butler and quickly schooled his features back to blankness.

'Can you wake up Mrs White?' Will asked. Mrs White was the housekeeper. 'We need a room made up for Miss Dorman. She will need night clothes, as well. And a dress for the morrow. And any other items essential for her care and comfort.'

'Right away, sir.' Bailey bowed in Miss Dorman's direction. 'Miss Dorman.'

She nodded in return.

In the light of the hall, Miss Dorman looked pale and fatigued, as if she might collapse in a heap at any moment.

Will took her arm. 'Come into the library. You can sit there. I should have asked Bailey for refreshment. You look like you are spent.'

'Thank you,' she managed.

He led her to a comfortable chair and lit a taper from the sconce in the hall, using it to light the library lamps. 'I can have Bailey bring tea later. All I have here is some brandy.'

'Brandy would be most welcome.' She sat on the edge of the comfortable sofa near the fireplace as if wishing to bolt.

He took the decanter from a cabinet and poured two glasses, handing one to her.

She took a sip. 'I should not be here,' she said.

'Lord and Lady Dorman left you no choice,' he countered. 'A hotel would be worse. It would only generate more talk.'

'They would not let us explain.' She held the glass against her cheek for a moment, talking more to herself than to him. 'Do they really think so little of me?'

Will's anger rose again. Yes. How dare they simply leave her like that? He drained his glass and poured them both another. 'I will call upon them tomorrow. I will make them listen. They will have to listen to me.'

The brandy was having no effect on him. Certainly not calming his anger. He paced the room.

Mrs White entered, still in her nightcap, robe wrapped around her thick waist. Bailey stood behind her.

'I am here, m'lord,' Mrs White announced. 'The room is being readied. Everything is being done.'

Will's shoulders relaxed. For the first time this night someone else seemed to take the reins from his hands.

She approached Miss Dorman. 'Miss Dorman, is it? I am Mrs White, the housekeeper. I will show you to your room. You look as if you need a nice rest.'

Bless the woman, Will thought. She knew nothing of what happened but was taking pity anyway. Neither she nor Bailey had asked any questions, even though, as old retainers, they well knew the animosity between the Dormans and the Willburghs. They'd been around when his father was killed by her father. Will owed them an explanation. Later, though.

Mrs White led Miss Dorman to the stairs, right across from the library door. At that moment, though, Will's mother appeared at the top of the stairs.

'I heard voices,' his mother said, then saw Mrs White and Miss Dorman. 'What is this?'

Anna looked up at the woman who, in her eyes, caused her papa to die.

She'd seen Lady Willburgh before at a distance, an always

elegant figure, still beautiful in her fiftieth year even in her nightcap and robe. How Anna resented her! She'd lured her papa into a seduction. If only he had resisted her.

'Who is this creature, Mrs White?' Lady Willburgh demanded. 'Why is she in my house?'

Willburgh came to the doorway. 'I will explain, Mother.' He climbed the steps to her. 'This is Miss Dorman who must stay the night as our guest.'

'Dorman!' Lady Willburgh's voice rose. 'Violet Dorman?'

'Anna,' Anna replied.

'The orphan?' The woman's voice was scornful.

Yes, Anna thought. Orphaned because of you.

Willburgh spoke. 'I will explain, Mother. But let Mrs White show Miss Dorman to her room.'

'I will not have a Dorman in my house!' she responded indignantly.

'It is not your house, Mother,' Willburgh said evenly.

Anna, still at the bottom of the stairway, lifted her gaze to the woman and tried to keep the animosity out of her voice. 'I am sorry to intrude, ma'am. Believe me, it was not by my choice.'

'Not my choice either!' Lady Willburgh sniffed. 'She cannot stay.'

'She *will* stay.' Willburgh took his mother by the arm. 'Come back to your room and I will explain.'

He escorted her away.


'Unhand me, Will.' His mother's arm felt surprisingly frail in his hand.

He led her to her bed and lit a candle from the fireplace.

'She is *his* daughter!' she exclaimed, standing her ground. 'How could you bring her here?'

Will faced her and made her listen while he told the whole story, starting with Miss Dorman's abduction.

When he finished, her eyes flashed. 'Those Dormans. They are nothing but trouble!' She glared at him. 'You should have left her to her fate! Likely she wanted that man to— to—'

'Mother.' Will admonished. 'What sort of man would I be not to intervene? Besides, I had no idea who she was until we were in the shelter. And then it rained.'

She pursed her lips together.

'I will call upon Lord Dorman tomorrow,' he assured her. 'I will straighten this out. Do not fret another moment about it.'

He smoothed her covers and helped her sit on the edge of her bed.

She fussed with her nightdress. 'You say others heard Dorman's accusations?'

'I am afraid so,' he admitted.

Her eyes narrowed. 'Then there will be a scandal. More scandal, because of *them*.'

At the time of the duel, tongues had already been wagging about the younger Dorman's affair with Will's mother. The duel set the scandalmongers on fire. It had taken until he was old enough to take his seat in the Lords for it all to die down enough for his mother to show her face during the London Season.

'I believe we can nip the scandal in the bud. Try not to dwell on it.' It all depended upon Lord Dorman's cooperation.

He lifted the covers and his mother crawled under them. 'I will not sleep a wink, knowing a Dorman is under my roof.'

Will placed a kiss upon her forehead and tucked her in like his nurse used to do for him when he was very young.

He blew out the candle and left the room, hearing her continue to grumble to herself about the Dormans.

Will understood that even knowing about this incident would have set his mother off. Any mention of the Dormans tended to do that. He'd never have mentioned it to her if only the Dormans had been reasonable, which, of course, they were not.

According to family lore, the Dormans had never been reasonable. The feud had existed for generations, beginning with that land dispute, land that abutted the Dormans' property at the Willburgh estate in Buckinghamshire. The land was potentially valuable, but, because of the dispute, it had gone undeveloped for over one hundred years. Before his father's death, Will had thought the dispute a frivolous one, surmising it only required some sort of compromise each side was too stubborn to propose. It was not the land but the death of his father for which Will could never forgive any Dorman. Even *the orphan*, as his mother had called her.

He'd heard that Lord Dorman had initiated another search for a clear deed to the land. Well, now Will would be damned if Dorman would procure rights to it. Will would contest it with all his might. He'd also heard that the Dorman finances were precarious, no doubt due to the excesses of each family member, Lucius especially.

The hypocrite. Lucius was quick to accuse his cousin of indiscretion when it was widely known Lucius spent a fortune on his latest lady-in-keeping—and the other women he saw behind her back.

But Will must damp down these feelings. He must approach the Dormans with a cool head.

He continued down the stairs in search of Bailey to again explain the events of this terrible night.

# *Chapter Three*

Lucius Dorman arose much earlier than was his custom and dressed more quickly, having been summoned by his father *in no uncertain terms*. He entered the breakfast room where his parents were already seated, stern expressions on their faces.

'Good morning, Father. Mother,' he said, gauging that his expression should not be too cheerful.

'About time you got out of bed,' his father barked. 'I swear you'd sleep the day away if you could.'

His father was correct. He'd much rather sleep all day. The night was so much more interesting, but then, he was like his father in that respect. And his mother. But it might be prudent not to make that point at the moment.

'I rose as soon as I heard you needed me, as I would do any time.' Lucius chose a slice of bread and ham from the sideboard. After the evening's festivities, his stomach was not in its finest shape. He poured himself a cup of coffee, adding much cream and only one lump of sugar and settled himself across from his esteemed father and mother. Why they were in a pet was beyond him.

Unless it had to do with the utter betrayal of his cousin. Cavorting with Willburgh. The insult was unbearable.

The Meissen clock on the mantle ticked loudly as he waited for his father to speak.

The man finally roused himself. 'Do you realise what a bramble bush you've landed us in?'

'I?' Lucius was affronted. It was all Anna's doing as he saw it—if that was to what his father referred.

'You know that we need that girl,' his father said. 'You will have to marry her.'

Lucius straightened. 'I'll do no such thing! I'll not marry the leavings of *Viscount* Willburgh. You cannot ask it of me.'

'We will need her money,' his father responded.

Lucius countered. 'I'll marry someone else rich.'

His mother smiled patiently. 'You know you cannot attract an heiress. Your father's title is not so elevated. A wealthy merchant's daughter you might manage, perhaps, and if you find one of those before Anna is twenty-one, you will not have to marry her.' She glanced away thoughtfully. 'Of course, Anna has aristocratic blood and that is very important. And she is so eager to please, she would make an acceptable wife.'

Anna's mother was the daughter of an earl, although the title was now extinct. The family was anything but prolific. All gone now, with only Anna left. The family's considerable fortune was bequeathed to her alone but only if she did not marry until twenty-one, only a few weeks away. If she married before twenty-one, her fortune would go to any children she might bear and with the same restrictions.

Lucius's parents had always let it be known to him that he might need to marry her. He hadn't minded so much—until seeing her with Willburgh.

'You expect me to marry the chit after she's been with Willburgh?' Surely they would not ask that of him.

'It pleases me no more than it does you,' his father responded. 'But we are in dire straits. We must cajole her back to us. If we can find her, that is. I've sent two of the footmen to search for her. We will have to concoct some story to counteract the scandal.'

His mother groaned. 'I am certain tongues are wagging as we speak.'

'She'll come back to us,' his father mused, mostly to himself. 'She has nowhere else to go.'

And she knew nothing of the fortune that awaited her at age twenty-one if she remained unmarried. Lucius's father had kept that information from her so she would feel even more beholden to the family for taking her in. Keeping the secret of her inheritance kept the whip in his father's hand. Besides, the allowance the family trust provided her was a nice boon for the rest of the family. Anna knew nothing of that either.

Lucius and his parents often laughed about Anna being his bride. They joked that she was their secret gold mine, only to be fully mined when she came of age. Lucius had no doubt he could charm her into marriage. He flattered himself he could charm any woman. Besides, it was not like Anna would have any other choices.

Although how the devil had she come into Willburgh's sphere? He must have targeted her somehow. Lucius burned with rage just thinking of Willburgh with her.

Willburgh, his most detestable enemy, had been ahead of him in school, as well as being ahead of him in almost every other way. In contests of strength. In success in his studies. In cleverness and courage. Lucius, though, had always bested him with women. That was why Willburgh seduced Anna, Lucius was sure. To thumb his nose at Lucius.

The droning voices of his parents interrupted these thoughts.

'You must secure her hand, Lucius,' his father was saying. 'Grovel to her if you have to. Put on that charm of yours.'

Lucius would never grovel! Not for Willburgh's used goods.

'Are you heeding your father?' his mother asked.

Lucius glanced from his mother to his father. He'd play along with them for the time being. And if he had to marry Anna, he'd find ways to punish her for letting Willburgh have his way with her.

'I will do as you say,' he told them. 'As I always do.'

Anna did not sleep well, even though the bed was more comfortable than her bed at the Dormans' townhouse, and the nightdress Mrs White provided her was woven of cotton softer than any Anna owned. Even the room was larger than her bed chamber and was beautifully furnished.

A pleasant but obviously very curious maid came to help her dress. Anna had no idea what, if any, explanation of her presence would be given to the servants, so she said nothing. The maid addressed her as Miss Dorman, so the girl knew that much—that she came from the camp of the enemy. The maid was trained well enough that she did not ask any questions of Anna, except regarding what was necessary to help her dress, but, even with that constraint, the girl was chatty.

'Mrs White said I was to bring this day dress for you,' the maid said. 'It was Lady Willburgh's, but she never wore it, really. Said the colour washed her out.'

Anna was to wear a dress of the woman who caused her papa's death? That held little appeal. It was a print fabric, fawn with darker brown vines, leaves and flowers on it. How the woman chose such a fabric in the first place was a mystery, but, at least Anna would not have to wear that awful Red Riding Hood costume. The dress needed stitching here and there to fit her. Anna, apparently, was slimmer than Lady Willburgh. 'Less womanly,' Violet would have said.

Violet.

Last night Violet could have spoken up for her, but, typically, she didn't. Violet usually found ways to blame Anna for her own transgressions. No doubt last night Violet had engaged in an assignation precisely like the one for which Anna had been falsely accused.

The maid piled Anna's hair high atop her head and managed several curls to cascade down, a far cry from the simple chignon Anna usually wore. Somehow the beige and brown of the dress complimented her nondescript brown hair and seemed to emphasise her light brown eyes.

When she walked down the stairs to the first floor a footman greeted her. 'Good morning, miss. They are waiting for you in the breakfast room.'

He directed her to a sitting room at the back of the house and opened the door. Willburgh and his mother were seated at a table. Both looked up at her arrival.

Willburgh rose. 'Miss Dorman. I see Mrs White has found you something to wear. Come have some refreshment.' His tone was devoid of emotion, neither welcoming nor repelling. 'I trust you slept well.'

Of course she did not sleep well! 'The room was very comfortable.' She nodded respectfully towards Lady Willburgh. 'Thank you for the dress.'

The older woman harrumphed. 'I loathe that dress. You might as well keep it. I'll never wear it again.'

Because Anna wore it?

The butler she'd met the night before attended her. 'What may I serve you?'

Anna did not think her stomach was up for the kippers and cold meat on the sideboard. Or even the blackberry preserves or sweet cakes. 'Some bread and butter will do,' she said. 'Thank you.'

After the butler placed the bread and butter on her plate and poured her a cup of tea, he left the room.

When Anna lifted the cup to her lips, Willburgh spoke. 'I will call upon Lord Dorman this morning.'

Anna took a sip and placed the cup back in its saucer. 'I will accompany you.'

His brows knitted. 'That would not be wise. Best to leave it to me.'

She shook her head. 'This is about me. For me, and I will hear what is said of me.'

Tossing and turning all night did not exactly help her decide a specific course of action. She still did not know what she should do.

But deep inside her, she knew what she would not do.

Lady Willburgh's hand shook. 'The scandal will be terrible.'

'Terrible for me, certainly,' Anna responded.

'And for our family!' Lady Willburgh shot back. 'No respectable mother will allow her daughter anywhere near Will after this! And the *ton* will take great delight in the fact that he has compromised *you*.'

Because they were enemies.

Anna faced the woman. 'I presume your son told you the truth of what happened.'

Lady Willburgh waved her hand. 'The truth. The truth does not matter. Society will much prefer the fiction.'

'Mother,' her son admonished. 'This is not helpful. I will go to Lord Dorman and fix this.'

'And I will go with you,' Anna added.

Henrietta Street, where the Dormans' London townhouse was situated, was only a few blocks away, a tad less fashionable and a bit smaller, which meant nothing to Will, but probably rankled Lucius Dorman. Lucius had always made such comparisons, a part of the rivalry between them, Will supposed. Although before the duel, Will had never paid much mind to Lucius, especially at school. Lucius was a nuisance, nothing more. After Will's father was killed, though, Will could not help but despise all things Dorman, including Lucius. It was only then that he noticed Lucius's lack of character, his shirking of responsibility, the excesses of his vices—gambling, drinking, and whoring. Lack of loyalty, too. Lucius had been vicious to his cousin—a Dorman— when he should have been protecting her.

Or was Will merely resentful of Lucius's freedom? Not that Will ever wished to be as dissolute as Lucius. But, after his father's death, Will never had a day without responsibility, never possessed a chance to simply do whatever he wished.

Now he must call upon the Dormans. He'd rather swim in a cesspool than call upon them, but he must.

He ordered his curricle, even though it made more sense to walk the short distance. Riding in the curricle lessened the chance his society neighbours would see him escorting Miss Dorman to Henrietta Street. They would know what that meant.

Will did not want her company on this errand, though. Better he discuss the issue man to man with Lord Dorman, distasteful as that was. Although if they resolved the matter this morning, he could leave her there and have no more to do with the lot of them. That was one advantage he could see. The only one.

Mrs White had somehow found a proper bonnet for Miss Dorman and a paisley shawl that complemented the dress she wore. She'd even found Miss Dorman a reticule. Why the woman needed a reticule was a mystery to Will. She had nothing to carry in it.

As they approached the Dorman townhouse, Will spoke to her. 'I will direct the discussion with Lord Dorman. It is best you leave it to me.'

'I cannot do that.'

He gaped at her reply.

'I will speak for myself. I believe I am the best judge of what I need.'

It was just like a Dorman to counter him.

Will shrugged. 'As you wish, but it will be a mistake not to allow me to handle this.'

They reached the Dorman townhouse and his tiger, who had been riding on the back of the curricle, jumped down to hold the horses.

Miss Dorman faced Will. 'Do you expect me to trust you to have my best interests at heart? How can I trust any of you?'

She had a point, Will conceded, but only to himself. Will *was* trustworthy, though. It was a point of honour with him and it did not matter if you were enemy or friend, if he gave you his word, he would keep it. When countless people depend upon you, like all the people who depended upon the Viscount Willburgh for their livelihoods, their food, clothing, and shelter, it would be dishonourable not to be trustworthy.

Since she was a Dorman, of course, he wanted to have the last word. 'I am a man of my word.'

'As any dishonourable man might say,' she added.

So much for having the last word.

Will climbed down from the curricle and extended his hand to help Miss Dorman.

He called to his tiger, 'Toby, walk the horses if they need it. I am not certain how long we will be.'

Will and Miss Dorman approached the door. Will sounded the knocker.

A butler answered. His face broke into a relieved smile when he spied Miss Dorman. 'Miss Anna! You are safe! What wonderful news!' He glanced at Will and frowned. Recognised him, no doubt.

Will handed the man his hat and gloves. 'Announce us, please. I wish to speak with Lord Dorman.'

The butler sputtered, as if uncertain of what to do.

Anna stepped forwards. 'Announce us, Sedley. We will wait in the drawing room.'

'Yes, Miss Anna.' The butler bowed and headed for the breakfast room where she presumed Lord and Lady Dorman would still be, lingering over their tea.

She gestured for Willburgh to follow her up the stairs to the drawing room.

They entered the familiar room, which for some odd reason seemed foreign to her. 'You may sit, if you wish,' she told Willburgh, but neither of them did.

Anna walked to a window and peered out to where Willburgh's tiger held the horses. From behind her she could hear Willburgh drumming his fingers on some piece of furniture. Anna's insides twisted in anticipation. What would it feel like to be in their presence again? After the things they'd said to her the previous night. After they'd walked away leaving her at Vauxhall Gardens alone?

Except for the company of the enemy.

The Dormans did not keep them waiting. After only a few minutes Lord and Lady Dorman burst into the room, followed by Lucius.

'Anna! My dear child! You've come home!' Lady Dorman embraced her.

Anna stiffened. An embrace from Lady Dorman was the last thing she expected.

Uncle Dorman also came to her, taking one of her hands in his. 'Our prayers have been answered. You are here. We are much relieved. I sent all the footmen out to search for you. Was it one of them who found you?'

'No one found her. We came on our own,' Willburgh said.

Her uncle ignored him and kept hold of her hand. 'I think we went a bit mad last night. Were we not, Lucius?' He turned to his son.

'Indeed,' Lucius replied, although his voice was dry.

What game were they playing? Acting so glad to see her? Their words from the night before echoed in her ears. She believed in their rejection, not their welcome.

She pulled her hand away.

Dorman patted her on the shoulder. 'We will not speak again of your little indiscretion, my dear. Fear not.' He glared at Will. 'We know who is to blame.'

Willburgh stood impressively tall and strong as he faced Lord Dorman. 'You have no idea who is to blame, sir, as you refused to hear us. The only indiscretion was your own, sir, to unfairly accuse your niece. You will hear us now—'

Dorman waved his hand dismissively. 'Whose ever fault it was matters not, I assure you. The important thing is that our dear Anna is in the bosom of our family again.'

'You gave us such a fright!' added Lady Dorman.

'So you left her all alone at Vauxhall?' Will protested.

'Not alone, my dear fellow,' Lucius drawled. 'She was in *your* company.' He turned to Anna. 'I suppose you spent the night with him, Anna.'

Anna had heard rumours of Lucius's conquests of women—actresses and the like. How dare he accuse her of loose morals!

'She spent the night at my townhouse,' Willburgh answered Lucius. 'With my mother in residence.'

Anna's anger rose. Lord and Lady Dorman and Lucius offered no apology. No acceptance of their responsibility in the event.

'You gave her no other choice.' Willburgh sounded angry, now, as angry as she felt.

Lady Dorman put her arm around Anna. 'Come sit, my dear. I've ordered some tea.'

Her touch felt revolting. Anna pulled away. 'I prefer to stand.'

'Then come with me to your room,' the woman persisted. 'I am certain you are eager to change that atrocious dress. I suppose it was one of Honoria's.' This last was said in a disdainful tone.

Anna supposed Honoria was Will's mother.

'I will stay here until this is sorted out, ma'am,' Anna retorted.

'Here. Here,' Lord Dorman broke in. 'There is nothing to sort out. You are home. That is all that matters.'

She swung around to face him. 'Home? Home?' Her eyes flashed. 'The place I am no longer welcome? That was what you said last night, was it not, sir?'

The man's expression turned ingratiating. 'Now, now. You know I did not mean it. Heat of the moment and all that.'

'You called me a trollop.' Anna, her temper lost, turned towards Lady Dorman. 'You accused me of having an assignation with this gentleman.'

'But you did have an assignation!' cried Lady Dorman.

Ever since Willburgh's father killed her papa, Anna knew her welcome at the Dormans' was on thin ice. She coped by being of service in any way they required. She always knew they valued her only because she was useful as Violet's companion, someone they could trust to behave in a moral and upright manner and who could try to make Violet behave so.

It took nothing at all, though, for them to think the worst of her.

Violet appeared at the door. 'What is all this talking? You woke me up.'

Anna strode over to her. Violet could have defended her the night before. She knew Anna was not sneaking off to bed Lord Willburgh. 'And you, Violet. You said I'd run off when you of all people knew I'd done no such thing.'

Violet, still in her dressing gown, looked at her haughtily. 'But you did run off, Anna.'

Lucius broke into this confrontation, his voice placating. 'Anna, it makes no difference to us if you ran off or if you were enticed away.' He tossed a scathing look at Willburgh. 'You know how fond we all are of you. This family cannot do without you. It was merely who you chose to be private with that shocked and surprised us so. You cannot put yourself in a compromising position with a Willburgh and expect us not to lose our senses. But we forgive you. We care about you so very much that we do forgive you.'

'You gave us such a turn!' cried his mother.

Lord Dorman readily agreed. 'That is so.'

Violet Dorman rolled her eyes.

Anna was appalled. Not one apology. From any of them. Not one acknowledgement of the wrong they'd done her.

Violet's gaze swept over her parents and brother. 'Have you all become beetle-headed? She's been with *him*.' She pointed to Willburgh. 'You disowned her for good reason.'

Lucius took Violet's arm and led her a few steps away. 'We have welcomed her back *for good reason*,' he said, enunciating each word.

But Anna could not fathom what that reason might be,

especially after all the horrid things they'd said to her the night before. It did not matter, though. Nothing would entice her to spend another day under their roof.

She drew an audible breath. 'Enough. I am done with this. I came to pack my belongings and leave. Please have a trunk brought to my room immediately.'

'Pack your belongings?' cried Lady Dorman. 'You are leaving?'

'Come now,' Lucius cajoled. 'Where will you go?'

Violet laughed dryly. 'Do not be a dunderhead. She's going with *him*.'

'You are correct, Violet,' If they persisted in believing the worst of her, Anna would not disappoint them. 'I *am* going with Lord Willburgh. You stated it all so publicly last night, right near the Turkish Tent in Vauxhall Gardens. Loud enough for everyone to hear. You said that I have been compromised with Viscount Willburgh. What other choice do I have?' She walked up to Willburgh and threaded her arm through his. 'What must a compromised lady do? I must marry him.'

# Chapter Four

$\underset{\displaystyle\sim\!\!\sim\!\!\sim\!\!\sim\!\!\sim\!\!\sim}{}$

Will stiffened in shock. What the devil? Who said anything about marrying? She was the last woman in existence he would ever marry.

The Dormans reacted more loudly. Shouts of 'No!' and 'You must never!' and 'Traitor!' and 'Turncoat!' sounded in his ears.

This was not what Will had expected. He'd expected to see Lord Dorman alone. He'd expected Lord Dorman would listen to the account of what really happened, then the man would apologise to his niece and agree to her return. Once that was done Will expected they would discuss how to minimise the scandal they'd created.

He should have known the Dormans would muddle up everything.

In a guise of being reasonable, they'd persisted in blaming her. They still had not allowed Will to tell them what really happened. Instead they'd thought the worst and refused to acknowledge that they left that young woman at Vauxhall Gardens, alone and friendless.

Except for himself, that was. He was no friend, though. It was only because he was a man of honour that he'd not deserted her, as well.

This was how she thanked him? By threatening to marry him?

Well, he would see about that.

'You ungrateful wretch!' cried Lady Dorman. 'After all we have done for you, you betray us this way? Marrying a Willburgh? You could do nothing worse!'

Will agreed. There could be nothing worse than a Willburgh marrying a Dorman.

Miss Dorman stood firm. 'The trunk to my room, please.'

Lord Dorman's face turned bright red and his hands were curled into fists. 'I will not allow you to dishonour our family in this manner. You will not marry him.'

Lucius scowled, but his expression suddenly brightened. 'Father. You can stop her. She is your ward. She cannot marry without your permission.'

Lord Dorman brightened. 'That is right. My permission.' He glared at his niece. 'I will never give my permission. You will never marry this Willburgh.'

Good. That much was settled.

She shot back. 'Then we will elope.'

*No!* Will cried silently.

'No!' Lord Dorman shouted. 'I'll keep you prisoner here. I won't let you out. I swear I won't.'

This was getting way out of hand.

Will held up a quelling hand. 'Lord Dorman, you will not keep her prisoner. That will make more trouble for yourself than you can imagine. Just have the trunk brought to her room so she can pack her things and leave.'

Will supposed he would have to take her back to his townhouse and after that he did not know what he would do with her.

Amidst protests from the others, Lord Dorman summoned the butler and made the arrangement.

Will walked at Miss Dorman's side up the stairs. He was angry with her—angrier at the rest of the Dormans—but definitely angry at her.

'Don't get in a lather, Willburgh,' she whispered.

What did she expect of him? To be happy?

Marriage was indeed the usual solution when a gentleman compromised a lady. If the gentleman did not marry the lady, the lady would be ruined. Not much happened to the gentleman in such a case, though. But he and Miss Dorman could not marry. They despised each other.

They entered a small bed chamber, little more than a closet. Miss Dorman retrieved a key from a hiding place and unlocked a drawer in the dressing table.

She took out a small box. 'My mother's pearls and locket.' She slipped the box in the reticule.

A servant brought in a very small trunk and a maid came to help Miss Dorman pack a few dresses and other necessary items. She left a good deal behind.

'What about the other dresses?' The maid lifted a ball gown, the same one Will had admired her in weeks ago. Before he'd learned who she was.

'I do not want them, Mary,' Miss Dorman said.

The girl set it aside. 'But you've only four dresses!'

'They will be enough.' Miss Dorman looked around the room. 'I think we are done.' She turned to Will. 'What shall I say to do with the trunk?'

This was her plan; she should know, he thought, but said, 'It should fit on the curricle. We may need ropes to secure it.'

She turned to the maid again. 'Will you get one of the footmen to carry it down to the curricle and get ropes, if needed?'

'Yes, miss.' The maid curtsied and started for the door. Before she reached it, she spun around and rushed back to Miss Dorman, giving her a heartfelt hug. 'I will miss you, Miss Anna,' the maid cried. 'I do not know what it will be like without you!'

'Oh, Mary!' She returned the hug. 'I will miss you, too. You have been such a treasure.'

The girl rushed out of the room.

Miss Dorman gave the room one more look. 'I am ready.'

Will let her pass through the doorway ahead of him. 'Did you foresee all this?' he asked. It seemed well thought out.

She shook her head. 'No, but I knew I could never return. Anything would be better.'

Even marrying him, he supposed. But that would never do. Every day the mere sight of her would remind him that her father killed his father.

They walked down the stairs together. The Dormans appeared in the hall and yelled curses at them until they were out the door.

Will stood with her on the pavement as the footman and his tiger fastened the trunk on the back of the curricle.

'I will not marry you,' Will said through gritted teeth.

She responded without facing him. 'And I will not marry you.'

Now he was truly puzzled. 'Then why announce that you would—we would? To *them*?'

She smiled. 'Petty revenge, I'm afraid. Me, marrying you. Lord Willburgh. The enemy. They will be at sixes and sevens for days.'

Will could not help returning a smile. 'Well, it serves them right. If they'd had an ounce of sense, they would have listened to us and kept the whole matter quiet. We could have gone on as before.'

'I could never have gone on as before,' she said.

The trunk was secured and Will helped Miss Dorman into the curricle.

He called down to his tiger, 'I am driving back to Park

Street. Not a far walk for you.' There was no room for the tiger to ride with them.

'I expect I will arrive there before you, sir,' the tiger, a small but spry man in his forties, responded. He set off on foot. Will signalled the horses to start moving.

'You are taking me back to your townhouse?' She sounded surprised.

'Until we can figure out what to do next.' Of which he had no idea.

'Take me to a jeweller,' she insisted. 'Or somewhere I might sell my mother's pearls and locket. So I have funds to find a room to let somewhere.'

'A room to let?' What the devil was she talking about now.

She stared ahead. 'I need money. My jewellery will give me funds until I can secure some sort of employment.'

Employment? What sort of employment could she find? Impoverished ladies might become a lady's companion or a governess, but this whole Vauxhall Gardens event was certain to cause talk. Who would recommend her? Who would hire her?

He blew out a breath. 'You do not have to sell your jewels.' She seemed to have pitifully few of them. 'I will give you whatever funds you need.'

She turned to him. 'I am not asking you to do that.'

He turned onto Duke Street. 'Believe me. The money is of no consequence to me.'

As a youth he'd had little regard for money. There always seemed to be an abundance of it, always more than he needed. After his father was killed, though, he'd learned that finances were not that simple. He'd managed to preserve his father's wealth and to build upon it, but the lessons he'd been forced to learn so quickly took their toll. At least he could honestly say that supporting her would indeed be of no consequence to him.

There was more traffic on the streets than when they'd left for the Dormans', men on horses, people in carriages, people walking on the pavement. Mayfair was too much like the village back in Buckinghamshire. Small enough that everyone knew everyone else, and they all could see that Lord Willburgh drove Miss Dorman in his curricle.

When they pulled up to Will's townhouse, he noticed the neighbour's curtains move. No doubt it would be noticed that he brought her to his house, trunk and all. Toby, his tiger, was indeed waiting to take the horses and as Will alighted, two footmen came out to get the trunk.

Will helped her down and they hurried into the house.

His mother was in the hall waving a newspaper in her hands. 'Did you see this? Did you see this? It is in the newspapers!'

He ought to have guessed. Spreading the tale word of mouth was not enough. 'Well, let us go to the drawing room.' The butler was attending the hall. 'Bring some tea, Bailey.'

'We are ruined!' his mother wailed. 'What are we to do?'

He was not about to discuss it on the stairs.

They entered the drawing room.

Having just been in the Dormans' drawing room, Will could not help but note the contrast. He'd resisted his mother's desire to remodel the principal rooms of the townhouse. This room remained much like it had been when he was a youth—before his father died—serene with its pale green walls, plasterwork and striped upholstery. The Dormans' drawing room was all that was new in garish shades of red, gold, and blue.

Will needed this serenity today.

'Mother. Miss Dorman. Please sit.' He gestured to the

chairs and sofas. 'I cannot bear all of us pacing the room.'
Like they had at the Dormans'.

Miss Dorman chose an armchair. His mother perched
on the edge of an adjacent sofa, as far away from the young
woman as possible. Will chose the sofa opposite his mother,
placing himself in between.

'Here.' His mother shoved the newspaper into his hands.
'Read it.'

It took him some time to find it.

*At Vauxhall Gardens last night, Miss D— was caught
by her guardian, Lord D and his son, in a private assignation with their sworn enemy Lord W—. A loud
altercation ensued, Lord D— leaving his ward with
W—, disowning her.*

That left nothing out.

But the truth.

'May I see it?' Miss Dorman extended her hand.

He handed the paper to her, pointing to where the words
were on the page.

She handed it back to him.

His mother glared at her. 'This is all your fault! I cannot bear it.'

'Leave it, Mother.' He put his head in his hands.

He did not know what to do. What solution was a good one?

Miss Dorman spoke. 'I'll accept your offer of money. I
will move away.'

'Oh, that will be lovely,' his mother said scathingly. 'Then
everyone will say you disappeared because Will got you
with child.'

'Then I won't move away,' she countered. 'We can pretend to be betrothed and after several months, I'll cry off.'

Society said a woman could break an engagement to be married, but if a man did so it would be considered a breach of promise.

Will brightened. 'That might work. My reputation might suffer a little, but the *ton* will get over it.' A man with a title and money rarely stayed outside the *ton*'s good graces for long.

Of course. *His* reputation might survive, but what about hers? With scandal, no funds, and no family to back her, what prospects would her future hold? She'd indeed be ruined.

He wished he hadn't realised this.

'It is not you whose reputation concerns me the most!' his mother wailed. 'No match you make will ever be as good as it would be without this scandal, but you will recover. A man always recovers. It is your sister I am worried about.'

His sister, Ellen, was sixteen, on the cusp of being presented to society and entering the marriage mart.

His mother's voice rose. 'She already suffers from the scandal your father created—this will put her beyond the pale. How will she ever make a good match now?'

He might remind his mother that it was her affair with Miss Dorman's father that started the whole thing. True, she'd only wanted to get his father's attention by inviting Dorman's addresses. Indeed, his father had noticed and the result was disastrous.

Bailey, the butler, appeared at the door with the tea service and a plate of biscuits. He set them on the table, then quietly spoke to Will. 'May I see you outside for a moment, m'lord?'

'Certainly.' Will rose, asking leave of his mother and Miss Dorman. He stepped outside the room. 'What is it?'

His butler pulled a piece of paper from his pocket and handed it to Will. 'One of the footmen discovered this handbill being sold.'

Will skimmed the paper. It was a scandal sheet showing a drawing of two people, looking vaguely like him and Miss Dorman, *in flagrante* and a very embellished account of what happened at Vauxhall Gardens.

'It was selling quite well, I am afraid,' Bailey said.

'Deuce.' It had taken no time at all for someone to profit from the event. Will inclined his head towards the door. 'I'll have to tell them before someone else does.'

He re-entered the drawing room.

'More bad news, I fear.' He showed them the scandal sheet.

His mother dropped her head into her hands. 'We will never recover from this! This is the end of all for us.'

Will walked over to the window and looked out. He knew what he must do. The clarity of it struck him like a blow to the chest. He ought to have known it from the moment he opened the door to Lucius and Lord Dorman at Vauxhall Gardens. Will must do what any gentleman of honour would do to salvage his reputation and the reputation of the lady. Miss Dorman herself had hit upon it. Only one way society would forgive this imagined transgression.

Will turned to Miss Dorman. 'We must marry.'

'No!' Anna shot up from her chair. She would not marry him. She would not! 'Just tell me where I might sell my jewellery. I'll find a room to let and trouble you no more.'

Was it her impulsive threat to marry Willburgh at her uncle's house that gave him this idea? That she was willing to marry him? She would never do so. She'd despised him for ten years, even without knowing him. If only she'd never met him!

If she had not met him, though, what would have happened to her at the hands of that vile creature at Vauxhall Gardens?

'Do not be foolish,' Willburgh said. 'Money from two pieces of jewellery will never be sufficient. You'll say you'll find employment. What employment? Who would employ you? You have no one to recommend you. Even a servant needs references.'

His words rang true, but she did not want to heed them. She lifted her chin. 'I will find something.'

He stood toe-to-toe with her, glaring into her face. 'Do you know the sort of employment left to a single woman of no means and no references? Such women walk the streets at night.'

Violet's governess had told them stories about street-walkers, women reduced to selling their bodies in order to survive. These were meant as cautionary tales of what can happen if a young lady does not protect her virtue.

But Anna had done nothing unvirtuous.

'Then pay to support me,' she snapped. 'You said the money would be of no consequence!'

'It would not be—' he began.

His mother interrupted. 'No, Will! You mustn't. Having her in your keeping will only cause more talk. Consider your sister...'

His face stiffened in pain. With his back to his mother, he spoke only to Anna. 'My sister. Ellen is sixteen. An innocent. Most of her life has been tainted by scandal. My mother is right. This does not affect only you and me. I must consider her.'

Anna knew of Ellen Willburgh, but never gave the girl a moment's thought. But she remembered herself at sixteen. So worried for what the future might bring. Could her hatred of the Willburghs extend to this innocent girl? Anna remembered the scandal the duel caused.

She could imagine ladies of the *ton* whispering together of how Willburgh had to send away that poor ward of Lord Dorman's, how it must mean there was a baby. After her papa was killed she'd overheard ladies whispering about him. She remembered suddenly that they'd speculated about her, too—and her mother. She'd made certain, then, to always behave with complete decorum.

Even so, the sins of one member of a family always tainted the whole family.

Anna raised her gaze, looked into Willburgh's face, and spoke in a pained voice. 'I do not want to marry you.'

'I do not want to marry you either.' His voice reflected hers.

'Must we elope?' she asked.

'Without your uncle's permission, it is the only way,' he responded.

# Chapter Five

They set off the next day in a post-chaise.

The decision to hire a post-chaise rather than take one of Willburgh's own carriages had been a topic of much debate, mostly with his mother—Anna's opinion was not sought, not that she had one in this particular matter, except that she'd rather not go at all.

His mother prevailed.

'Good gracious,' she had exclaimed. 'Is there not enough gossip? Someone is bound to recognise the crest on your carriage. They will know you are going to Gretna Green and soon it will be in papers all over the country.'

Anna doubted that much interest in them existed.

In any event, Willburgh, Anna's future husband, opted for the post-chaise. To make the changes at coaching inns as simple as possible, they each brought luggage small enough to carry by hand. Anna's portmanteau was reluctantly lent to her by Lady Willburgh and contained one change of clothing. Toby, the tiger who'd ridden with them to Henrietta Street two days ago, was the only servant to come with them. He rode on the outside of the chaise.

The fastest route apparently was the mail route. Mail coaches with their ability to travel day and night could make the trip in three days. Anna and Willburgh did not require that level of speed, however. It would take them seven days.

The longer the better, thought Anna. More time meant more of a chance to come up with a different way out of this predicament.

They had little conversation as the streets of London opened into country scenes and glimpses of small villages. Anna could not simply gaze at the fields and hedgerows they passed and pretend Willburgh was not with her, though. He sat next to her on the one seat and Anna could not ignore how tall and broad-shouldered he was. Every bump in the road pressed his body against hers. His long legs knocked into hers. His warmth and strength had its effect on her. When had she ever been so close to a man and for so long a time? And such a man. The sort who would turn heads wherever he went.

Except for short breaks to change teams and one longer one for a midday meal, Anna spent eight hours enveloped by Willburgh's presence, yet raging against being forced to marry him. It was exhausting and unsettling.

When dusk fell, they pulled into a red brick, thatched roof inn with a sign posted of a fox and hound.

'Where are we?' Anna asked.

'Northampton,' Willburgh responded tersely. 'We'll spend the night.'

An ostler opened the door of the chaise and Willburgh disembarked first. He turned and offered Anna his hand to assist her.

Her legs were stiff and aching from sitting, but she managed to descend from the chaise. Toby spoke to the stable workers then followed them carrying their luggage.

'Remember who you are,' Willburgh whispered to her as they entered the inn

He had decided they should travel under false names to protect them from more gossip should the handbills and newspapers have reached this far.

'Welcome,' the innkeeper greeted them.

'I am Mr Fisher,' Willburgh announced. 'I would like two rooms. One for me and one for my sister. And accommodations for my coachman.'

The innkeeper's brows rose at the word *sister* and his mouth twitched. 'Very good, Mr Fisher. We can accommodate you and your *sister*.' The man cast a meaningful look at Anna. 'And your coachman.'

She managed to appear composed, pretending she hadn't noticed. It was discomfiting, to say the least.

Willburgh signed the register. 'May we arrange a private room for dining as well?'

'It will be done, sir,' the innkeeper said.

'We will freshen up and desire our meal in one hour. Will that be possible?'

Anna thought Willburgh sounded every bit a viscount in his imposing tone. The innkeeper had already tagged her as not being a sister; the man likely figured out Willburgh was not a mere mister.

'It will indeed, sir,' the innkeeper said. 'I will show you to your rooms directly. Do you need servants to attend you?'

Willburgh turned to Anna. 'You will likely desire a maid to assist you at bedtime. Do you want assistance now?'

'No,' she replied. 'I will manage.'

The innkeeper gave them rooms right next to each other. Toby carried their luggage to the rooms and excused himself, assuring Willburgh all would be ready in the morning to continue their trip.

Anna luxuriated in the sensation of being entirely alone, away from Willburgh—except she could hear him moving around in the other room. She sighed and walked over to the basin to wash her hands and face and ready herself for dinner.

Will paced his room trying to release the pent-up tension of being cooped up in the chaise for long spells of time. And sitting next to Miss Dorman.

He was well aware of crowding her, though she did not complain and did not try to shirk away. Her scent filled his nostrils, and it was impossible to miss the loveliness of her profile, the soft femininity of her figure, especially when his body was jostled against hers. His senses were filled with her. How was he to endure a week of this close proximity?

A lifetime.

He shook off that thought. It did no good to think about marrying her. He'd learned after his father's death that it was best to think about the next task in front of him. The enormity of the whole picture always froze him in place.

He washed his face and hands and shaved the stubble off his chin, brushed off his clothes and waited until an hour had passed, then left his room to knock on her door.

'I am ready,' she said.

They ate a typical coaching inn meal of mutton stew and bread and drank ale instead of wine. Perhaps after she retired for the night Will would come down to the public rooms and have something stronger. They hardly spoke.

They'd hardly spoken to each other all day. What was there to say, after all? They both knew they did not want to marry.

But Will forced that thought away. Handle the next task. Only the next task.

He escorted her back to her room after dinner. A maid awaited her there to attend her.

At her door, he said, 'We'll leave early in the morning.

Breakfast at seven. Order a maid to wake you early and help you dress.'

'As you wish,' she responded.

As soon as her door closed Will returned to the public room and ordered a glass of whisky. And a second.

The next day of travel was much like the first. Passing towns and villages. Stopping to change teams. Enduring the close quarters and desolate silences. As the sun dipped lower in the sky, they entered a town larger than the ones they'd passed through.

Will broke the silence. 'We'll stay the night here.'

'What town is this?' Miss Dorman looked out the window with some interest instead of blankly staring at nothing in particular.

'Loughborough,' he responded.

'Loughborough?' Her interest seemed to increase. 'The Loughborough where the Luddites attacked the lace factory?'

'Yes.' He was impressed that she'd heard of it. As a member of the House of Lords Will had been completely informed. 'The attackers came from Nottingham, not from Loughborough. They attacked the watchmen, destroyed fifty-five frames, and burned the lace.'

Their chaise passed by a three-storey building with the name *Heathcoat and Boden* on it. The building looked empty and neglected.

'That is the lace factory, I suppose.' Miss Dorman gestured to the building, an imposing structure made of the same red brick as their inn the previous night. She added, 'I do not know to whom I should owe sympathy. The owners and workers in the factory or the men whose livelihoods disappeared because of the machines.'

'There was a great deal of suffering on both sides,' Will agreed.

They stopped at the Old Bull Inn and their evening was much like the previous one, although their discussion of the Luddite attack and the economic hardships that spawned it gave them conversation across the dinner table. Miss Dorman asked many questions and seemed interested in hearing how the Lords had discussed the situation. They debated the suspension of the Habeas Corpus Act which allowed persons to be imprisoned without bail, in Will's view the most important issue of the day.

The third day brought them into Nottingham and led to conversations about Robin Hood and debate about stealing from the rich to give to the poor and whether there had indeed been a Robin Hood or had he been a fictitious legend.

In addition to being almost irresistibly alluring, Miss Dorman was also an intelligent woman of good education and thoughtful opinions. Many of the young women thrown in his path to court had little to say of substance at all. Miss Dorman told him she, along with her cousin Violet, had been given typical lessons in proper behaviour, stitchery, piano, and other feminine skills. She also loved to read and had been permitted to read whatever was in Lord Dorman's library.

As long as she was in no one's way.

When Will settled down to sleep that night, he allowed himself to be a tiny bit hopeful about marrying her. Perhaps there could be something more between them than the grievances of the past.

Will had just fallen asleep when a knock on the door awakened him. It was Toby, looking alarmed.

He gestured for the man to come in. 'What is it, Toby?'

'Sir.' His tiger was out of breath. 'I was in the public

rooms having a pint when three men came in, asking the innkeeper and others if there was a Lord Willburgh staying here. I believe it was young Mr Dorman, sir. And a fellow he called Raskin and another fellow.' He swallowed. 'I lay low in case they'd recognise me, but they wouldn't. That sort don't take notice of men like me. Any road, I decided I'd better tell you right away.'

Lucius. Looking for him. Planning to thwart their elopement, Will was certain. He was glad he'd used a different name, but they'd figure out who Will and Miss Dorman were quickly enough. Dorman had obviously guessed that they would head to Gretna Green using the quickest route, the mail route.

Will would be damned if he'd allow Lucius to stop him.

He paced the room, thinking, then stopped and turned to his groom. 'Here's what we will do, Toby.'

The knock on Anna's door woke her. It took a moment for her to remember where she was. And why.

She went to the door. 'Who is it?'

'It's Will. I need to talk to you.' He used the name his mother called him. Will. He'd never done that before.

'One moment.' She hadn't packed a robe but did have a shawl, so she wrapped that around her, almost covering all of her shift, which she wore to sleep in so as not to pack a nightdress. She opened the door.

He was dressed more like his groom than a viscount. Before she could ask why, he burst into the room and shoved a dress at her. 'Put this on. We have to leave now.'

How dare he order her like that. 'Leave? What time is it?'

'I do not know,' he answered. 'Five, perhaps. Heed me. Lucius is here, staying in this inn. And Raskin and some other fellow. My groom heard them asking for us.'

Anna felt the blood drain from her face. 'Lucius? Why would he?'

'It foxes me,' Willburgh replied. 'To stop us, can be the only reason. We have to leave. Are you able to dress yourself?'

Would Lucius truly want to stop her? Why? After the things he said to her—that all the Dormans said to her— why were they not glad she was gone?

'I am able to dress myself,' she responded. 'But why this dress?' The dress was plain, like a maid's dress.

'Toby has hired a man and woman to impersonate us. One of the ostlers agreed to do it. With his wife. This is her dress. They will dress in our clothes, carry our luggage, and ride in our post-chaise. Toby will go with them. With any luck Lucius will believe they are us.' He shoved a cap into her hands. 'Wear this, too.'

'But I need things from my portmanteau,' she protested.

'We'll purchase whatever we need. It is a market day, I'm told, so all we need should be available.' He made it sound so easy. 'Hurry. I'll wait outside your door.'

Good thing she'd left anything she cared about in London at Willburgh's townhouse.

Anna dressed as quickly as she could. Fixed her hair in a simple chignon, covered it with the cap, and opened the door.

He gestured her to come with him. They walked quietly down the hallway and the stairs and out into the yard. Willburgh's groom was waiting for them. He and Willburgh spoke again about the arrangements and the groom directed them to the market square.

As they set off, the sun was sending its first rays into the new day. Even though it was June there was a breeze that chilled the air. The market was not open, of course but they found a place to sit out of the wind. They sat on the stone pavement which sent cold right through Anna's clothes.

She shivered. 'The first item I wish to buy is a shawl.'

Willburgh gazed at her. 'You are cold.' He changed positions. 'Here. Come sit in front of me. I'll warm you.'

He sat cross-legged so that she wound up sitting on his legs instead of the cold stone. He leaned her back against him and put his arms around her.

His body did indeed warm her, but also sent a strange thrill throughout. Her cheeks flamed. It was scandalous for him to hold her like this, but since they were dressed as they were, the few people who arrived to set out their wares paid them no heed. When the food booths opened Willburgh bought them loaves of brown bread and hot salop, a sweetened sassafras tea.

'I've never tasted such things,' Anna remarked. 'They are lovely.'

Willburgh smiled, which only made his handsome face more handsome. 'I am glad.'

By the time they'd finished eating and returned the wooden bowls to the vendor, more and more booths were filling with wares. They wandered through them until discovering one selling shawls. Some were beautiful paisley shawls worthy of a Bond Street shop, but Anna chose a plain woollen one in a brown shade not unlike the dress Lady Willburgh had lent her.

Had that only been three days ago?

'Good choice.' Willburgh nodded.

'The plan is to not be noticed, correct?' she responded.

'You have grasped it.'

Surprisingly, his approval pleased her.

Next they purchased two portmanteaux, one for each of them and spent another hour or more finding toiletries and used clothing. In the end they looked very much like a labourer and his wife and nothing like Viscount Willburgh and the lady he was to marry.

They sought respite in The Bell Inn, right on Market Square.

'What now?' Anna asked as they sat drinking tea and eating pasties. 'How do we proceed?'

'That is what I am turning over in my mind.' He pulled out a map and a copy of *Cary's Coach Directory*, two items he'd just purchased. He laid the map on the table. 'We should not follow the mail route, that is certain.'

Using the mail route must have been how Lucius almost found them.

'We'll stay east.' He pointed to the map. 'It will take longer, but we can avoid Lucius and his companions that way.' He looked up. 'There was a third man with Lucius and Raskin. I wonder who he was.'

She curled her hand into a fist. 'A—a companion of Raskin's abducted me. Could he be the third man?'

He blinked in surprise. 'I assumed that man had been a stranger. He was someone Raskin knew?'

'I was not given his name.' Her heart pounded with the memory. 'I do not think I was supposed to.'

'Lucius knew him as well?' His voice deepened.

'I cannot say.' She glanced away. 'I would hate to think Lucius would…'

But she feared both he and Violet had set her up. Perhaps without knowing what the man would do or perhaps it was their idea of a joke. Lucius did seem to know precisely where to find her after the rain.

What horrible men they all were. So unlike this man whom she'd called her enemy. Even though he despised her, he'd protected her. And was doing so still.

She met Willburgh's gaze again and held it.

# Chapter Six

Will's anger flamed. He'd half a mind to seek out Lucius and show the man precisely what he thought of him. With bare fists, preferably. The lady seated across from him surely did not deserve such treatment.

She was proving more game than he'd anticipated. Uttering not one word of complaint the entire trip, even through this morning's trials. Not a word about wearing plain clothes, nor of giving up her own dresses. He knew she could not be happy about any of this.

He needed to get back to the task.

'How we should travel, I cannot decide,' he said, breaking the silence that followed talk of Lucius. 'Whether to hire another post-chaise, or take the stage coach, or even purchase a vehicle and horse.'

Her brows rose. 'You have enough funds with you to purchase a vehicle and horse?'

He cocked his head. 'I might arrange it.'

At that moment a youth approached their table. Will glanced up at him.

'Are you Mr Fisher, guv'nor?' The boy could not have been more than fourteen.

Willburgh looked at him suspiciously. 'Who asks, if you please?'

If Willburgh wished to portray a labourer, he sounded precisely like a viscount.

'Name's John.' The boy gave a little bow. 'I am to tell you that the gentlemen have gone.'

Willburgh nodded, but still looked askance. 'And why did you think I was Mr Fisher?'

The boy pointed to the hat Willburgh had placed on the chair next to him. 'M'brother's hat. M'brother's the one you hired to be you and his wife to be your wife.'

Miss Dorman winced when the boy called her Will's wife.

The boy went on. 'Yer groom paid me to find you after he left with m'brother and the gentlemen left soon after.'

Willburgh relaxed. 'Thank you, John.' He reached in a pocket and pulled out a coin to hand to the boy.

The youth took it and wrapped his fist around it. 'If you do not mind me asking, sir, if you have any other work to be done? I'm good around horses and I'm clever in a pinch, if you get my meaning.'

Willburgh stared at him, obviously thinking.

Finally he said, 'I have need of a groom to accompany us the rest of the way to Scotland.'

The boy hopped from one foot to the other. 'I am your man, sir. I can be a groom. I've been around horses all m'life. M'father was an ostler. And m'brother.'

Willburgh gestured to a chair. 'Sit, John, and hear what I have in mind.'

The boy sat. Willburgh called to the servant to bring the boy some tea and a pasty, which the servant brought right away.

When the servant was out of earshot, Willburgh said, 'I wish to hire another post-chaise, but to take a different route to Scotland. I do not want those gentlemen to know where we are or where we are heading. They must not find us.'

'Do not worry, guv,' the boy said after biting into the pasty. 'M'brother will fool them.'

'Can you assist in hiring the post-chaise? Or any available vehicle?' Willburgh asked.

'Yes, sir,' the boy replied, his mouth full. 'But if you do not mind me saying, you are not dressed like riders of a post-chaise usually are dressed.'

'Because labourers would not hire a carriage like that,' Miss Dorman broke in. 'We will have to dress more prosperously.'

So she and Will returned to Market Square and the clothes dealers and found clothes that were not too rich, nor too poor. John, Will's new groom, went to talk to the head ostler at The Bell Inn, to hire a carriage for them.

By noon Anna and Willburgh were riding in another post-chaise with their luggage secured and Willburgh's new groom, John, on the outside. The forests made so famous in the Robin Hood legends gave way to rolling countryside with stone fences and sheep grazing. They also glimpsed tall chimneys of smelt mills and spied mining villages.

The seat to this carriage was more spacious so Anna did not have to sit with Willburgh's body touching hers, except when the road caused the carriage to ram them together. Perhaps she was getting used to it, because it did not bother her as much as before.

They had more conversation than before, as well, conferring on the route they were taking, commenting on what they saw outside the carriage window. By sitting in the Lords, Willburgh knew things, such as the state of the mining industry, the challenges to farming, the hardship the war had caused some of these villages, the fomenting of unrest in the country. Anna liked learning of such things.

At dusk they entered Sheffield, a town unlike any Anna had seen before, dirty, grimy, its streets ill paved. It was a town full of industry, known for making cutlery, the place silver plate was created, a lead mill, a cotton mill. Smoke. Poverty.

And yet they passed by a beautiful church with a tall spire.

Willburgh seemed as aghast at the conditions as Anna was.

'I will remember this town,' he murmured, although she did not think he was speaking to her.

The chaise pulled into the King's Head Inn and ostlers jumped to tend to them. John carried their luggage like a proper groom, although he did not have the livery. Anna thought that befitted the roles they were playing—shopkeepers, if anyone asked.

They entered the inn and met the innkeeper who asked their name.

'Oldham,' Willburgh said.

'Mr and Mrs Oldham,' repeated the innkeeper handing the register to Willburgh.

Anna waited until they were standing in the room and John and the innkeeper had left. 'You put us in the same room!'

He faced her. 'It is best.'

'It is not best for me!' she scoffed. 'We are not married yet!'

'Heed me.' He sounded angry now, too. 'We have Lucius and—and his disreputable friends chasing us. Maybe there are others. This is better for our disguise. Besides, this town looks dangerous. I can protect you.'

'I can take care of myself,' she huffed.

They went to dinner in silence.

Anna declined a maid even for after dinner. He left when she was readying herself for bed. Only one bed in the room.

Where was he going to sleep? He had better not take any liberties with her. When they were married, she'd endure it, but not now.

Although his arms around her that morning to keep her warm were extremely pleasant. Even thrilling.

She needn't have worried, though. When he returned to the room she pretended to be asleep. He approached the bed but all he did was remove a blanket. He stripped down to his shirt and drawers, a sight she could not help watching. She also watched him settle into a chair, his legs on another chair, the blanket around him.

How was he to sleep in that position? And, even if he could sleep, how would it be for him to feel cooped up in the carriage all day tomorrow?

'Willburgh?' she cried softly.

He startled at the sound of her voice. 'What?' He tried to straighten in the chair, scraping the one that held his legs on the wooden floor.

'You cannot sleep on that chair,' she said. 'I should. It will fit me so much better.' She sat up to trade places with him.

'You will not sleep on the chair.' His voice was firm in the darkness, the sort that brooked no argument.

She argued anyway. 'You will be miserable and cross in the carriage. Not to mention aching bones.'

'No matter. You will not sleep on the chair.' His voice grew louder.

She persisted. 'The floor, then. I should do nicely on the floor with a blanket and pillow.'

He sat up. 'Are you daft, woman? I would not take the bed and leave you on the floor or a chair or wherever else you contrive. Leave it.'

'As you wish, then,' she retorted in clipped tones.

Anna lay back down under the covers, turning her back

to him, but the creak of the chairs every time he moved kept her from sleeping. It was impossible to endure another person's discomfort. Totally against her nature.

She rolled over to face him. 'Willburgh?'

'What now?' he snapped.

She could not believe what she was about to say. 'This bed is big enough. We can both sleep in it.'

His silence was palpable.

'I have given up propriety, if that is your concern.' She swallowed. 'They took that away from us days ago.'

'Propriety is not the only concern,' he responded, his voice quieter.

She forged on. 'You must not touch me, though. I draw the line there.'

The chairs scraped and she watched him stand up. Blanket in tow, he walked towards the bed. She scooted to the far side tucking some of the bed linens around her like a shield. The bed dipped as he climbed in. They were face-to-face for a moment before they each rolled away. Anna was more awake than before, acutely aware of the warmth of his body so near to hers, of the cadence of his breathing. Of the scent of his soap and of him, now becoming so familiar to her.

Of that strange thrill she'd experienced when his arms were around her that morning.

When Will woke the next morning his arm was around her and she was nestled against his chest. His first impulse was to push away from her, but he checked himself in time, not wanting to wake her.

And she felt so good against him, so soft and round and smelling like the lavender water they'd purchased the day before.

He closed his eyes and tried to bring back the memory of

pistols firing and his father falling to the ground. Her father stood a moment longer, a look of triumph on his face, before he, too, collapsed. The emotion of that day came back, but when he opened his eyes he could not attach any of it to her.

He did not mind her company. Could no longer blame her for their predicament. No. It seemed as if they were facing this together. The two of them against the world.

Her eyelids fluttered and soon he was looking into her eyes, the colour of a fine brandy, still warm and sleepy. Her eyes widened, though, and she pulled away from him. He moved away as well, climbing out of the bed and gathering his trousers.

She rose and wrapped her shawl around her. They'd replaced the drab brown one they'd chosen at first with this muted green one, embellished with embroidered flowers. Neither of them spoke until they were dressed and ready for breakfast.

Before they sat down to eat, Will sent a servant to alert John to ready their carriage. They breakfasted in a private dining room, attended by one servant girl.

When they were alone, she broke their silence with each other. 'Did you sleep well?'

He felt his face flush. He actually had slept better than any night since Vauxhall Gardens. Even before. 'Quite well,' he responded. 'And you?'

Her eyelids fluttered. 'Very well.'

The stiffness between them was unlike when they'd started this journey, but Will missed the growing ease between them.

The servant returned. 'Mr Oldham, your groom wishes to inform you the carriage will be ready within an hour.'

'Thank you,' Will replied.

After the servant left, the silence between him and Miss Dorman filled the room again.

Will broke it. 'I was thinking that we should agree on how I should call you, should I need to use a name. I do not wish to slip and call you Miss Dorman.'

She looked up at him over her cup of tea. 'I cringe when you say Dorman. Call me Anna.'

'Anna,' he repeated, liking the sound on his tongue.

He ought to tell her to call him Will. But, no. Not yet.

Travel the next two days and nights was as pleasant as could be expected. John proved adept at finding the equipage needed when the post they hired could not continue any longer. Some carriages were more comfortable than others, but Miss Dorman—Anna—was as uncomplaining as ever.

Their days were filled with the changing scenery. Fields. Mountains. Lakes and rivers. Villages and towns of all sizes, each with its unique character. Their nights grew more comfortable. They shared a room and a bed and slept snuggled next to each other.

As much as Will tried to tell himself their physical closeness was no different than it had been when he'd used his body to warm her in Nottingham, his senses demanded more. In the darkness he was consumed with the desire to join her body to his, but he'd somehow kept to his promise. He held her but no further liberties. Will did not know what their nights would be like after marriage; he could only trust that eventually he could make love to her the way his body demanded. That she seemed to welcome his arms at night and smiled at him more during the day, fed that trust. He could almost believe their marriage could be more than tolerable. It might even bring great pleasure.

Then he'd remember who she was and how it came to be that they shared a bed together. Then hope vanished.

They'd spent those two nights first in Skipton; then, Orton

and before Will knew it their latest post-chaise was pulling into the Bush Inn in Carlisle. The Scottish border was less than ten miles away.

This was the most vulnerable part of their journey thus far, though. They were back on the mail coach route where they'd sent their decoys. If there was anywhere to encounter Lucius and his companions, this would be the place.

'We'll stay in the carriage until we know,' he told Anna.

'And be ready to leave quickly if Lucius is here.' She was always quick to comprehend.

Will sent John to make enquiries and to look around the inn and stable yard. He'd seen Lucius, Raskin, and the other man back in Nottingham. He would recognise them.

Not more than a half hour later John walked back to the carriage with none other than Toby!

'Toby is here,' Will prepared to exit the carriage.

'I hope that is good news,' she said as he helped her out.

John spoke straight away. 'Those gentlemen are not here.'

'But they are waiting for you,' Toby added. 'At the border.' He turned to Anna and tipped his hat. 'G'day, miss.'

'I am glad to see you are in one piece,' she responded.

They settled into a private dining room Toby had arranged. Refreshment was ordered and Will, Anna, and Toby sat down to plan the next step while John saw to their luggage.

Toby filled them in on his part of the journey.

He and John's brother and the wife managed to remain a few hours ahead of Lucius. They avoided the coaching inns that the mail coaches used but once had to make a run for it when Lucius showed up asking for them. They reached Gretna Green before they were discovered, but since they had no information of Will and Anna's plans, there was nothing Lucius could learn from them.

'Mr Dorman was hopping mad, too,' Toby said. 'Cursing and pounding his fists. The ostlers ordered him to compose himself or leave. Right before I slipped away, I heard him say they would wait for you at the border and hire more men to stop you. I wouldn't put it past him to have followed me, though, so you cannot stay here.'

Will spread his maps on the table. 'Then we must find another way. Another route. Gretna Green is not the only Scottish town where we can marry.'

It was too late in the day to try to make it into Scotland if they had to go farther out of their way.

'We could take another day,' Anna said. 'Find the next best place to cross the border west of here. No matter what, I do not want to encounter Lucius.'

The map showed a route to a village called Canonbie that was right over the border but east of Gretna Green.

'What if they guess we have gone east? Canonbie would be the first place they would look.' Anna pointed to a town marked a bit north of there. 'We should go a little farther still. Here, perhaps.'

She pointed to Langholm.

There was a knock on the door and John entered.

He was out of breath. 'A post boy coming from Mossband told me a gentleman was looking for Lord Willburgh's groom, supposedly who'd been on horseback. That'd be you, right?' he asked Toby.

'Me.' Toby frowned.

Will started to fold up the maps. 'John, get us something to take us out of here right away, but we won't leave from the yard. Meet us somewhere.'

'There's another coaching inn on this street,' John said, although how he knew, Will could not guess. 'The Angel

Inn. I'll run ahead and get something from there. You can meet me there.' He started for the door.

'Wait,' Will said. 'Let us make them think we are staying the night here. I'll procure a room and you can make a pretence of taking the luggage there. Then go to the inn. We'll meet you at the other inn as soon as we can sneak out of here.'

'I'll stay here,' Toby said. 'If they find me, I'll make it seem you are here, as well.'

Will and Anna went with John to arrange the room. Will went so far as to order dinner and paid for it all right away. After John brought the luggage and left, Will and Anna were out on English Street within a half hour. Will carried their luggage.

By the time they made it to the inn, John had a post-chaise ready for them and they set out east for Brampton, a market town about nine miles east of Carlisle. They pulled into a white stucco inn, The String of Horses.

Thwarting whatever plan Lucius had for chasing them to Scotland drove out of Will's mind the realisation that he would be married on the morrow. *Focus only on the next task.* When he settled in the bed next to Anna, though, the thought came back to him, both with anticipation and misgiving. What would bedding her be like next he lay beside her?

For that alone he hoped he'd keep Lucius at bay.

# Chapter Seven

Anna woke as the first rays of daylight shone through the window. This would be her wedding day.

She gazed at the sleeping face of the man who would be her husband. It was a handsome face, almost boyish in repose. It had also become a familiar one over these few tumultuous days since he removed his mask at Vauxhall Gardens.

But she did not know him, really. She knew the Dormans' version of him, especially Lucius's version. A haughty man. A selfish one. One who could not be trusted. That version had been ingrained in her over the last decade.

Ever since his father killed her papa.

She supposed she could call him haughty, but could that merely be his anger over being forced to marry her? He was not selfish, though. His own interests seemed to never count in any action he undertook. That was true from the moment he rescued her in Vauxhall.

Could he be trusted? All she could say was he'd not given her any reason not to trust him.

If only she could forget what his father did, she might even look forward to marrying him. She knew the *ton* would consider him a catch. He was a viscount, after all.

He murmured in his sleep and rolled over. Anna slipped out of the bed without disturbing him. She padded over to the wash basin and poured fresh water. Taking advantage of his sleep, she washed herself as thoroughly as she could and splashed on the lavender water. Its scent calmed her. Reminded her of her mother. Of when she had a home, when the three of them, she, her mother, and her papa lived together in an exotic house in India. She remembered the warm breezes, the scent of spice in the air. And her mother's lavender water.

She was a far cry from that idyllic childhood. When her mother caught a fever and died, Anna and Papa took the long trip to England, where she'd been told she was *from*, but had never set foot. She'd lost everything but Papa and, then, within a year, she'd lost him, too.

That wound was still painfully deep.

Blinking away tears, she dried herself and checked to see if Willburgh was still sleeping. She changed into a clean shift and put on her corset, tying her strings as best she could. She'd been wearing the same dress since Nottingham, but the night before had unpacked her only other dress, a carriage dress of dark blue. Most of the wrinkles were out of it this morning. Such a dress would have been fashionable over five years ago. It was made of corded muslin which gave it the effect of white fabric with thin blue stripes running on the bias. Its collar nearly touched her chin, but the buttons down the front made it easy to put on herself. The ribbon sash at her natural waist made it particularly old-fashioned.

Anna held her breath as she put it on, hoping it would fit. She released a relieved sigh when she was able to button every button. She checked herself in the dressing mirror. The sleeves were a bit too long and the bodice a little loose, but it would do.

Willburgh's voice came from behind her. 'The dress looks well on you.'

Anna turned around, surprised he was awake and even

more surprised at how pleased she was at the compliment. 'I did not know you were awake.'

'I just woke up.' He swung his legs over the side of the bed and continued to gaze at her. 'You made a good choice on that dress.'

It would not do to grin in gratification of his words, but she could not suppress a small smile. 'It is hardly *à la mode*.' Lady Dorman and Violet would have perished before wearing such a garment.

As he rose from the bed, Anna's memory flashed with how warm and comforting it was to sleep next to him. As if she were not alone in the world.

Would they sleep together as a married couple? Would he wish to perform the marriage act with her? Her senses flared at that thought. Did that mean she wanted him to or she did not want him to?

While he washed and shaved and dressed, she brushed out her hair and, to be a bit fancier, braided it first before winding it into a chignon. Not that it mattered, though. She covered her hair with a bonnet.

Willburgh had arranged a private dining room for their breakfast. The less they showed themselves the better, in case Lucius had tracked them this far. John reported that there had been no sign of them, however.

After a quick breakfast they were again on the road, this time on the final leg of their journey. John called down to them when they neared the Scottish border. Anna held her breath. Both she and Willburgh scanned the surroundings to see if Lucius would appear or if anyone would try to stop them, but their passing the border was uneventful.

Willburgh turned to Anna at that moment. 'We've made it to Scotland.'

She could not tell if he were pleased or disappointed.

'Willburgh, this is what we must do, is it not? We have no choice, do we?'

He looked deeply into her eyes. 'We have no good choices. This is what we decided was the best of them.'

She held his gaze. 'I am sorry it has come to this.'

Will glanced away.

Was he sorry? When he woke that morning and watched her buttoning her dress and looking at her image in the mirror, he'd been aroused by the intimacy of the sight and the situation. She was lovely and he wanted nothing more in that moment than to remove that dress and take her back to bed. As the coach rumbled on, though, the old feelings of resentment and frustration crept back in. He was not marrying by choice. He was marrying the enemy.

By noon they entered Langholm, the destination they'd chosen. Most of its buildings were built of a grey stone that lent the town a dismal, depressing air. What's more, the sky was also grey and the air heavy with signs that rain was imminent.

How fitting that rain should have forced them together both now and at Vauxhall.

When they pulled into the Crown Inn, fat droplets started to fall. John went off to sort the post-chaise and the luggage, Will and Anna dodged raindrops to dash into the inn.

And found nobody.

Will paced the hall, waiting for the innkeeper to appear, to no avail. This was exasperating. 'Where is the innkeeper?'

Laughter sounded from another room. Will followed it with Anna right behind him.

They entered the tavern where a half dozen men were drinking, three seated and two leaning against a bar behind which one was wiping a glass. Every single one of them turned their heads to look at them.

The man behind the bar gestured for them to approach. 'Well, now, I dinna hear you enter the inn. I'm the innkeeper. You'll want a room, I expect.'

'We do.' Will wasted no time. 'We also want to be married—'

Collective laughter responded to that.

'Do y' now.' The innkeeper thrust out his hand for Will to shake. 'Name's Armstrong. There are plenty of us Armstrongs about, so they call me Armstrong of the Crown.' The man laughed as if he'd said something funny.

'A pleasure, Mr Armstrong,' Will accepted the handshake. It would have been an impudence for Armstrong to presume such familiarity of a viscount, but the man could not know Will was a viscount. That had been the whole point of their disguises. 'Can you please tell us where we might find someone to marry us?' Will's patience was wearing thin. Better to get this over with as soon as possible.

The man came out from behind the bar, with a bottle and two glasses. 'Come sit and have a drink and I might tell you.'

This was annoying, but so the Scots could be to Englishmen. Will pulled out a chair for Anna to sit. He sat next to her. Chairs scraped as everyone turned to face them.

Was an Englishman such a novelty? In a border town?

Armstrong poured them each a glass. 'Have a whisky.' He waited for them each to take a sip. 'Now, for a guinea each for my friends here and me, I'll tell you what you want to know.'

Will had been told to expect to show his coin to anyone even peripherally involved in a Scottish wedding. He reached in his pocket and paid the outrageous amount.

'Who is it who is after being married?' the innkeeper asked.

'We are.' Will gritted his teeth.

Armstrong rolled his eyes. 'I meant your names, lad.'

All Will wanted was directions to where to find someone to marry them, but he felt he had no choice but to play along.

'I am Neal Willburgh.' He gestured to Anna. 'This is Anna Dorman.'

Anna spoke up then. 'Anna Edgerton. I am Anna Edgerton.'

Will gaped. This was the first he had heard of this. 'Not Anna Dorman?'

'No.'

The innkeeper quipped. 'Have the two of you met, by any chance?'

The room broke out in laughter.

She wasn't a Dorman? Not a real Dorman? Something loosened inside Will, like a knot untwisting.

The innkeeper went on. 'And I gather the two of you are of age.'

'I am twenty,' Anna said.

'Twenty-eight,' Will added, pointing to himself.

Armstrong grinned. 'And you truly want to be married?'

One of the men seated at the other table shouted, 'Heed what you are doing, lad! Before it is too late!'

The others laughed.

The innkeeper chuckled, but turned to Anna. 'Miss, do you truly want this man to be your husband?' He spoke as if it was a poor idea indeed.

'Yes,' said Anna.

Will's patience was lost. 'Perhaps you could merely tell us where we might find someone to marry us?'

The innkeeper held up a hand. 'Do you truly want her as a wife?'

'Do not do it!' another patron called out.

'Yes, I want to marry her,' he snapped.

'And nobody's forcing you?' the man asked.

Anna looked as if she was suppressing a smile. 'No one.'

Will was less amused. 'Of course no one is forcing us. Can you direct me to the proper person—'

The other men snickered.

'First I must fetch a piece of paper.' The man disappeared behind the bar again.

To bring them directions, Will hoped.

When Armstrong returned he placed the paper on the table along with an ink pot and pen. 'Fill this in, my lad and lassie. As soon as I sign, and two of these witnesses sign, you are married!'

The room broke out in guffaws and the innkeeper filled everyone's glass from the bottle. 'Let's drink to their health!'

Will glanced at Anna whose eyes were sparkling. 'You guessed.'

'Not at first.' She smiled.

Will dipped the pen in the ink pot and filled in his name. He handed it to Anna.

'We do not fuss about in Scotland,' Armstrong explained. 'All you need is to be of age and to declare you want to be married of your own free will. Simple, eh, lad?'

Will managed a smile. 'Simple indeed.' He downed his glass of whisky and the innkeeper poured him another.

All the signatures were completed and the paper returned to Will. He folded it and placed it in his pocket. He was not certain if what he felt was relief or bewilderment. He downed the second glass of whisky.

'I'll record it in my ledger, as well,' Armstrong said.

The other men came up and clapped him on the back, giving him various warnings about married life.

'Do as she says, whatever she says,' one man told him. 'Won't never go wrong.'

The others groaned at that one.

They were more gallant towards Anna, bowing to her or kissing her hand, all of which she accepted with good humour.

John entered the tavern, looking stunned at the revelry. 'I've brought your bags, sir.'

Will managed a smile. 'Congratulate us, John,' he said. 'We are married.'

Anna smiled through the impromptu celebration. The Scots in the tavern seemed very ready to be joyous and their merriment was infectious. The whisky helped as well, its warmth spreading through her chest and making her mellow.

She was glad it was done, the marriage. No more uncertainty. The die was cast. She was even happier at her impulsive reclaiming of her name. Her real name; the name given at birth.

She'd used the Dorman name since a baby, her mother had explained. Now, after how the Dormans had treated her, she was glad to claim another, even for only a few minutes.

Because now she would ever be a Willburgh, the name she'd once learned to hate. Armstrong poured her another drink. The lovely whisky floated all her tension away, all the tension of the last ten days when her life again changed for ever. She watched the Scotsmen tease Willburgh about being a married man and about not knowing her name. It made her laugh.

The innkeeper wagged his eyebrows. 'I ken it is time to show you to your room.'

The other men hooted.

Anna finished her third glass of whisky and stood. And swayed. 'Oh. Goodness,' she said. 'I felt dizzy for a moment.'

The innkeeper pushed Willburgh towards her and he put his arm around her to steady her.

'Follow me,' the man ordered. He turned to John who had also consumed a glass or two. 'Bring the bags.'

'Yessir. They're in the hall.' John walked ahead of them.

In the hall, Armstrong had Willburgh sign the register. 'Be sure to write Mr and Mrs Willburgh,' he bantered.

When they started up the stairs, the man looked over his shoulder. 'I'll be giving you the best room in the inn.'

Anna's legs felt like jelly. She held on fast to Willburgh's arm. Behind her John tripped on a step and dropped their portmanteaux.

'Pardon,' he said.

The room was tucked away at the far end of a hallway. Armstrong opened the door with a key and they entered. Anna noticed a large bed with four carved posts and an intricately carved headboard. It was made of the same dark wood that panelled the tavern. There was also a dressing table and other tables and chairs.

Armstrong lit a fire in the fireplace and took John by his collar and pushed him out of the room, closing the door behind the two of them.

'I think you had better sit.' Willburgh guided her, not to a chair but to the bed. He sat her on the edge. He unlaced her half boots. 'Your shoes are still wet.'

And it still rained. She could hear the rain patter against the window.

'It was a funny wedding, was it not?' Her head felt so light. In fact her whole body felt as if it might easily float to the ceiling.

'If we are married, perhaps you should call me Will.'

Anna took his head in her hands and lifted his face, looking into his eyes. How had she never noticed his eyes were a piercing blue?

'We are married, Will.' She blinked. Gazing at him left her feeling giddy inside. And wary. Was he happy about being married to her?

Of course he was not.

# *Chapter Eight*

$\sim\!\!\!\sim\!\!\!\sim\!\!\!\sim$

Will was drawn closer to her, closer to tasting her lips, but she pulled her hands away as if she'd touched a hot poker.

As the innkeeper had led them up to the room, Will's excitement grew. He knew what Armstrong and his friends teased him about. They expected him to consummate this marriage. Post haste.

And he wanted to consummate this marriage. He was on fire to do so. The whisky had stripped away all his resolve. His mind could not keep hold of family enemies and duels and death. All he could think of was how she felt in his arms at night and how that delight promised greater delights. Now that he could bed her. Should bed her. Wanted to bed her.

He'd drunk too much and so had she.

He slipped off her half boots and stood.

'I know what is supposed to happen between a husband and wife,' she said, slurring her words. 'And I know you do not want to do it. You did not want to marry me, but you had to and you are angry at me. You do not like me. *Sins of my father* and all that.' Her upset was building with each word.

He sat beside her and turned her to face him. 'You, Anna, have had too much whisky.'

She lifted her chin. 'I've only had three.'

He nodded. 'Three.' That was sufficient for her good sense

to fail her. 'And I have had a great deal more than that. I know precisely what we should do.'

'What?' She sounded combative.

He took off his coat and waistcoat and pulled off his boots. 'We should rest.'

She blinked at him. 'In bed?'

'In bed.'

A grin grew on her face. She tried to unbutton her dress, but could not manage it. Will was not certain he could either, but he managed the first one, then the next. Excitement grew inside him. Arousal.

He undid all her buttons and pulled the dress over her head.

She turned her back on him. 'Unlace me,' she murmured.

He managed to untie her laces and she slipped out of her corset. He recalled how she felt wearing only her shift and he yearned to rid himself of that flimsy barrier, to throw off his shirt and feel her naked skin against his.

But he wouldn't. Instead he lay her down in the bed and moved next to her, to hold her like he'd done the past two nights.

With a sigh she settled against him. And fell asleep.

When Will woke the room was dark except for the glow of the coals in the fireplace. They'd slept until night apparently, the whisky and the several days of acute stress knocking them out. The day before was a blur, but he remembered one thing. They were married.

They'd thwarted Lucius's efforts to stop them and they were married. They'd achieved that goal. Never mind that it was a goal neither of them wanted; it was still a goal achieved. He was glad of that.

He tried to recall the wedding ceremony, but it was a

jumble, possibly because he had not known it was happening until it was all done.

She'd caught on much before him. She was clever. Uncomplaining.

And not a Dorman.

Will laughed at himself for being glad of that.

He rose from the bed and poured some water to rinse the foul taste from his mouth. Another gift from the whisky, along with his foggy mind. He turned to look for a lamp or a candle to light before he crashed into something and woke her. Lord, he was hungry. They had not eaten since breakfast. Perhaps there was a lamp on a table.

There was a table right inside the door, in a particularly dark corner. He gingerly felt his way to it, hoping he would not topple a chair or something in its path. He groped the surface of the table. His fingers touched a candlestick. Excellent. He groped his way to the fireplace and rubbed his hand on the mantle. A taper, as he expected. Will lit the taper from the one glowing coal in the fireplace and touched it to the candle, blinking as the flame came to life.

He could now see the room better. To his relief, the candle illuminated a plate of bread and cheese and a teapot on the table by the door. He placed the candle on the table and helped himself to a piece of hearty oat bread and a generous slice of Caboc cheese.

He poured a cup of tea and gulped it down, not bothering with milk or sugar. The tea was tepid. Will did not care. He poured himself another cup and drank it, as well.

The refreshments had not been there when they first entered the room, Will would swear. That meant Armstrong or someone else must have come into the room while they were sleeping. That was distressing. Someone had entered and he did not wake.

What if it had been Lucius?

Lucius was no longer a threat, though. Will and Anna were married.

Will helped himself to more bread and cheese and washed it down with a third cup of tepid tea.

Anna stirred and Will turned towards her, just able to make out her face.

Her eyes opened. 'Willburgh?'

'Will,' he corrected. Who else did she expect?

'Will,' she repeated. 'I could not see you in the dark. What time is it?'

'I am not certain.' There wasn't a clock in the room, not that he'd found at least. 'Middle of the night.'

She sat up and groaned. 'My head aches.'

Why did he feel disquieted around her suddenly? Why sound so churlish?

He tried to soften his voice. 'That's the whisky.'

She pressed her fingers against her temple. 'How much did I have?'

'Plenty.' He'd lost track of how many times his glass was filled. 'You said three, I believe.'

She sighed. 'I don't remember that. I don't remember coming up to this room. Did we miss dinner?'

'We did,' he responded. 'Are you hungry? There is bread and cheese and tea.'

She groped around until finding her shawl. She wrapped it around her and walked over to him.

He pulled out a chair for her. 'Have a seat and I will cut you some.'

'Some tea first please.' She sat in the chair. 'My mouth is so dry.'

He poured her tea and handed it to her. 'It is no longer hot.'

'I do not care.' She drank it as quickly as he had done.

He cut her a piece of bread and a slice of cheese and sat across from her. She ate as eagerly as he had.

She took a sip of her second cup of tea and lifted her gaze to his. The candlelight softened her face. She looked vulnerable. And alluring.

'Did—did we—?' she asked.

He knew what she meant. 'No. We didn't.'

She glanced away. 'I—I want you to know that I will understand if you do not want to. I—I know you did not want this marriage. I know you may not want to bed me.'

Will's first impulse was to snap back at her and accuse *her* of not wanting to bed *him*, but she looked so forlorn, he pushed that impulse away, remembering her growing distress the day before, saying that he did not like her and that he blamed her for her father's actions. He did like her—or was growing to.

He lowered his voice. 'We are man and wife. To think of what we wanted before is useless now. I expect us to have—marital relations.'

She faced him again.

He went on. 'We—we do not have to—to consummate our marriage tonight, though. I make you a promise that I will not touch you until you are ready.'

She peered at him. 'I cannot tell if your words mean you want to or you do not want to, because I certainly do not wish it if it is abhorrent to you.'

He met her eye. 'It is not abhorrent to me.' Good God, his body was already humming with desire for her.

She glanced away again. 'I—I am not sure if it is abhorrent to me.'

Who might have discussed such matters with her? Young women might have such instruction right before their wedding day. No one would have had that conversation with her, though.

'What do you know of it?' he asked.

She gave a wan smile. 'Cautionary tales from the governess. Titillating tales from some of the maids. I know what happens.' Her brows knitted. 'I believe it must give pleasure, otherwise would men seek it out so; would women engage in affairs?'

That was an intelligent deduction. 'I will do my best to give you pleasure, Anna.' He meant that. 'Whenever you wish to try.'

She inhaled a deep breath. 'Tonight? Best not to wait, I think.'

Will stood and extended his hand.

Anna put her hand in his and let him lead her to the bed.

Her knees trembled. She was afraid, yes, but it was a fear she was eager to face, much like when she was young and afraid to ride horses but wanted to more than anything. Of course, riding a horse was exhilarating, something that gave her great pleasure. Could she trust that the marital act brought pleasure? Having heard a description of what happens between the man and the woman, and having seen animals copulate, she could not imagine pleasure from it. Perhaps it would merely be gratification from conquering the fear.

When they neared the bed, he swooped her into his arms and gently placed her on it. Anna felt giddy. It was so unexpected. So playful.

She'd not imagined that Willburgh could be playful. She sat on the edge of the bed and watched while, in the same playful spirit, he removed his trousers. Only his drawers remained. She was used to seeing his drawers. He'd kept them on when they'd shared a bed.

She smiled. 'Did you fall sleep in your trousers?'

'I must have.' He took off his drawers, as well.

Now he wore only his shirt, but it covered his body nearly to his knees.

He undid the ribbon at the collar, but paused and his expression sobered. 'We may do this clothed or not. What do you prefer?'

She hardly knew. Except, once she'd learned to properly mount a horse, she'd wanted to gallop.

'Unclothed,' she said.

He crossed his arms and grasped the hem of his shirt. In one fluid motion, he lifted the shirt over his head. He was naked.

Anna could not take her eyes off him.

'Have you seen a man unclothed before?' He tossed the shirt aside.

'I've seen statues.' But statues did not prepare her for this male physique.

He was broad-shouldered with rippling muscles all the way to his waist, like a statue of Hercules she'd once seen in Lord Lansdowne's house. His waist was narrower, though, and his skin was spattered with hair and glowed in the dim light in a way cold marble could never do.

Would she ever tell him that he compared favourably with Hercules? She doubted it, but it made her smile.

Standing naked in front of her, he twirled a finger in her direction. 'And your clothes?'

Her breath came faster. She wore only her shift.

'I'll take it off for you, if you like,' he murmured.

She'd never heard his voice sound like that. Like a purring cat. It added to the thrill.

'Very well,' she managed.

He came closer and took the thin fabric in his hands, easing it up her legs. As his hands came close to her female parts, her body seemed to throb. She wriggled, freeing the garment from beneath her. He'd moved slowly before, but now pulled the shift over her head as swiftly as he'd removed his shirt.

His gaze swept up and down her body, his blue eyes darkening.

The modiste that dressed Lady Dorman and Violet and altered their castaways for her always complained that her breasts were not large enough to fill a dress properly and that she was too tall. She was not round and luscious like Violet.

'I am a disappointment, I know.' She scooted onto the bed and covered herself with the bed linens.

He peeled them away. 'Not a disappointment at all.'

He was being kind.

He climbed in the bed next to her and she rolled on her side to face him.

Her nervousness returned and she could hardly get a breath to speak. 'How do we start, then?'

How was he to start? Will wondered. How was a man to give a woman her first experience of the marital act, especially when she'd been forced to marry?

It had been a long time since he'd lain with a woman, but the lack had not overly bothered him. There always seemed to be too much to do and too much required of him to pursue any amorous adventures like his old schoolmates were fond of doing, the friends who'd convinced him to go to Vauxhall Gardens that night.

That lifetime ago.

His head might not have felt the lack of female company,

but his body certainly did. He'd kept it in check the three nights he'd shared a bed with Anna.

But just barely.

Now, with barriers gone and expectations high, his body wanted nothing more than to surge on, the fastest and hardest that he could go.

But he would not do that to Anna.

Their truce was fragile. The trip to Scotland had given them time to become acquainted with each other. She proved herself more intelligent, more resourceful and more forbearing than he ever would have imagined. And she seemed as willing as he to see if they could make something good out of this forced marriage.

He could ruin that by rutting like some bull in a field of cows.

Which was precisely what his body wanted to do.

Will began carefully by touching her cheek. She tensed, but he simply stroked her skin with the back of his hand. She relaxed. He put his hand on the back of her head and lowered his lips to hers.

*Gentle kiss*, he told himself. *Barely touch her.*

When he moved away, she sighed.

'I'm going to touch you,' he said. 'I'll tell you what I'm going to do before I do it.'

She nodded.

'You can tell me to stop any time.'

She nodded again.

He stroked her cheek again and her neck and slid his hands down her arms.

'Now your breasts.' He started by stroking the skin above her breasts.

'They are too small, I'm told.' Her voice was forlorn.

He guided her face so she would have to look him in the

eye. 'Your breasts are lovely.' He covered one with his hand. 'See? They fit perfectly.'

She laughed. 'Now you are making sport of me.'

He made her look at him again. 'No, I am not.'

He caressed her breasts again, but instead of relaxing her, her back arched and eager sounds escaped her mouth.

Could she be aroused?

'A kiss,' he murmured and placed his lips on her nipple, then dared to taste it with his tongue.

She writhed in response, but she did not say no.

He continued caressing her, running his fingers down her abdomen, sweeping his fingers down her legs. The force of his arousal intensified, becoming more and more painful and demanding by the moment. He could not wait much longer.

'I must prepare you now,' he told her. 'If you feel you are ready—'

'For goodness' sake, Willburgh,' she rasped.

'Will,' he corrected.

'Will,' she repeated. 'I am not made of glass. Gallop already.'

He eased up enough to look at her. 'Gallop?'

'I meant I am ready.' She pulled him down.

That was all the permission he needed. He moved atop her and she opened her legs and arched her back. He knew she was unschooled in this; her body must be doing its own demanding. His body urged him to thrust into her, but he had enough restraint to go slow. When his male member touched her, she flinched, but immediately rose to him.

'This—this might cause you pain,' he managed.

'I assure you, I will deal with it,' she responded.

*As you wish*, he thought. He wanted to give her pleasure this first time—or at least not cause her too much pain. He eased himself in slowly.

She gasped and tensed around him. He moved slowly at first, creating a rhythm that she quickly matched. They moved faster and faster together.

Galloping, he thought, right before crossing the border between reason and desire.

Anna had not thought it would be like this. She had not imagined the want, the need, that propelled her forward, to ride with him as far and as fast as he could take her. Into some unknown place that she suddenly was desperate to discover.

His kiss had surprised her with its gentleness. His touch had soothed and excited her. His consideration of her, though, unsettled her. When, since her papa had died, had another person been concerned about how she would feel?

The only sound in the room was the clapping of their bodies coming together and their gasping breaths. His thrusts came faster and with more force, but that only intensified the need inside her. That first stab of pain quickly became inconsequential in light of the ride he was taking her on. She did not know the destination, where want and need would be fulfilled.

But she wanted to get there as rapidly as possible.

When her pleasure burst, she cried out. She had not expected this.

His came right after. He tensed and trembled inside her. Spilling his seed? It must be.

The next moment he collapsed on top of her and rolled off to lie beside her, panting.

'So that was all?' she said, as if disappointed.

'What do you mean, "that was all?"' he shot back, rising enough to glare at her.

Anna laughed. 'I am jesting with you. It was really quite—' How to describe it? 'Quite nice.'

He lay back again. 'Nice. That is damning with faint praise.'

'Indeed it is not,' she countered. 'If so, I would be implying it had fault.' She turned to face him. 'And it really was quite perfect.'

Her gaze captured his and held, perhaps saying more than words could convey.

He closed the distance between them and touched his lips to hers again, as gently as he had done before, but not tentative.

Affirming.

He tucked an arm around her and pulled her against him. His skin was warm against hers and slightly damp. With her head against his chest she counted his heartbeats. And reprised every moment of the lovemaking in her mind. He'd been her enemy for so long, but now she could not imagine any other man touching her, kissing her, joining with her.

She pressed her lips to his skin. 'A fortnight ago would you have dreamed you would be here? With me?'

When he responded she felt the words rumble in his chest. 'I would have wagered a fortune against such an idea. I would have lost.'

She dared another question. 'Are you sorry about it?'

He laughed. 'Not at the moment.'

# *Chapter Nine*

The next morning Will woke when sunlight poured in the window. He glanced at Anna, still asleep, looking young and innocent and beautiful.

He'd bedded her. Twice. And had found it a profound experience, so why were his emotions in a jumble this morning?

He closed his eyes, but instead of sleep, visions of his father's duel with her father flew into his mind. He again saw them lifting their arms and firing, the smoke bursting from the barrels of both pistols. His father fell, his shirt turning red with his blood.

A mere fortnight ago, Will could go weeks without remembering—reliving—that scene. Since that night at Vauxhall he'd relived the memory nearly every day. Was he doomed to think of it every time he looked at her? He was married to her. Bound to her for the rest of their lives.

But he had not relived the memory the day before. Or the past night. That was a puzzle. From the moment he married her, in that manner so casual he almost missed it, he'd been caught up in revelry. Making love to her had been—he had no words to describe it. Only that he'd felt—whole. As if he did love her and wanted to marry her. As if they belonged together.

But her father killed his father.

The memory returned.

He rolled over in bed and sat up, too restless to remain there.

She woke up and stretched. 'Good morning,' she murmured and he remembered the delights of the night they shared together.

He remembered how good it felt to touch her, to teach her about lovemaking, to make it comfortable for her, to make certain to give her pleasure. Gazing at her and remembering, he wanted to repeat the experience.

But it was madness to care for her. To actually like her. To want her comfort and happiness. Her father killed his father.

But no. The day before she'd given a different name.

'Tell me something,' he said as he picked up his clothing from the floor. 'Tell me why you said your name was Edgerton.' His voice had an edge to it.

She covered herself with the bed linens. 'The man who fathered me was named Edgerton.'

'He was not Dorman?' He put on his drawers.

'No.' There was tension in her voice.

Because he was sounding churlish, no doubt. 'But you were called Dorman. Lucius's cousin.'

'It was the only name I knew.' She paused. 'Until my mother told me my real name. On her deathbed.'

Will knew her mother had died when Dorman and she came to stay with Lord and Lady Dorman.

Her expression turned pained. 'My mother told me about Edgerton. She'd been married to him before she married Bertram Dorman.'

He tried to mollify his tone. 'What happened to him?'

'He died,' she said. 'When I was a baby. He was a soldier in the East India Company army. He was killed at Seringapatam. In the battle.'

'In India?'

'In India.' Her voice was taut, as if her words were difficult to speak. 'That was where I was born and lived until my mother died.'

How little he knew of her. She'd been born in India? Lived there before coming to the Dormans? Of course, he'd been at Oxford at that time and had been totally absorbed in his own interests and desires.

'I called Dorman Papa,' she went on. 'He was the only father I knew. When my mother died, I was afraid, because I did not really belong to him. I dared not talk to him or to anyone about it. What if he would leave me as well?'

The Bertram Dorman Will knew of was reputed to gamble and drink to excess. Worse, he was a womaniser who loved to toy with a woman's affections, as he had done with Will's mother. Her fears had merit.

'A vile man,' Will muttered as he completed dressing.

She got out of bed and put on her shift and corset before speaking again. 'He was not a vile man,' she said with feeling. 'He was generous and fun and kind to me. It was a blow to learn he was not my father. A worse blow when he was killed. I will not hear ill spoken of him!'

Will would not hear him praised. 'He seduced my mother.'

'The Dormans said your mother seduced him!' she cried. 'I do not care. He was good to me and when he died I had no one.'

Will could not stop himself. 'You obviously had the Dormans.'

She turned her back to him, stepped into her dress, pulled it up, and buttoned it.

She faced him again. 'Eventually Lord and Lady Dorman decided I could stay, but after my—my papa—was killed, it was not a certainty. You might say I was *allowed* to live with the Dormans. They found many ways to let me know I was there only out of the goodness of their hearts.

The Dormans had always let Anna know she did not truly belong there, but lived with them at their whim. Did she belong anywhere, to anyone?

Last night, when Will so gently and daringly made love to her, she'd felt perhaps she'd found where she truly belonged. This morning, though, he became like the man with whom she'd been caught in the rain at Vauxhall. Disagreeable. Disdainful. Despising her.

She put on her stockings and sat at the dressing table to comb her hair into some semblance of order. She could hear him moving around behind her but she was hurt and angry and wished he would leave.

She plaited her hair, wound it into a chignon and covered it with a cap. Married women wore caps, did they not? Even if married to a disagreeable man.

He became so quiet that she wondered if he had left the room.

She jumped when he did speak, but his voice was still clipped.

'Forgive me,' he said. 'I spoke unkindly.'

She turned around to look at him and their eyes met. Her senses leapt at the sight of him. She could not help it. How was she to guard her emotions when the mere sight, sound, and scent of him affected her so?

Perhaps he apologised out of duty. He'd married her out of duty, had he not? Had he made love to her out of duty? No. No. That must have been real. It had to be real.

A knock at the door broke into her thoughts.

'Who is it?' he asked.

'The maid, sir.'

He glanced at Anna as if to ask if the maid should enter. She nodded.

'Come in,' he called through the door.

The maid looked no more than a girl. She wore a crisp, clean apron and a plain dress.

'My da—Mr Armstrong—sent me to tell you there are three gentlemen to see you.'

She was the innkeeper's daughter, then.

'Gentlemen?' Will frowned. 'What are their names?'

'I do not know, sir,' the maid replied. 'My da dinna tell me. They are *English*, though.' She spoke the word *English* as if it left a bad taste in her mouth.

'Is it Lucius, do you think?' A new worry. Anna shoved Willburgh's manner aside. Who else could it be? 'Or perhaps Toby or John?'

'Not Toby or John,' he replied, his brow knitted. 'They would not dress as gentlemen and there would not be three of them.' He turned back to the maid. 'Tell them I will come directly.'

'Yes, sir.' The maid curtsied. 'Da says they will be waiting in the tavern.' She left the room.

Anna's heart raced. 'It must be Lucius. And—and—what if the other one is—is *that man*.'

'The one who abducted you? Why do you think so?' he asked.

'I—I am just afraid that he is. The man spoke to Raskin before Raskin disappeared with Violet.'

'Raskin and Violet ran off together?' Willburgh's expression darkened. 'I will see what they want.'

'Wait.' She hurriedly put on her half boots. 'I will go with you.'

\* \* \*

Will thought it unwise for her to go. If it was Lucius and the others, they were likely up to nothing good. But after he'd acted so churlish towards her, he could not deny her wishes.

He did not like himself very much at the moment. She'd done nothing to deserve his ill manners. Her behaviour had been faultless this whole trip. She deserved better than him snapping at her.

He suspected it was not memories of his father's duel that made him pull away from her. He knew she was not at fault. God help him, though, he was petty enough to be glad she was not really a Dorman. The man who fathered *her* was not the man who killed his father. He could no longer use that as an excuse.

What was it, then? Was it that he'd told himself—and his mother when she pushed—that he was not ready for marriage. He needed to master being a viscount first and he was far from perfecting that role. It consumed him. He did not want to be like his father, so enveloped in other duties that he neglected a duty to a wife.

He opened the door for her and the two of them walked down to the tavern.

When they entered, Armstrong was behind the bar.

He broke into a grin at the sight of them and wagged his brows. 'Well, well, well. Mr and Mrs Willburgh, good morning to you.'

How pleasant it was to be greeted by a friendly face. 'Good morning, Armstrong. I hope you are well.'

'No' too poorly, thank you.' He winked at Anna. 'And you, Mrs Willburgh? How do you fare?'

Anna's cheeks turned pink, but she smiled at him. 'No' too poorly, sir.'

Armstrong laughed.

'I understand we have visitors,' Will said.

The innkeeper frowned. 'That lot. *English*, y'know.' He sounded just like his daughter.

'We are English, you realise,' Will reminded him.

'Aye,' Armstrong cocked his head. 'But there are English and then there are *English*.'

Will thought he could agree with that statement, although he'd been acting the disagreeable type to Anna.

'I put them in the private dining room,' Armstrong said. 'So they won't upset the guests.'

His hand swept the room, but only three men were seated at a table who might have been disturbed, the same three men who had been present at the wedding and celebration after.

They all lifted their glasses and Will gave them a friendly wave.

He turned back to Armstrong. 'Show us the way.'

Armstrong draped a towel over his shoulder and led them to the dining room door and opened it.

Will stepped in before Anna.

It was Lucius, Raskin, and another man seated at a table, tankards of ale in front of them. The third man, Will recognised as one of Lucius's old schoolmates. Millman. Millman was precisely the sort of degenerate who would force himself on a lady. Will clenched his fist, wanting nothing more than to plant it in Millman's face.

They looked up, but none of them stood.

'This is a surprise,' Will said, although he was not surprised. 'You are a long way from London. What are you doing here, Lucius?'

Lucius looked from Will to Anna. 'I see we are too late.' He looked daggers at Anna. 'We came to bring you home, Anna. Where you belong. But you have betrayed the family thoroughly, I see. With a Willburgh. You've had your Scottish wedding, I presume.'

'I have.' Anna lifted her chin. 'But you have it wrong, Lucius. I am where I belong now. It was you, your parents, and Violet who betrayed *me*.' She glared at Raskin. 'You and Violet left me alone at Vauxhall, so you are a part of it as well, Raskin.'

'Me?' Raskin put on an innocent face. 'I would never do such a thing.'

Millman leaned on the back two legs of his chair, smirking at everyone. Before Will knew it Anna walked around the table and yanked the back of his chair. The man fell sprawling to the floor with a loud crash.

*Well done, Anna,* Will said to himself.

He had to admit he liked that fire in her.

'That is for what *you* did,' Anna cried.

The man protested as he fumbled to his feet. 'I did nothing.'

She leaned into his face. 'I know what you did. What you tried to do.'

His face turned a guilty and angry red. He lifted his hand as if to strike her, but Will was there in a flash. He seized the man's arm and twisted it behind his back.

'See here!' Lucius protested.

Gripping the man closely, Will spoke into his ear. 'You stay out of my sight, Millman. And if I hear of you repeating with any woman what you tried to do to *my wife*, I'll be coming for you.'

Millman scurried out of the room.

'Not too hospitable of you,' Raskin drawled.

Will whirled on him. 'Do not get me started on you.'

'There you go, Willburgh,' Lucius piped up. 'Always throwing around your superiority. Here we've raced across the country, trying to save Anna from you, and this is how you treat us.'

'Your efforts would have been unnecessary if your father would have cooperated,' Will said. 'Or if any member of your family had had the decency to listen to her.'

'It was dear Anna who did not cooperate,' Lucius countered. 'Who would not listen. We were willing for her to come back to the family with all forgiven, but look how she thanked my parents for all those years of taking care of her. Marrying the enemy.'

Anna broke in. 'Do not speak of me as if I am not here.'

Lucius made a conciliatory wave of his hand.

Anna's eyes flashed and she pointed towards the door. 'You both left me with that worm. And then your parents abandoned me altogether. I want nothing to do with you.'

Lucius gave a slimy smile.

'This is a waste of our time,' Will said. 'Come to the point of why you wanted to speak to us. You could have guessed you were too late to stop us.'

'Oh, yes.' Raskin sneered. 'That delightful barbarian, Armstrong, told us.'

Lucius stood. 'You are right, Willburgh. Although I cannot believe I am saying that. This is a waste of time. I only wish I could be there when you both discover just how foolish this elopement was.' He glowered at Anna again. 'My dear, you will regret choosing a Willburgh.'

Raskin rose as well and gave them an exaggerated bow. With one final glare Lucius and Raskin left the room.

Anna lowered herself into a chair. Her knees were shaking with anger.

Willburgh leaned against the back of another chair. 'You were magnificent, by the way.'

She glanced at him.

Some of the anger inside her could be laid at his feet.

But he did defend her.

She took a breath. 'It was *him*, was it not? Millman?'

'Guilt was written all over him,' Willburgh responded. 'Lucius and Raskin knew his reputation. Everyone did. And yet they left you with him?'

'Lucius had left already, before Raskin came with—with *him*.' She pressed her fingers into the table. 'After Violet and Raskin disappeared, he approached and offered to escort me back to my aunt and uncle. Well, you know what happened after that.'

Willburgh blew out a breath. 'I hope we are rid of them for good.' He pushed himself away from the chair and walked to the window.

It seemed he stood there a long time, before he turned back to her. His expression had softened. 'Shall I arrange breakfast?'

Any appetite she'd possessed had been swallowed up with emotion—starting with her waking to a colder Willburgh. 'If you so wish.'

'I do wish. I am famished.' His brows rose. 'Are you not hungry?'

She shrugged.

'We should eat. I'll let Armstrong know.' He left the room.

When the door closed, she moved the tankards of ale to a sideboard. She did not want to think of whose hands and lips had touched them. She opened a window as if to release the room of their every essence.

The air was crisp and clean and a breeze did its job of scouring out old smells. The sky was a vivid blue, a beautiful day so in contrast with her mood.

What had Lucius meant when he said she and Willburgh

would discover what a mistake this elopement was? Had Willburgh already discovered the mistake?

Willburgh returned with two generously large bowls of porridge. He ate greedily, precisely how you'd expect a famished man to eat. Anna forced herself to eat a spoonful or two, and it sparked her hunger. She finished the whole bowl and looked up at him, waiting for him to make some scathing remark.

Instead, he asked, 'Do you wish to travel back today?'

Be trapped in a post-chaise with him?

Her answer must have shown on her face, because he quickly answered his own question. 'No travel today, then.'

She felt her cheeks flush. She'd thought she was more skilled at hiding her thoughts. 'Did you wish to start back?' she asked.

He held up a hand. 'Believe me, I have no need to be cooped up in a small carriage if it is not absolutely necessary.'

So he did not want to be trapped with her either. Yes. Their lovemaking must have been a fluke.

She rose and walked over to the window.

He joined her. 'What would you wish to do if you could do anything?'

Her mind went blank. Who'd ever asked her such a question since her papa died?

She flung it back to him. 'What would you do?'

He stared out the window for a moment before speaking, 'It is a fine day for riding.'

She gaped at him. Again her face betrayed her.

He smiled. 'Ah. You agree with me.'

She turned away. 'It is impossible. We have no horses. No saddles. I have no riding habit or proper boots or a proper hat.'

He cocked his head. 'We are in a large enough town. What

did I hear Armstrong call it? *Muckle Toon*. Such problems might be easily remedied in a town of this size.'

She peered at him. 'I do not understand what you mean.'

'Anna.' He met her gaze. 'I have the funds. We merely purchase what we need.'

Willburgh was true to his word. He purchased everything they needed.

A visit to a bank provided the funds. Mr Armstrong directed them to where they could find what they needed. Armstrong even knew a horse breeder with stock to sell.

Willburgh purchased *three* horses. *Three*, when he probably had a stable full of horses on his estate.

Anna found it difficult to fathom.

It took the rest of the day and visits to several establishments to accomplish everything else. Anna was able to see much of Langholm and to assist in each aspect. Goodness! Willburgh even sought her counsel on selecting the horses. She picked the horse she would ride. Imagine. Before this she'd ridden whatever steed Violet or Lucius did not want to ride.

Anna selected a lovely and very sweet grey Highland pony she named Seraphina. Willburgh chose a brown pony for John and a bay dun for himself. Anna named his pony as well as John's. She could not resist naming Will's Armstrong and John's Crown, after Armstrong's inn. Amazingly, they had no difficulty finding saddles that fit them, a riding habit that fit her well enough, and boots, hats, and gloves.

As they left the last shop, Willburgh said, 'I was thinking. Since we purchased the horses, we might as well ride them as far as we are able. Would you agree? We could ride them all the way to London if we so desired.'

She stared at him, astonished. Not to be jostled in a post-chaise with no room to move? Instead to be on horseback in the fresh air? Every day?

Again her face must have shown her thoughts.

He smiled. 'There it is, then. We ride all the way to London if we like.'

'Is it what you desire?' she asked.

He was confusing her again. Why would he go to such lengths merely to please her? He had turned kind and generous again. Like the night before. Why would he do so, when he woke so unhappy with her?

It must be that this was what *he* wished to do. She just happened to desire it, as well. That would make sense.

The day, really, in spite of how it started, had been a joy.

They ate dinner in the tavern and all the men who had been there the day before, the ones who witnessed their wedding, were gathered there again. It felt like they were among old friends.

And then the day was over.

And they were faced with going to bed.

# *Chapter Ten*

$\mathcal{O}\!\!\!\!\!\sim\!\!\!\!\!\mathcal{O}$

$W$hen they readied for bed, the air was filled with tension, such a contrast to how the day had been after they'd rid themselves of Lucius and his cohorts.

Will could not remember when he'd last had such an enjoyable day not spoiled by some burdensome task or another hanging over his head. How could he feel guilty for giving himself over to the pleasure of the moment, when she'd been giddy with excitement when choosing her horse?

'A horse of my own!' she'd cried. 'I've never had anything so grand!'

His chest had burst with joy at her words.

And why should he not feel joyful? Purchasing whatever they wanted—whatever *she* wanted—had been a delight, even more of a delight, perhaps, than their passion-filled night before. Will did not want these feelings to end.

Now that they were back in the room in the inn, though, it was as if all his disagreeableness of the morning had returned.

Will wanted the joy back.

Anna climbed into bed much as she'd done when they stayed at the other inns and he'd promised not to touch her. Will joined her. He moved close to her, spooning her in front of him. But her body did not quite melt under his touch as it had the night before. She felt distant even though she was in his arms.

He gathered his courage and whispered in her ear, 'I want to make love with you again. Will you permit it?'

He felt her muscles tense, but she said, 'If you wish it.'

'I do wish,' he replied with feeling. 'But only if you wish it, too.'

She needed to share in the pleasure, like when they'd purchased the horse, or it meant nothing.

It seemed a long time before she answered. 'I wish it.'

He removed his drawers and threw them aside. She sat up and he lifted her shift over her head. One candle was still burning, bathing her lovely skin in a soft glow. His need for her flared, but he touched her carefully, relishing in the silkiness and warmth of her skin.

She was not indifferent to his touch, stirring beneath his fingers. He leaned forward and placed his lips against hers, hoping he could erase the words with which his lips had wounded her. She softened.

They lay down then, but he contented himself with the pleasure of stroking her skin. What harm to give himself to this pleasure? To give her this pleasure as well? They had no difficulties to face, no plans that needed to be made, and none of his duties back home could press him here. Was this not what he'd once lost? To simply enjoy himself?

His body's needs grew stronger and her response urged him on. He rose above her and entered her with ease. Her body was ready and it felt like a welcome, like forgiveness. All Will could think at the moment was that he loved her and was glad he was married to her.

In the next moment his primitive urges drove all thought and emotion from his mind. He moved faster and faster and she met him, stroke for stroke. Together they came to the brink of pleasure and carried each other over it. He felt her release burst and his followed. He slid off her and held her in his arms. They did not speak. Eventually her breathing became even. She was asleep.

Sleep came later for him as he savoured the joy for as long as he could.


They rose early in the morning and dressed for riding. While they ate breakfast John saw to the horses. Their portmanteaux had been exchanged for saddlebags, now all packed and ready to go.

Mr Armstrong insisted on wrapping up bread and cheese— and three bottles of cider—for their trip. He and his daughter and the tavern regulars were there to wave them off as if they were old and dear friends.

Will helped Anna onto her horse, but turned to shake Armstrong's hand before mounting his own.

'Thank you, Armstrong.' He handed the man his card. 'If I may ever be of service to you or your family, write to me.'

Armstrong glanced at the card. 'I'll be a—you are a lord?' He turned to his friends. 'The lad's a lord!'

'G'wan!' they cried.

Will clapped him on the shoulder. 'Do not hold it against me.'

Armstrong shook his head in disbelief. 'First one I met who wasn't *English*.'

Will laughed. 'I am English but, from you, I will take that as a compliment.'

Armstrong turned to Anna. 'So you are a lady, then, lass?'

Anna smiled graciously. 'Ever since you married us, sir.'

Armstrong waved his arms. 'Be off with ye before I charge you an extra guinea or two for the room.' Will had already paid him generously.

They said their final goodbyes and were on the road.

As the inn receded in their sight, Anna said, 'I believe I will miss them.'

Will thought she said this more to herself than to him but he responded, 'As will I. They were decent people, the lot of them.'

It was another fine, clear day, not too hot for June. A perfect day for a ride and Will was determined to enjoy it.

John rode a few feet behind Will and Anna. Will rode next to her, but they did not talk much.

It was difficult to endure her distant silence, especially since he wanted her to share in the freedom from all responsibility that he felt. On this ride back to London, they could take all the time they wished. They could indulge every whim without any care. He'd be patient with her. He could not expect Anna to trust he would not turn churlish again merely because he felt the opposite.

He was determined to be amiable, though.

'You ride well,' he said as they left the town and entered the countryside.

She turned to him and he was gratified to see her smile. 'I enjoy it.'

He smiled, as well. 'Then I am glad we are making this trip on horseback.' He wanted to keep the conversation going. 'We should make it to Carlisle by noon, I should think.'

Their first destination was Carlisle, to find Toby.

She merely nodded.

Once out of the town they rode past fields rich with crops and green pastures dotted with sheep or cattle. Stone fences or thick hedgerows crisscrossed the lands. Will wondered how many of the barriers were a result of the Clearances, where large landowners took over the land, driving off the tenants whose animals had grazed over the pastures for generations.

Another topic Will met with ambivalence. He also was a landowner who needed to increase the productivity of his farms, but he could not help feeling more was owed to the common people who were displaced.

There was nothing he could do about it at the moment, though. He filed such thoughts away for a later date and merely relished how beautiful was the land.

Anna took in a deep breath of the crisp countryside air. Coils of tension deep inside her since Vauxhall Gardens loosened a bit. The scenery itself was calming. To be riding, even at this sedate pace was a joy. She was already in love with her pony, who seemed completely at ease.

She glanced at the man riding beside her, so tall and comfortable in the saddle. She smiled to herself. He looked too big for his Highland pony although the animal seemed perfectly content to be carrying him on its back.

She thought of the night before. His lovemaking had been as gentle and kind as the first time, and she'd given in to the pleasure of it. He'd been exceptionally kind the whole of this trip, but in a sudden instant he'd turned back into the enemy—antagonistic, disagreeable, churlish—much like he'd been when they first removed their masks at Vauxhall Gardens. She did not know what to trust. The kind man or the ill-natured one?

At least riding her lovely pony amidst the beauty of the countryside and breathing the fresh country air mollified her emotions. She could forget for long stretches of time that he might not be the strong, handsome, loving man that first night of lovemaking—and the one following—promised him to be.

Whatever he was, though, the die was cast and she must lie in the bed she'd made for herself. Or what had been made for her.

They reached Carlisle when the sun was high in the sky. Noon or near to it, and they found Toby at the Bush Inn where they had left him. With him were John's brother and his wife, Lottie.

Willburgh requested a private dining room and they gathered there as equals for refreshment and to trade tales of their separate experiences.

'You should have seen when the gentlemen discovered us was us,' John's brother, Adams, said. 'The one was hopping mad.' He grimaced. 'They thought they could get the better of me, but I was bigger and stronger.'

Anna gasped. 'Did they fight you? Did you get hurt?' She had not wanted anyone to come to harm because of her.

John's brother grinned. 'No, ma'am. They did some pushing and shoving, but I put a stop to that right off.'

His wife gave him a proud look.

'I am so very grateful to both of you,' Anna said.

The brother's wife waved her words away, then said, 'I have your dresses packed for you.'

Anna touched the young woman's arm. 'I would like for you to have them, Lottie.' They had come from the Dormans and Anna did not want them anyway.

Her eyes brightened. 'Thank you, ma'am.'

Their meal was leisurely and pleasant, but as it went on, Willburgh asked Adams, 'Are we keeping you from your work?'

The young man shrugged. 'The stable let me go. But you paid me plenty. We'll be all right and something will come up.'

Willburgh looked towards Toby. 'We should have something at Willburgh House, do you not think?'

Toby nodded. 'Looks to me like you have three more horses need tending to. An extra hand will be welcome.'

'And there is always need for an extra pair of hands in the house.' He glanced at Lottie. 'If you like. It means leaving your home, though.'

'This isn't our home, sir,' John said. 'We came for the work.'

'We'll gladly work for you, m'lord,' his brother said.

While they discussed arrangements, Anna watched Willburgh. Here was another surprise. Such a generous offer. He hadn't been required to make it; he'd paid them well, after all. He offered them security.

When the horses were rested and their repast over, she and Will returned to the road. Toby, Adams, and his wife were to travel by coach directly to Buckinghamshire where Willburgh's country estate was located. Anna knew the house and property, of course. She'd glimpsed it many times while riding with Violet and Lucius. It was grander than Dorman Hall, the Dormans' country house. The Dormans' property abutted Willburgh's at that parcel of wooded land to which each claimed ownership. Part of the feud between the families.

When she and Will left Carlisle behind and were back in the open countryside, Will had ridden ahead. Anna urged her horse to catch up to him.

'Willburgh?' she called.

He turned around and waited for her. Her horse came to Willburgh's side.

He smiled—a bit sadly, she thought. 'It's Will,' he said.

She felt guilty for deliberately not calling him by his preferred name. 'Will,' she repeated. 'I wanted to say—' She didn't know how to say it. 'I wanted to say that it was good of you to hire John and his brother and wife.'

His smile brightened. 'A mere trifle.'

She remained next to him, while John rode behind. She made an effort to talk to him, to comment on the sites they passed or the other travellers on the road. They avoided the busy routes with their wagons of goods and speeding coaches. They were no longer dependent upon coaching inns and post horses and could stop and rest their horses at any village inn they wished. They rode the smaller roads and were often the only ones in sight. It was quiet and peaceful and her coils of tension loosened even more.

They stopped at one such village inn to spend the night, registering as Mr and Mrs Willburgh. Their room was small and Anna's legs were aching from the day in the saddle. The bed, though, was comfortable enough to make love. After Anna again experienced that exquisite burst of pleasure, she relaxed in Will's arms. The wall she'd constructed over her heart cracked a little. Anna fell asleep as the crack allowed a glimmer of hope to seep into her heart.

The next day Anna's heart opened a little more, each time Will treated her or someone else well. He was truly the best man she'd ever known and her heart leapt at the mere sight of him.

The frantic travel by post to reach Scotland could not have been more different than the leisurely return trip. They stopped as often as they wished or whenever the horses needed rest. They avoided the larger towns but happily explored whatever smaller village they fancied, villages with names like Newbiggin, Bollington, and Goosnargh. When staying at inns, Will always signed them in as Mr and Mrs Willburgh and no one questioned that. They wore ordinary clothes and rode ordinary horses and were simply assumed to be ordinary people.

On fair days they picnicked by clear blue lakes and explored crumbling ruins. They rested in the inns on rainy days, playing cards and making love during the day. When the roads were dry and the air was fine, they let the horses gallop, the wind tugging at her hat. It felt like flying.

Anna told Will about India, about her *ayah* and the other beloved servants she left behind, about the sights and sounds and smells. Will regaled her with stories about his school days, about the mischief he and his friends engaged in, about the oddities of his tutors. They remarked on what they saw along the road and the people they met. At night they let their bodies speak and the lovemaking only got better and better.

Throughout the trip neither of them spoke about fathers or duels or Dormans or duties or even what arriving in London would bring.

After almost a fortnight, though, they faced the end of their idyll. The roads became thick with wagons, horsemen, and carriages. The fields and woods and tiny villages gave way to factories and workshops and crowded tenements. Finally they reached the neat streets, shops, and townhouses of Mayfair where passers-by dressed in fine fashions eyed them with curiosity and dismay. Anna suddenly saw herself through their eyes. Her clothes, full of the dust of the road, were the worse for wear after almost two weeks of travel.

When they turned onto Park Street, Anna's spirits sank. They were at the end. At the door of Will's townhouse.

Anna, dirty and shabby, looked like she ought to be using the servant's entrance; Will, like a labourer seeking work. John appeared more like his companion than his groom.

Will helped her dismount and John held the horses while Will sounded the knocker. Bailey answered the door.

The butler's shocked expression quickly became composed when he welcomed Will's return and quickly summoned a footman to tend to the horses and another to collect their bags.

Before leaving her pony, Anna stroked the horse's neck. 'Thank you, Seraphina, for carrying me so far,' she murmured.

She was rewarded with a nuzzle back.

Anna reluctantly stepped away. 'See she's taken good care of,' she pleaded.

The footman bowed. 'Yes, m'lady.'

Anna blinked. Right… *M'lady.* She was Lady Willburgh now.

Will introduced John to the footman. 'He is our new groom,' Will explained. 'Show him the stables and introduce him to the head groom. He is to be welcomed and given every consideration. Let them know. He can be in charge of these horses.'

'Yes, m'lord,' the footman said.

Anna approached John before he was led away. She clasped his hand. 'Thank you, John. You must let us know if you need anything at all.'

'I will, ma'am,' the youth said.

Will escorted Anna into the hall where the butler eyed her with some distress. She hoped it was merely due to her dress.

'Bailey, you saw John, our new groom,' Will said.

'I did indeed, sir,' the butler replied.

'Check on him later, if you will,' he went on. 'I want to make certain he is treated well. He was invaluable to us.'

How like Will to be concerned about John, Anna thought. The young man *had* been invaluable to them.

'I will, sir,' the butler replied. 'And Toby? Is he with you?'

'I sent him on to Willburgh House.' He handed Bailey his old hat and worn gloves. 'Is my mother at home?'

'She retired to the country a few days after you left, m'lord,' Bailey responded.

'Probably for the best,' Will said, as if to himself.

Anna could just imagine what her new mother-in-law would have thought of her present appearance.

'Are there rooms ready for us?' Will's voice sounded different. Like a viscount's. He even stood differently. Stiffer. With an air of command.

Had her affable, relaxed new husband disappeared?

'Yes. Your room and the one adjoining it for the viscountess.' The butler looked a little disturbed. 'Some of the servants have the day off, it being Sunday and we did not know to expect you today, but I will find your valet, sir, and a maid to tend to—to the viscountess.' He turned to Anna. 'The belongings you left here are in the room, unpacked, m'lady.'

At least they'd thought of her.

'Very good, Bailey.' Will spoke before Anna could acknowledge him.

Will offered his arm and walked with her up the stairs to the bed chamber that had been Lady Willburgh's. His mother must not have been pleased at being so displaced, Anna thought.

'There is a connecting door to my room.' Will opened it to show her. 'Is there anything I can do for you before a maid appears?' His voice sounded so formal.

Anna looked around at the beautifully decorated room. How could his mother not resent her use of it?

'I will not need you.' She echoed his formal tone.

What she did need was for it to be only the two of them in a simple room in an inn, helping each other, not waiting for valets and maids. Those days—and nights—would never return.

She removed her hat and pulled off gloves, placing them both on a chair. Still feeling like an intruder, she opened drawers and discovered her clothes were indeed there, as

Bailey had said. She took out a clean shift and corset. It would be glorious to change into them. It would be glorious to clean off the dirt of the road.

In a corner of the room behind a spectacular hand-painted screen was a lovely French wash stand with ornate marquetry. Inside its cabinet were soap and towels. The pitcher was filled with water. It did not matter to Anna if it was fresh or not. She stripped off her riding habit and underclothes and washed the dirt of travel off her body. It would be lovely to wash her hair as well, and even to have a tub bath, a nice long tub bath with nice hot water. Would it be offered to her? she wondered.

Or could she, now Lady Willburgh, simply order it done? This she could not imagine.

After she dried herself and put on her clean shift and stockings, there was a tap at the door.

'It is the maid, m'lady.' It was the chatty maid who had served her before. She entered the room carrying Anna's saddlebags. 'I've brought your luggage. Mr Bailey also said I was to help you dress or whatever you wish me to do. I'm not a lady's maid, though.'

'You helped me well enough before,' Anna said. 'What is your name?'

'I am Hester, m'lady.' Hester was little more than a girl, smaller than Anna with a riot of blond curls escaping her cap.

Anna nodded. 'Hester, I found my underclothes, but I have not yet found my dresses.'

The girl walked over to the wall covered with Chinese wallpaper. She found knobs cleverly blending in with the wallpaper and opened a cabinet, a clothes press built into the wall. 'Your dresses are in here, m'lady.'

Anna could not help but laugh. 'I would never have found them.'

'Which dress, ma'am?' Hester asked.

Anna glanced inside the cabinet where three dresses were neatly folded on shelves, one of which was the dress Will's mother gave her. She selected that one.

'This is the one Lady Willburgh gave you,' Hester exclaimed. 'I must say it looked better on you than it did on her.'

'It wasn't her colour,' Anna said diplomatically. She touched her hair. 'Before I dress, I should like to brush my hair. I have a brush and comb in the bags over there.'

Hester went to the dressing table and opened a drawer. 'There is one here, as well.'

Anna joined her. 'Someone thought of everything.'

'His Lordship wrote a letter saying you would come soon,' Hester said. 'He told Mr Bailey to tell Mrs White to make sure you had everything you would need.'

Anna had not known that.

'But you need more dresses,' Hester added as Anna sat at the dressing table and she removed the pins from her hair. 'You don't have nearly enough.'

When her hair was arranged, the maid said, 'Before I forget, I am to tell you to meet His Lordship in the drawing room when you are ready.'

Yes. She'd be meeting *His Lordship*, not her Will.

# Chapter Eleven

Will sat at his desk in the library, piles of mail and other papers in front of him. It would take an age to attend to it all. A quick riffling through the pile showed many notes from his peers in the Lords. Two or three letters from his mother. Bills from various shopkeepers. Letters from the managers of his various estates. A summons to come see his men of business. Charities seeking donations. Relatives seeking funds. Relatives writing to chastise him for compromising Anna. Others warning him not to marry her.

He wanted to chuck the lot into the fireplace and watch it burn to ashes. He wanted to be with Anna, free to ride down country lanes, explore new villages, revel in the delights of sharing her bed. His mind refused to focus, yet all this correspondence was vitally important. Countless people depended upon him meeting his responsibilities.

His idyll was over.

Staring at the endless piles was achieving nothing, though, and he'd told Anna to meet with him. Will left most of the letters unopened and walked out of the library to go to the drawing room where Bailey was just setting down a tray of tea, biscuits, and sandwiches.

'Thank you, Bailey.' Will took two of the sandwiches off the tray. 'I did not realise how hungry I was.'

'I suspected it, sir,' the man replied.

Will sank down in one of the chairs. 'Before you go, tell me. What has it been like here?'

'Well, sir.' The butler straightened. 'About as dreadful as one could imagine.'

Will groaned. 'Tell me.'

'The printers seemed to be attempting to outdo each other. Several handbills were released embellishing the tale. Some made you out to be a terrible villain, preying on an innocent. One could have been written by Lord Dorman, all about how his ungrateful ward betrayed the family by consorting with you, merely to hurt them.' He dipped his head. 'I saved them for you. They are on your desk.'

They must have been at the very bottom of the piles.

'Your mother received some nasty letters,' he went on. 'And all the invitations she'd received hitherto were withdrawn.'

'She was wise to leave town, then.' And Will had been glad she'd gone.

His feelings towards his mother were ambivalent at best. Although he'd resolved not to ignore her as his father had done, he did not believe she was wholly innocent in the affair that caused his father's death even though she attempted to paint herself as ill-used. Especially when she tried to manipulate him to get her own way. She was often the most burdensome of his chores.

Bailey added, 'She was quite distressed.'

As well she would be. Will was glad he and Anna were spared that at least. It would all die down now they were married.

'Is that all, sir?' Bailey asked.

Will stood and walked over to the cabinet. 'Is there brandy here?'

'There is, sir.'

Will opened it and took out the carafe of brandy and a glass. 'Then nothing more. Thank you, Bailey.'

The butler bowed and left the room.

Will poured himself a glass of brandy and drank it in two swallows. He wished he had taken Anna straight to Dover and hopped on a packet to the Continent. Think how exciting it would be to explore France, Italy, Spain, and Greece with her?

If only he could. He'd merely neglected his duties for three weeks and his work had turned mountainous. Payment for choosing enjoyment over a rush back to duty.

He poured himself a second glass of brandy.

Anna entered the room.

It had been almost two weeks since Will had seen her dressed in anything but her riding habit, a simple dress—or her shift. She took his breath. She wore that dress his mother gave her, the one that complemented her colouring so well. Her skin glowed with the health a week spent in fresh air would do. Her light brown eyes captivated him. She looked stunningly beautiful.

All he wanted was to take her in his arms and carry her back to his bed chamber. And remove that lovely dress.

Instead he stood. 'There is tea. And refreshments.'

She gestured to his glass. 'What are you drinking?'

He lifted the glass and peered at it as if noticing it for the first time. 'Brandy. Would you prefer a glass?'

She looked at him with questions in her eyes, but merely said, 'Please.'

Did she realise he sought out brandy when stressed?

He put his glass down and turned to the cabinet to get one for her. 'Is the room and service meeting your satisfaction?' Lord. He sounded stiff-necked.

She took the glass from his hand. 'Of course it is.' She spoke with a touch of irritation.

At him, he supposed.

She lowered herself into a chair. 'Hester has been a help.'

Will sat, too, and passed a plate of sandwiches to her. 'I am glad. She is a good worker.'

He took a couple of biscuits and berated himself. This was not what he wished to say to her. It was as if they were strangers again.

His thoughts were consumed with her. How was he to accomplish all that needed doing?

She sipped her brandy and seemed to be watching him carefully. 'Hester tells me I need a new wardrobe.'

He remembered the urgency of their purchasing old garments from the market in Nottingham as well as the pleasure of shopping for her riding habit in Langholm. Think how delightful it would be to comb the second-hand clothing shops on Petticoat Lane with her.

But, no. A viscountess must have her clothing made by a modiste.

'Buy whatever you want,' he said. 'Have the charges sent to me.'

'And a new riding habit?' She smiled wanly.

'Of course. A new habit.' He answered automatically, thinking how deprived of enjoyment he felt not to be ordinary enough to shop on Petticoat Lane.

A minute later he realised she'd meant him to remember how excited they'd both been when the garment fit her. The moment had passed.

He also realised he'd answered her exactly how his father answered his mother when she attempted to talk to him about something she desired to buy. '*Buy whatever you need,*' his father would say, as if he'd wished not to be bothered.

Or maybe his father was simply preoccupied by work. Will could understand now. Will was overwhelmed at how much he needed to do.

But somehow his father never seemed to yearn to be free of responsibility. When his father said duty comes first, he almost always sounded glad.

Anna finished the glass of brandy. She might as well have been alone. Will was preoccupied. He was also almost formal with her, more like he'd been those first days when they were nothing but enemies. It was as if he'd turned from being her Will of their travels into the viscount as soon as they crossed this house's threshold.

She put her glass on the table. 'What is it, Will? You are not attending.'

He shook his head as if dislodging more important thoughts. 'Forgive me. You said a new habit. New clothes. I could unearth the name of my mother and sister's modiste, but you may not want to use her.'

'I'd rather not,' she admitted. 'I certainly do not want to use Lady Dorman's modiste.'

'No, indeed,' Will looked distracted again.

She tried again. 'Will, what is wrong?'

He met her gaze. 'Wrong? Nothing.' But he finished his brandy and stood. 'I am sorry to do this, but I must leave you.' He seemed in a hurry to do so. 'I need to tend to a desk full of correspondence in the library.'

'Oh.' He was leaving her alone? 'Is there anything I might do to assist?' Anna wanted his company, even if he seemed a million miles away.

He shook his head. 'You are free to do as you wish, though. If you need anything, call a servant.' That felt like a dismissal. 'I will see you at dinner.'

He left.

*He left?* How could he leave her so abruptly? Not that he seemed like much company the last few minutes. What had happened?

The room turned deadly quiet except for the ticking clock. She must do something at the moment or go mad.

She placed the empty plates and the glasses on the tray that held the untouched tea things. She could at least carry the tray down to the kitchen.

As she descended the stairs to the lower floor and emerged in the hallway to the kitchen, Mrs White, the housekeeper, met her. 'M'lady! I was coming to you. You are not to be carrying trays. I will take that.' She almost pulled the tray out of Anna's hands.

'I thought I would help,' Anna explained. 'I knew some of the servants had the day off.'

At the Dormans' she'd often perform servants' tasks when asked.

'You are not to help, m'lady,' the housekeeper scolded. 'You must ring and we will come to see what you need.' The woman started to walk away.

'Mrs White?' Anna called. 'What were you coming to see me for?'

'The dinner menu. I will meet with you in a moment.' She turned away again.

'Shall I follow you?' Anna called after her.

The housekeeper turned back. 'Goodness, no.' Her voice softened. 'Lady Willburgh never came down to the kitchen. I will come to you.'

'Where shall I meet you?' asked Anna.

Mrs White looked a bit pitying. 'M'lady, you must tell me where you wish me to be.'

There was nowhere in this house Anna felt comfortable.

'Would the bed chamber do?' She could not call it *her* bed chamber.

'That will do nicely,' the housekeeper said. She bustled away with the tray.

Anna paced the bed chamber until the housekeeper came. There was very little to discuss about dinner, as it was obvious Mrs White and the cook knew precisely what they wished to serve.

'What else might you need, m'lady?' Mrs White asked as she readied to leave the room.

'Nothing at the moment. Thank you.' What she really needed and wanted was a return to the gambol of the past two weeks with Will.

After the housekeeper left, Anna paced the room again, until she could stand it no longer. She wanted to be with Will even if he was busy. She'd go down to the library and park herself there. Read a book. Or even better, assist him.

She descended the stairs and entered the library without knocking.

Will stood. 'Anna!' He did not sound overly glad to see her. 'I was just about to come to you.' He straightened a pile of papers on his desk. 'I just this moment learned I must leave you. Lord Lansdowne and Lord Brougham have sent for me to meet them and others at Brook's. There is to be a vote tomorrow to suspend habeas corpus. It is important we discuss the matter beforehand. I must go.'

'You must go now?' she asked.

'I must.' He straightened another pile.

'And you will be gone tomorrow?' she managed.

'Tomorrow. Yes.' He hurried past her. 'I am sorry. I will miss dinner. And I may be late. These things take time.' He turned back to her. 'Choose any book you like. The library is yours.'

And he was gone.

And she was alone.

She stood at the window and watched him rush out of the house and hurry down the street.

The vote on habeas corpus was important, she knew. It protected citizens from imprisonment without proof that they had committed a crime. The government thought its suspension would help control the unrest that was fomenting across the country and to prevent the sort of revolution France had endured.

If Will had simply spent a few minutes talking with her about it, Anna might be more forgiving of his abandoning her. She'd have felt important to him, not excluded. Instead, it seemed like he'd been eager to be away from her.

She was mystified at this change in him, but had she not experienced this once before? He'd become haughty and disagreeable the morning after their wedding. She was mystified but also angry. She had done nothing to deserve this treatment, to be left alone with virtually no regard for her feelings. She might as well be back with the Dormans for all the consideration she received from him.

One thing was different, though. She was not entirely powerless. She was Viscountess Willburgh now and a viscountess could sometimes have her way.

Anna turned on her heel and strode out to the hall, but it was unattended at the moment. She wasn't about to ring bells and wait, no matter what Mrs White thought of her. She marched down to the lower floor and found Mrs White and Bailey conversing in the servants' hall.

'M'lady,' Mrs White began. 'I said you must ring—'

Anna interrupted her. 'I did not wish to wait for bells. This is what I want. I want a bath. As soon as it might be accomplished. I want to wash my hair. Bring dinner to my room when it is convenient and I do not care what Cook fixes. She need not fuss. Anything will do.'

Without waiting for a response, Anna turned around and hurried off, before her emotions exploded. On her way to her bed chamber, she stopped by the library and pulled three books at random.

'*Choose any book,*' he'd said, as if that made amends.

Anna's bath was arranged right away and Hester attended her. Since Anna was not intending to leave her room, she dressed in night clothes afterwards. She sat at the dressing table while Hester combed the tangles from her hair.

The maid remarked, 'M'lady, your hair curls nicely.'

'Curls?' Anna remembered that this maid had arranged curls in her hair before, when Anna had first stayed here.

'Yes, m'lady. Especially if you bunch it up in your hands as it dries.' Hester took a lock of Anna's hair and demonstrated. 'See? It curls.'

Indeed when she released her hair, the curls remained. Anna was used to pulling her hair straight, although she did remember having curls when she'd been a little girl.

Hester bunched up another lock of hair.

'You made my hair curl before,' Anna remarked.

'Those weren't what I call curls. Want to see curls?' Hester removed her cap. 'See my hair? It is too curly. But yours will be nice curls.'

'Hester, your curls are lovely,' Anna said.

The girl sighed. 'More like a trial, ma'am.'

Hester's good-natured company was giving Anna some comfort. She certainly needed it.

'Hester, you said I need new clothes. Do you know where

I might find a good modiste? I do not want to use the one the Dormans used.'

Hester sniffed. 'You certainly can do better than that one. My cousin says she is not very skilled and she charges too much. And she is not really French.'

Anna suppressed a laugh. 'I suspected that. Your cousin knows her?'

The maid stopped with the comb in mid-air. 'My cousin sews for a modiste who dresses the daughters of merchants and cits. She wants to have her own shop someday.'

'Do you think your cousin might sew for me?' Anna asked.

Hester dropped the locks of hair she was bunching. 'Do you mean that, m'lady? I'm sure she would love to. My goodness! She'd be making clothes for a viscountess!'

'I'm not sure she would want to advertise that it was me,' Anna responded. 'Not with the scandal, but Lord Willburgh would pay her well, I am certain, especially if she could make some clothes quickly. Could she see me tomorrow, do you think?'

Hester put the comb down and bunched more curls into Anna's hair. 'I could go to her now and arrange it. If I have permission to leave, that is.'

'Who should I speak to arrange permission for you?' Anna asked.

Hester giggled. 'M'lady, you need not seek permission. If you say I can leave, I can leave.'

The meeting at Brook's dragged on until near midnight. Will might as well have missed it. He could barely attend to the discussion let alone contribute. His mind was filled with Anna. He missed her company. His body ached for her.

This would not do. He needed to pay attention in meetings like this. He needed to contribute.

Lord Lansdowne offered him a ride home in his carriage and Will was forced to continue their discussion as the carriage made its way to Park Street.

How was he to go on? He had his responsibilities. His duty. He could not spend his hours mooning over her like a lovesick calf.

The carriage stopped and a groom opened the door. With Lansdowne still making one more point, Will paused before climbing out and bidding the man goodnight.

He entered the house. The hall was being attended by a sleepy footman who took his hat and gloves. Everything was dark and quiet.

Will hurried directly upstairs to his bed chamber, catching his valet dozing in a chair.

'Beg pardon, sir.' The man jumped to his feet.

'No need,' Will responded. 'It's late, I know. Is everyone asleep?' He meant had Anna retired or was she waiting for him?

'I expect so, sir,' The valet helped him off with his coat and boots.

'I'll tend to myself from here, Carter,' Will said. 'You can go to bed.'

'Very good, m'lord.' Carter bowed and, carrying Will's coat and boots, left the room.

As soon as he left, Will went to the door connecting his room with Anna's. He opened it a crack and listened, but all was quiet. There was a light, though, so he entered. It was a candle on a table near the bed, burning itself almost to a nub.

It left enough light, though, to see that Anna was in bed, eyes closed, breathing evenly.

'Anna?' he whispered, but she did not stir.

He stood watching her for a long time, yearning to strip off the rest of his clothes and join her, but reluctant to disturb her peaceful sleep. Eventually, he turned around and returned to his own bed chamber.

Anna opened her eyes and watched him walk away.

She'd already heard a clock strike twelve so she knew it was later than that. Had he thought her asleep? Why did he not come to her anyway?

It wounded. And angered her.

If he had only joined her in her bed, she might have forgiven him for staying away so long. Instead he walked away.

She rolled over and hugged a pillow, but sleep did not come easily.

# *Chapter Twelve*

The next morning Will woke early, acutely aware that he was alone in the bed, alone for the first time in over a fortnight. He missed her. He greatly missed her.

His valet was as prompt as ever in appearing to help him dress. Will had half a mind to send Carter away and see if Anna was still abed. Perhaps there was still time to make love in the morning like they'd done on their journey, but if he did that he'd keep his valet waiting and the maid serving Anna might have to wait, as well. Will made it a point of honour to be considerate of the servants and to appreciate the services they performed for him.

So he let his valet dress him, and as soon as Carter left, Will went to the connecting door. He opened it and listened, but all was quiet. He walked in as quietly as he could.

The bed's linens were smoothed and everything appeared neatly in order.

She had arisen early. Earlier than he.

He hurried down to the breakfast room and found Anna there, sipping tea and reading the *Morning Post*. She wore the same dress as the day before, the one his mother had given her, but her hair had been transformed into cascading curls that framed her face and bounced at her slightest movement. He was entranced.

She looked up. 'Good morning, Will.' Her voice was flat. And chill.

'Good morning.' What was he to say to her?

He wanted to tell her she looked beautiful. Wanted to beg her forgiveness for leaving her alone the day before and tell her they could spend this entire day together. But that would mean neglecting some correspondence that must be answered this day and missing the meeting his men of business had deemed of the greatest importance. Afterwards he must make his way to the Old Palace of Westminster for the House of Lords session and the vote. His day was filled.

He gestured to the newspaper. 'I arranged to have a notice of our marriage put in the papers.' One of the tasks he'd accomplished the previous day. 'It will be printed tomorrow.'

She lowered the newspaper and simply stared at him. Or perhaps *glared* was a better word, although no specific emotion seemed to be reflected in her expression.

None that he could read, at least. He selected his food from the sideboard and sat across from her. 'I am afraid I will be gone most of the day today.'

She stared at him again, pausing before she spoke. 'And what shall I tell Cook about dinner?'

He hated his reply. 'I will not be here for dinner.'

She returned to the newspaper.

By the time Will finished his breakfast, he'd convinced himself her coolness towards him was a good thing. He needed to do his work and the sooner she realised that took precedence over everything else, the better. His could not be a life of enjoyment and spontaneity. The mountain of papers on his desk was testimony to that.

Because he wanted what he could not have. The freedom to enjoy her company.

* * *

Before Will settled down to his pile of papers, he wrote out letters with his seal indicating that the shopkeepers could bill him for any purchases Anna made. He could have had Bailey or one of the footmen bring her the letters, but he chose to deliver them to her himself.

He found her in her bed chamber, surprising her, apparently.

'Will!' She shut the drawer she'd been looking through. 'I—I did not expect to see you.'

He handed her the letters. 'Show these letters at any of the shops,' he told her. 'They will allow you to purchase whatever you like.'

She took them from him. 'Thank you,' she said in a low voice, but raised her head to meet his gaze. 'Because I will need clothing quickly, I expect to be asked to pay more than what is customary.'

He held her gaze and felt his resolve waver. He wanted to take her in his arms. Instead he said, 'Cost does not matter. Buy what you like.'

A faint smile flitted across her face. 'As you have often told me.'

He wished she'd not reminded him of their time together shopping. He'd never had such pleasure spending his money.

He hesitated a moment, still gazing at her, but then glanced towards the door. 'I have work to do,' he said. 'I wish you a good day.'

He left.

Will holed himself up in the library, putting pen to paper, hardly looking up until he heard voices in the hall. He rose and walked to the door, opening it a crack to see Anna and the maid leave by the front door. From the library window he watched them walk down the street. It lowered his spirits even more.

By noon he was forced to stop working on his correspondence and called for his carriage. As he climbed in he thought he ought to have told Anna to take the carriage. He could have caught a hackney coach. Too late.

His coachman drove him to Fleet Street and the offices of his men of business. Whatever they'd deemed so urgent wound up taking a little more than an hour. He had time to kill until he must appear at Westminster. He strolled up and down the street waiting for his carriage and stopped when a shop window caught his eye.

The shop was Rundell and Bridge, goldsmiths and jewellers to the king.

He went inside. Until this moment he'd not given it a thought. Anna had no wedding ring. He'd fix that forthwith.

The next morning Anna's humour was improved. The meeting with Hester's cousin had been unexpectedly diverting and productive. Anna even left with two new dresses she could wear right away. She and Hester also managed to buy two hats, three pairs of gloves, several pairs of stockings, and countless ribbons. They'd even gone to a tailor to be fitted for a riding habit and to a corset maker.

Hester and her cousin devised a brilliant way for Anna to build a complete new wardrobe quickly. Her cousin would ask as many modistes as she could think of if they had any dresses that were not paid for or not finished for any reason. If they would be of a near size to Anna's, Hester's cousin would propose buying the dress for her unnamed customer. Then the cousin and her seamstresses would alter the dresses so they would not be recognisable as the originals. 'So m'lady wouldn't be talked of for wearing someone else's discards,' Hester's cousin explained.

As if she would not be talked of for other reasons, Anna thought.

After Anna dressed and Hester arranged her hair she examined herself in the mirror. The pale lilac dress complemented her well. She looked the best she'd ever looked in her life.

Not that Will would notice.

He hardly took the time to say hello to her. What plans would take him away this day? she wondered.

This morning Will arrived for breakfast first. He stood when she entered the room.

She managed, 'Good morning.'

He stared at her, finally saying, 'Is that a new dress already?'

'It is.' Although the pleasure of it was diminished by his lukewarm response. 'Do you approve of it?'

His gaze flicked up and down her body. 'I do approve. You look very well in it.'

That was better, but not by much.

'Did you manage to buy all you needed?' he asked.

'Not in one day.' She sat across from him. 'I did order a new riding habit, though.'

He sat, as well. 'Very good.'

Even mention of riding did not elicit more from him.

She'd heard of marriages like this—or perhaps read of them in a novel—the courtship all filled with declarations of love only to turn into coldness or abuse after the wedding.

But she and Will had no courtship and she was confident he would never hurt her, at least not in a physical way.

After filling her plate, the footman left the room.

Will rose. 'I bought something for you.'

'Oh?' She poured her tea.

He walked over to the chair next to hers and took a small box from his pocket.

He placed the box in her hand. 'You should have had this on our wedding day.'

Anna opened the box and gasped. It was a ring. A beautiful ring with one large diamond in the centre and smaller ones encircling it. The diamonds were set in a gold band fashioned in a floral filigree design.

Her eyes flew to his face.

He took the ring from its box and slipped it on the third finger of her left hand.

Her heart beat so fast it took a long while before she could speak. 'You—you should not have—it must have cost a great deal—'

He continued to hold her hand. 'I wanted you to have it.'

She was awed. 'It is beautiful, Will.' Even more so because he troubled himself to buy it for her.

He smiled. 'Now our marriage is official.'

She leaned over and kissed him on the cheek. He gazed at her and reached up, touching her cheek so gently it sent waves of sensation throughout her body. She yearned to have him share her bed again.

He moved back to his original seat and handed her the *Morning Post*. 'The announcement is in it.'

She scanned the page until she found it.

'Does the wording suit you?' he asked.

'It seems adequate,' she responded.

She was more puzzled than ever. Right when she'd resolved herself to think him turning cold, he did something so lovely. Buying her a ring. Why was he so cold and formal with her? Why did he not come to her bed?

Bailey entered the room. 'Pardon, sir, this missive just

arrived for you. The messenger said it was important. He awaits your reply.'

Will read it. 'Tell the messenger I will come within the hour.'

Bailey left.

Will handed the message to Anna. 'This is from a man at Coutts Bank. It is about your trust.'

She looked up in surprise. 'My trust? I have no trust.'

'He says that you do and insists that I call upon him immediately.'

She perused the message. 'There must be some mistake. How would I have a trust, when I have no money?'

Will stood. 'I will go right now.'

She rose, too. 'I will go with you.'

'Women are not typically expected to go to—'

Was he going to say women were not welcome at Coutts? She cut him off and was adamant. 'I will go with you.'

'Very well.' He started for the door. 'I will call for the curricle.'


Within a half hour Will's curricle was brought around. He was surprised to see who held the horses.

'Toby, you are back from the country.' Will helped Anna into the seat and climbed up himself, taking the ribbons.

'I am, sir. All is well there.' He jumped into the groom's seat.

Anna turned towards him. 'How are John's brother and his wife settling in?'

The groom shrugged. 'As best they can. You know how it can be if you're from a different place.'

More to worry over, thought Will.

As they reached the Strand, Will wondered at the urgency of the summons to Coutts. What could be so urgent? And why did Anna know nothing about a trust in her name?

'Could the trust have been set up by your relatives?' Will asked her.

'My mother said we hadn't any relatives,' she replied.

'But there was your father.' Perhaps this was about her father.

'None on my father's side, my mother said. Or on her side.'

They passed Somerset House and St Clements and pulled up in front of Coutts Bank. Toby jumped down and held the horses.

Will helped Anna down. 'I do not know how long we will be,' he said to Toby.

'I'll walk 'em if need be, sir,' the groom replied.

Will escorted Anna into the building. He announced himself to the attendant at the door. Several men within earshot turned to look when they heard 'Lord and Lady Willburgh.' Anna was the only woman present.

'We are here to see Sir Edmund Antrobus,' Will said.

'Lord Willburgh,' the attendant said too loudly. 'Yes. Follow me. I am certain Sir Edmund will see you.'

As they followed the man, Anna whispered to Will, 'We are attracting a great deal of notice.'

'I can see,' Will responded.

They had to wait only a few moments for Sir Edmund, who was one of the partners at Coutts, second in importance to Thomas Coutts himself. To come without an appointment and be seen right away? What did it mean?

Sir Edmund bowed to Anna. 'Lady Willburgh. It is a pleasure. I did not expect you.'

'Indeed, sir?' responded Anna. 'This apparently concerns me.'

'Yes. Yes.' He gestured to some chairs. 'Please do sit. May I serve you tea?'

'Thank you, no.' Will glanced at Anna who shook her head. 'Tell us. What is of such importance?'

Sir Edmund did not sit until they both took their chairs. 'It was the announcement of your marriage that prompted me to contact you, sir. From the—um—information made available to us before this, we did not know for certain that you would be married.' That information being from the handbills, he meant? 'I must say that I would have strongly advised you to consult with us before taking that step—'

'Why would we consult with you?' Will asked.

'Why? Because of the trust.' He looked dumbfounded.

'What trust?' The man was making no sense.

'Why, Lady Willburgh's trust,' Sir Edmund said.

Anna spoke up. 'I have no trust!'

Sir Edmund turned to her. 'Oh, but you do, my dear lady. It was set up by your grandparents.'

'But I have no grandparents!' she cried.

'No.' Sir Edmund gave her a sympathetic look. 'Not now, because they died shortly after your poor mother. Your grandfather set this up before their deaths.'

'So what of this trust?' Will asked.

Sir Edmund turned back to him. 'What have you heard of her grandparents?'

'Nothing,' Will replied.

Anna broke in. 'That is because I know nothing!'

Sir Edmund continued to address Will. 'The grandfather was Norman Lyman, a nabob. Made a fortune in India, then retired to Croydon in Surrey. It broke their hearts when their only daughter eloped with that soldier, especially when she went with him to India. Her parents disowned her, but settled some money on her when she had the child.' He inclined his head towards Anna.

Will glanced at Anna. Her face was pinched with distress. No wonder. Sir Edmund told it in a manner so oblivi-ous of her feelings.

Sir Edmund went on. 'Then Edgerton died and she mar-ried Dorman. Mind you, this is all before her twentieth year.' He grimaced. 'Dorman must have been the only English-man to lose a fortune rather than make one in India. He went through her money like water through a sieve.' Sir Edmund chuckled. 'Dorman begged Lyman for more money after she died, but Lyman set up the trust instead, providing the child with an allowance, but no more.'

Will interrupted him. 'So Lady Willburgh inherits this trust?'

'No,' Sir Edmund said. 'That is why I wished to see you. To explain.'

'Then tell us.' Anna's voice was strained.

'Well,' Sir Edmund went on. 'The Lymans did not approve of either of the marriages. They blamed their daughter's age. They were determined to prevent the same mistakes being made by their granddaughter.' Again the man gestured to Anna as if Will would not know to whom he referred with-out pointing her out. 'So the will has a stipulation. If the heir marries before age twenty-one she forfeits the inheritance entirely and it reverts to her children when she dies, with the same stipulation and so on.'

Will leaned forwards, unwilling to believe his ears. 'Do you mean there is a fortune to be inherited, but Anna—Lady Willburgh—cannot inherit because she married—'

Anna broke in. 'I will be twenty-one within months.'

Sir Edmund attempted to look sympathetic. 'I am afraid you do not inherit, but your children, if you have any, will.'

'And what happens if she does not have any children?' Will asked, his voice rising.

'Then it defaults to a charity. I would have to look up which. The Church, I believe.'

Will turned to Anna who looked as if she was struggling to control her emotions.

'How much of a fortune is this?' Will asked.

Sir Edmund held up a finger. 'I looked it up this morning after I read the marriage announcement. Ninety-six thousand, five hundred and thirty-six pounds.'

Will saw Anna grip the arms of her chair. It was an astounding figure. Enough wealth to live very, very well.

Will swallowed. 'Is there any property?'

Sir Edmund shook his head. 'As the will directed, the property was sold upon the death of both Mr and Mrs Lyman.'

Will glanced at Anna again. She looked about done.

He felt a knot twisting in his stomach.

She would have been only a month away from a fortune large enough for her to live on her own terms no matter how much gossip flew around her.

If only he hadn't married her.

Will stood. 'There is nothing else to say.'

Sir Edmund rose, as well. 'We will continue to manage the trust and you are certainly welcome to ask for an accounting at any time.'

Will offered his hand to Anna. She let him help her from the chair, but she did not look at him.

Sir Edmund walked them to the lobby. 'You must tell us if you have children, of course. Each child will receive fifty pounds a year.'

'Fifty pounds,' repeated Will.

'Yes,' responded Sir Edmund. 'Each child—as long as they do not marry before age twenty-one.'

'But not me,' Anna said, her voice wounded.

'Oh, but you received it,' he said. 'Did you not know?'

She shook her head.

'Was it paid to Lord Dorman?' Will's tone was tense.

'Well, he was her guardian.'

So Dorman knew all this and did not tell her? Will fumed.

Sir Edmund's hand covered his mouth. 'We gave him the money not two weeks ago.'

Will's lips thinned. 'We were married by then.'

Sir Edmund nervously wrung his hands. 'I suppose we should try to get the money back.'

'It belongs to the trust,' Will responded.

They reached the lobby. Sir Edmund bowed politely, bade them farewell and quickly turned away, hurrying back to his desk.

Will and Anna walked outside.

'Anna—' Will began.

She interrupted him. 'I want to go back to the townhouse.'

He did not know what to say to her. It was his fault they married so quickly. They could easily have waited for her to come of age. What had he done?

# *Chapter Thirteen*

Toby came with the curricle and Will helped Anna into the seat. She could not speak. She felt as if someone had struck her in the face.

Betrayal. More betrayal.

By the Dormans, certainly. They could have told her she was an heiress. They could have let her know that she was not wholly dependent upon them. Fifty pounds was a great deal of money, enough for her clothing, pin money, food. She'd never been a burden on them.

Her stepfather—Anna could no longer think of him as her papa—could have told her, too. Why had he not if he'd truly cared for her?

Even her mother. Why had she not told Anna about her father and her grandparents long before she died?

And these grandparents she'd never known—they betrayed her, as well. They sent money after she was born, true, but they'd cruelly rejected her mother when she married her father. How her mother must have felt, no more than sixteen years old, to be shunned by her own parents? What if they had helped her instead? Maybe her father would not have had to stay in the army. Maybe he would not have had to go to India. Maybe he would still be alive. Her mother, too. Maybe she would not have caught the fever that took her life. Maybe Anna could have had a family who loved her.

And if her father had never died and her mother never married her stepfather, perhaps her stepfather could have found someone he truly loved. Maybe he would not have dallied with Will's mother and the duel would never have taken place. Perhaps Will's father would still be alive and Will would not have been so wounded.

She glanced at him. He was totally in control of the horses and was driving them skilfully through the busy traffic on the Strand. His expression was grim, though.

And why would it not be? Because of her he was trapped into a marriage that had been completely unnecessary.

Those days on the ride back to London were mere illusion. They were pretending they led other lives, lives without care, lives in which they could be happy, but all the while they'd not known the mistakes they were making.

The curricle pulled up to the Park Street townhouse. Will helped her down and she immediately rushed into the house. She passed the footman who attended the hall and hurried up the stairs to her bed chamber. The bed chamber that should have remained Will's mother's. She removed her shawl, her bonnet, and her gloves and flung herself onto the bed.

But she would not let tears fall. Some hurts were beyond weeping.

There was a knock at the door and Hester entered. 'Oh, my lady. Pardon me. I did not think you were napping.'

Anna sat up in the bed. 'I wasn't napping.'

Hester was clearly excited. 'I came to tell you that my cousin finished another dress and she has located several others for you to look at if you can come for fittings tomorrow.'

At least the search for a complete wardrobe was an excit-

ing distraction. Even though she could have afforded three
wardrobes if…if…

Anna blinked away those tears she refused to have fall.
'I am certain I can go to a fitting. Will you be able to accompany me?'

'Goodness.' Hester laughed. 'We'll merely tell Mrs White
you need me.'

Anna managed a smile. 'Then let us go in the morning.'


Will sat at his desk and tried to look through the mail
that had arrived that day. When he could not concentrate,
he paced the room.

It was no use. He strode out of the library and into the hall.

'My hat and gloves,' he said to the footman. 'I'm going out.'

'Yes, m'lord.' The footman rushed off and returned in
a trice.

Will put them on. 'I shouldn't be gone long.'

He walked the few blocks to Henrietta Street and sounded
the knocker at the Dorman townhouse.

When he was admitted by their butler, he demanded, 'I
wish to see Lord Dorman.'

'One moment, m'lord,' the butler said.

Will cooled his heels in the hall until the man returned.
'Lord Dorman will see you.'

The butler led him to the same drawing room where Will
and Anna had spoken to him before.

'Lord Willburgh,' the butler announced.

Will faced them all. Lord Dorman, Lady Dorman, Lucius,
and Violet. None of them looked pleased to see him. None
of them rose when he entered.

'What now, Willburgh?' Lord Dorman snapped.

'I have been to see Sir Edmund Antrobus at Coutts.' Will
did not need to tell them Anna had come with him. 'I know

what you have concealed from Anna all these years, what you knew when we called upon you before.'

Lucius laughed. 'Did I not tell you the elopement was foolish?'

Will glared at each of them in turn. 'Do you know how exceptionally cruel it is to have deprived Anna of her rightful inheritance? What sort of gentlemanly behaviour is that?'

Again it was Lucius who spoke. 'We did nothing of the sort. It was *you* who deprived her. By compromising her. By eloping with her. We tried to stop you. Why do you suppose I tore off to Scotland?'

'Do not say so, Lucius,' Will shot back. 'A word from any of you would have stopped it.' He turned his glare to Lord and Lady Dorman. 'And how badly done of you to conceal the truth of her fortune? She had a right to know. You made her believe she was accepting your charity. Her expenses were paid and you knew it.'

'She cost us more than a paltry fifty pounds!' Lady Dorman cried.

Violet laughed. 'It is such a joke, though, is it not? She was only a few short weeks from being rich.'

Lucius grinned at her.

Will regarded them all with disgust. 'I do not know more detestable people than you lot.'

Lord Dorman half rose. 'See here, Willburgh. I will not be insulted in my own house. You may leave.'

Will turned to go, but turned back again when he was in the doorway. 'I wonder how well a handbill will sell with the story of how Lord and Lady D fraudulently kept fifty pounds belonging to the trust when they knew Anna was married and they were not entitled to it?'

Lucius vaulted from his chair. 'You would not dare!'

Will gave them a sinister smile. 'Oh, wouldn't I? Give

me the name of the printer you used for the handbills you
had printed—'

'We won't tell you!' Lady Dorman was red-faced with
anger.

Will kept his smile. 'Thank you for confirming that sus-
picion.'

'Why you—' Lucius came at him, but Will walked out
before he even got close.

That evening Anna half expected Will to have arranged
some meeting or other so he would miss dinner, but he didn't.
She'd hoped to eat alone in her room again. She really did
not wish to see him, to see the disappointment on his face.
For marrying her.

Hester had convinced her to wear the new dress for dinner and to put her pearl earrings in her ears. It pleased the
young woman, so Anna did as she requested. The dress was
a Sardinian blue silk, but what Anna loved about it was that
Hester's cousin had replaced the full sleeves with white satin
inset with lace. She'd added matching lace to the neckline
and at the hem. It was versatile as well, appropriate for afternoon or for less formal events such as the theatre or dinner parties.

Not that Anna expected to be invited to dinner parties.

Besides the fact that Will was not going out, the dinner
was already planned. Mrs White had dutifully consulted
with Anna on the menu that morning which meant, really,
teasing out what dishes Cook wished to prepare.

Morning seemed so long ago. Before their visit to Coutts.

Will had just stepped out of the library door when Anna
entered the hall.

'Will,' she said, feeling she must greet him.

'Anna,' he returned.

They walked into the dining room together. The long table had been set with a place at each end, far enough away from each other that Anna might as well have dined alone.

Will frowned when he saw it. 'This seems odd.'

When Anna dined with Will and his mother, they'd been seated on each side of Will who sat on the end.

Bailey was attending the room. 'Is there a problem, sir?'

Will twirled his finger. 'Move the settings so we sit closer to each other.'

Bailey moved Anna's place to a chair adjacent to Will's.

As soon as they sat, wine was poured and soup was served.

Having Bailey in the room and a footman bringing the food put even more of a damper on conversation than had become typical with them. What did they have to say to each other that they would not mind the servants knowing? Surely nothing about the fortune she'd lost.

How was she to ever get through this?

'Were—were you able to address the piles of papers on your desk?' she asked. Might as well pretend to be a viscount and viscountess having a quiet meal at home—Pretending worked so well on their ride back from Scotland.

'Everything urgent is done,' he replied.

They fell silent for a while, except for the sounds of their chewing and swallowing and the crackling of the chandelier above them.

Will looked up from his plate and took a sip of wine. 'Your dress is quite nice. One of the new ones?'

'It is,' she replied. 'Hester's cousin sent it over today.'

His brows rose. 'Hester's cousin is the modiste?'

'No, she is a seamstress,' Anna responded. 'She sews for a modiste, but she is helping me and, I must say, she's ingenious about it.'

'Is she?'

Anna did not have any illusions that Will was truly interested in dresses or the cousin of one of his maids, but she described how clever Hester's cousin was in gathering a brand-new wardrobe for her. It passed the time until the meal was almost done.

As they were finishing their pudding, Will said, 'Hester's cousin ought to have a business of her own. There must be others who need clothes quickly or at less cost.'

'She is very clever,' Anna agreed.

'Have Hester come speak to me,' he added. 'Perhaps her cousin merely needs some investment to get started.'

Anna gaped at him. He truly was an extraordinary man.

When the meal was done they retired to the drawing room for tea. As soon as Bailey left them after bringing in the tea service, Will went immediately to the cabinet in the corner of the room and took out the decanter of brandy. Tea simply would not do for him, not after the day they'd had.

He held up a glass and gestured an offer of brandy.

'Yes. Please,' she replied with feeling.

He poured them each a glass and handed hers to her before seating himself in a chair near hers.

This had been one horrible day. First the visit to Coutts, then the one to the Dormans. That had been foolish. Useless. Although he did confirm that they were behind some of the printing of the handbills.

That had not surprised him.

He should not have called on Dorman, but he'd been so angry he had to do something. He needed to get a hold on his emotions or he'd never be clear-headed.

He glanced at Anna sipping her brandy, looking abstracted.

No need to tell her about calling upon the Dormans and distress her more.

But he had to say something about what they'd been through. 'What Sir Edmund told us. It does not change anything.'

He meant he would still do his duty by her, try to make her life as pleasant as possible. He understood, though, that it must change how she felt about this marriage. About him. She must resent him for pushing the idea of marriage. How could she not?

She took another sip. 'It does change things,' she insisted. 'It makes everything worse.'

He had to agree with her. He'd not rescued her. He'd not saved her reputation. If he'd simply agreed to what she wanted—to live free from the Dormans—she'd have a fortune in a few weeks and then could do whatever she wished.

He finished his brandy and poured another one. 'If we had waited a few weeks…'

'You would be free,' she finished for him.

She had it wrong. 'No, you would be free,' Will said. 'You would be a wealthy heiress.'

Anna emptied her glass and extended it for Will to refill. She put it to her lips and let the amber liquid warm her mouth and chest.

She stared into her glass for a long moment before raising her eyes to his. 'What is it about me that no one saw fit to tell me about this will?'

He didn't answer, but she did not really expect him to.

She twirled the glass in her hand. 'I thought my stepfather cared about me. But if he did why did he not tell me I could be rich someday?'

'Perhaps he thought you were too young,' Will responded.

'I was ten. That seems old enough to me.'

'Perhaps he would have told you in time.' If he'd not first been killed by his father, she figured he meant.

It had been a long time since Anna had thought about that and she'd rather not think on it now. 'Lord and Lady Dorman should have told me, then.'

He nodded. 'Indeed they should have.'

She fell silent, sipping her brandy. When she finished it, she placed the glass on the table next to her.

'No one was honest with me,' she said with feeling. 'My mother was not an orphan. I was not a charity case that the Dormans needed to care for. Even my pa—' She stopped herself when a sudden thought intruded. She turned to Will. 'Did my stepfather keep me with him because of the money?' Did he not care for her at all? Had anyone besides her mother cared for her?

Will looked at her with what seemed like sincere sympathy, but could Anna trust in him? Did he truly care for her or was he merely trying to be kind? He changed so unpredictably even before this revelation—that he need not have married her at all. It was nonsensical to believe he would not resent her.

An ache grew in her heart that all the brandy in the world could not soothe. She wanted him to love her. Desperately wanted it. Because he was truly the finest man she'd ever known and, briefly, she'd felt cherished and safe in his arms. As if she belonged with him always and yet their being together was merely a fluke. A mistake.

A mistake that need not have happened. She felt sick with grief. The magical life of her early childhood, her unhappy life as a Dorman, the illusion of a home with Will, all were lost to her. What was she to do?

Anna stood, unable to contain her emotions any longer

and not wishing to impose them on Will. 'I should like to retire now. If you will excuse me.'

'Of course.' He rose to his feet and appeared for a second as if he thought he must accompany her. She did not want him to, not out of obligation.

She walked out alone.

## *Chapter Fourteen*

The next day's visit to Hester's cousin was not as diverting as the one before, but Anna made an effort to hide the swirl of emotion that threatened to consume her. Odd how she could both actively engage about the dresses and, at the same time, puzzle out how she was to go on in her marriage.

These two young women were filled with enthusiasm about providing her with a wardrobe the likes of which neither of them could ever afford. Yet so much could go wrong for them. What if Will refused to pay for the dresses? What if he let Hester go without a reference? Will, of course, would do none of those dishonourable things, but other men did. Anna remembered Lady Dorman's modiste insisting on payment before making another gown for her. Or Lady Dorman nearly turning out one of the maids because Violet accused her of stealing an item Violet had merely misplaced.

Anna was so much luckier than they were. And luckier than many other women who'd been forced to marry. Will might not care for her; he might resent her, but he would never shirk his duty to her. She would always have everything she needed.

Except those glorious times when they were simply Mr and Mrs Willburgh.

She squared her shoulders and lifted her chin as Hester

and her cousin altered the dress to fit her. It was a muslin carriage dress in pale yellow with a matching spencer of corded silk. The lace that had festooned the original dress had been removed when Anna deemed it much too fussy.

After the fittings Anna and the two cousins visited several other shops and Anna purchased hats and gloves and scarves. Anna found a beautiful paisley shawl that Hester's cousin said would match all her new clothes. They even stopped at a shoemaker's shop to order shoes and a boot-maker where Anna was measured for some very fine riding boots and walking boots.

By the time Anna and Hester returned to the townhouse, it was late afternoon and Anna had spent a great deal of Will's money. She'd taken him at his word and he'd better not complain.

They stepped into the hall, the poor footman tasked with carrying their packages stumbling in behind them.

Will appeared in the doorway of the library. 'I would speak with you, Anna.' He sounded grim.

Anna turned to the footman. 'Please take the packages up to the bed chamber.'

'I had better go with you,' Hester said to the young man.

She gave the footman attending the door her hat and gloves and followed Will into the library.

He didn't ask her to sit, but put a handbill into her hand.

'A new handbill. Out today,' he said.

She read it immediately.

The handbill spoke about how she had lost her inheritance by only a month by marrying Will. It went on to make up a story about a violent fight between the two of them because he'd caused her to lose a fortune.

She crushed a corner of it in her hand. 'How did they even know of this?' She looked down at the handbill again.

'They must have known we spoke with Sir Edmund. Would Sir Edmund have told them?'

Will had a pained expression. 'Not Sir Edmund. Me.'

'You?'

'I called upon Lord Dorman yesterday,' he admitted. 'They were all there. I didn't tell you—'

She searched his face. 'But, why? Why call upon them?'

He averted his gaze. 'I was angry at them for what they'd done to you.'

Or what they'd done to him, perhaps. Getting him trapped into marrying her.

She felt sick.

On her shopping spree, she'd seen boys hawking handbills. Were those handbills about her? She'd also spied people staring at her and whispering behind her back. Shopkeepers' brows rose in recognition when they learned her name.

It was discomfiting to be talked about, to have one's personal affairs exposed to all.

'I am sorry, Anna.' Will's voice turned low.

She tried to shrug it off. 'Nothing to be done about it now.'

'We should go to the country,' he said. 'Leave London. We never should have come here in the first place.'

She looked at him. 'What about your duties in Parliament?'

He paced in front of her. 'I'll have to shirk that responsibility. In any event, I might prove a distraction from the real work that must go on.'

Surely they were not that important.

'We can leave tomorrow morning,' he went on.

A full day in a carriage with him? Anna imagined silence between them. And distance, trying not to sit too close. Like that excruciating first day on the trip to Scotland.

Before she fell in love with him.

'Very well.' She spoke firmly. 'But I want to ride. I want to ride Seraphina.'

He seemed to consider the idea. 'Have you your new riding habit?'

She shook her head. 'I'll wear the old one. I do not care. They can print a handbill about it, if they like.'

'Very well,' he said. 'We'll ride the ponies. It is not more than forty miles. We should be able to reach Willburgh House before dinner.'


They rose at dawn and were ready to leave an hour later.

Anna suspected the town servants were happy to see them go. She'd invited Hester to come with her and be her lady's maid, but Hester declined. She had family in London…and there was a certain footman in the house four doors away she had her eye on.

Anna would miss her.

Hester had mended and brushed her riding habit so that it looked as good as it could. Putting it on was like reuniting with an old friend. And like being enveloped in happy memories.

Hester promised to ship the new riding habit and all her new dresses to her when they were done. She had all the accessories they'd purchased and four dresses to take with her, including the blue one which could be worn at an evening party or even a ball. Anna did not think there would be any of those, though.

True to his word, Will rode his Highland pony even though Anna was certain he had a finer horse he could have ridden. Anna rode Seraphina and John accompanied them on the brown pony.

Just as they had done when leaving Scotland.

Will's coachman would carry both Anna's and Will's

trunks as well as Bailey, the valet, and the two footmen. The other grooms, including Toby, would bring the curricle and the other horses Will had stabled in Town. Luckily Will said he and Anna needn't stay with the carriages. They could ride as freely as they'd done before.

Except the pall of reality shrouded the journey. They'd been run out of town by gossip.

It was nearly five o'clock by the time they reached the wrought iron gate that led to Willburgh House. When Anna had been a girl, she'd passed by this gate and glimpsed the house a few times. The Dormans had filled her ears with disparaging remarks about the unfashionable baroque architecture and inferior red brickwork which they said had been made on the estate itself.

John dismounted to open the gate and closed it again after they passed through. The avenue leading to the house was lined with lime trees standing like soldiers on review. Off to one side she glimpsed an octagonal dovecote. On the other side, she could barely see a small lake behind cultivated landscaping.

As Anna rode closer, the house appeared even more impressive. Certainly it was not of the classical style that Lady Dorman insisted was the height of good taste, but it had tall, paned windows in abundance, a lovely symmetry and its red brick showed well, with Corinthian pilasters setting off the centre of the house from the two wings at its side.

Will slowed until his horse was next to hers. 'You've seen the house before?'

'Not properly,' Anna responded.

'What do you think of it?' He sounded uncertain.

'It is very pleasing,' she answered honestly. And daunting.

A satisfied smile flitted across his face and he rode ahead again.

John followed a little behind Anna. 'That's a big house, m'lady.'

She turned her head to answer. 'It is indeed.'

They'd given no forewarning of their arrival so undoubtedly the household would be in a dither. Will's mother was supposed to be in residence. What sort of reception would Anna receive from her? Anna doubted it would be welcoming.

Shouting could be heard from the house as they rode closer. Servants began to pour out of the doorway and line themselves in order of precedence to receive the return of their viscount. And their new viscountess.

Her appearance was certainly not typical of a viscountess, in her worn, ill-fitting riding habit that she was so fond of. She hadn't thought ahead about it.

Too late for regrets.

Will rode up to the front of the house and one of the footmen promptly took the reins of his pony, giving the animal a quizzical look. A servant Anna assumed was an underbutler spoke to Will as she reached the house. The servants were all eyeing her, but trying not to appear to be doing so. Anna knew she looked a fright and the expressions on the maids confirmed it.

Will quickly took her in hand and presented his staff to her, their names washing through her mind like water through sand. How was she to remember them all?

One face was familiar. John's brother's wife, who smiled shyly at Anna.

'My double!' Anna shook her hand. 'It is good to see you again, Lottie. I hope you are well and happy here.'

The young woman's smile faltered. 'I am quite well, ma'am.' She did not answer Anna's second question.

John stood awkwardly with the ponies who seemed to

receive the same disapproving looks as Anna had. Will noticed and introduced John to them.

He called over John's sister-in-law. 'Would you like to take John to your husband, Lottie? Tell the others that John is to care for these ponies.'

Anna's heart lurched. How good of him. To notice John. And to care.

He rejoined her at the door. The under-butler opened it and they entered a fine panelled hall, the painted ceiling two stories high depicting some classical scene and leading to an arcade of marble columns. But Anna could not take it all in. In the hall stood Will's mother looking like thunder and a very pretty young girl who looked sixteen. Will's sister, she presumed. Will walked straight to them.

'Mother.' He gave her a dutiful peck on the cheek.

'You could have let us know you were arriving today,' she complained.

'No, we could not,' he said casually, then turned to his sister with a grin. 'Hello, Lambkin.' He took her in his arms and swung her around. 'I've missed you.'

Anna approached Will's mother. 'How are you, Lady Willburgh?'

The older woman looked her up and down, but rather than return the greeting, turned to her son. 'This is very inconvenient, Will. You have put the house in an uproar.'

'We do not require a fuss, Mother,' he responded, leading his sister over to Anna. 'Let me present you to my wife, Anna.' He presented his sister proudly. 'My little sister, Ellen.'

Anna, still stinging from Lady Willburgh's blatant rebuff, smiled. 'I am delighted to meet you, Ellen.'

'Why are you dressed that way?' Ellen asked, eyes wide.

It was so spontaneous and what everyone else must have

wanted to ask that Anna laughed. 'These are the only riding clothes I had.'

'There is a tale about that,' Will interjected. 'We'll tell you all of it later.'

'Did you really elope to Gretna Green?' the girl asked.

'Not Gretna Green,' he responded. 'But we did elope to Scotland.'

The servants filed back in and hurried to their tasks. One footman held their saddlebags awaiting instructions. The housekeeper, whose name Anna could not remember, stood a few steps away. She was a formidable, thin-lipped woman with narrowed eyes that seemed to miss nothing.

'What rooms should we prepare, ma'am?' the housekeeper asked Lady Willburgh.

Will answered. 'We will occupy the lord and lady's chambers, Mrs Greaves.'

'As you wish, my lord,' she replied. 'It will take some time, though, to ready the lady's chamber. In what room do you wish us to put Lady Willburgh's belongings?'

'You mean the Dowager Lady Willburgh's belongings,' he corrected. 'Lady Willburgh's belongings will be placed in the lady's chamber.'

The housekeeper and Will's mother exchanged glances. 'I did understand you, sir.'

Anna was to displace Will's mother again.

Will blew out a breath. 'Really, Mother. Could you not have selected another room before this?'

She sniffed. 'I would have had you told us when you were coming.'

Anna broke into this. 'Please. At the moment all I need is a place to tidy myself and change clothes.'

'You may use my room,' Will's sister offered.

'Excellent idea, Ellen,' Will said. 'Will you show Anna where it is?' He gestured to the footman to follow them.

Ellen led her through the marble columns to an impressive oak staircase. 'My room is on the second floor,' she said. 'Mama's room—the one you will have—is on the first floor. They both face the garden, which you will like.'

When they entered her room, the huge windows revealed a lovely garden and park.

The footman waited at the doorway. 'Which...bag... m'lady?'

Anna indicated which was hers.

The footman brought it in and turned to leave.

'Would you summon my maid, please?' Ellen called after him.

One of the footmen helped Will change from his riding clothes to home attire. When he was done he asked the man to have his mother meet him in the parlour and to have tea served there. Now Will was seated in one of the more comfortable chairs in the parlour, eyes closed, weary from the long ride.

He heard his mother enter and rose.

'Really, Will,' his mother began. 'I am much put out with you, coming with no warning like this. This whole quagmire has taken a terrible toll on my nerves and it does not help that you spring all this on me without even a how do you do.'

Will was too weary for this. 'You make too much of it, Mother,'

She presented her cheek and he kissed it.

She glanced around and sighed. 'Do I need to ring for tea?'

He gestured for her to sit. 'I have already arranged it.' She selected a chair and Will sank back into his. 'Tell me how you have been,' he said. 'How are matters here?'

She fussed with her skirt. 'Well, it has been difficult to manage without Bailey. And Ellen has asked me why you had to marry if you had done nothing wrong. What was I to say?'

'What did you say?' he asked.

'Only that it would ruin all of us if you did not marry.'

'That was the truth of it.' Right. There had been some urgency to marry—to prevent the scandal from affecting Ellen. But they could have waited. Should have waited.

He certainly was not going to tell his mother that they need not have married at all.

His mother rubbed her brow. 'I cannot bear it that you had to marry into *that* family?' She gestured in the general direction of the Dorman property which abutted theirs, albeit acres away.

'Actually she is not a Dorman.' Perhaps it would ease his mother's nerves to know this. 'She had a different father. Her mother was widowed before marrying Dorman.'

She averted her face. 'That is not what he told me,' she said in a barely audible voice.

'What did you say?' Will demanded.

She faced him. 'That is not what Bertram Dorman told me. He said she was his daughter.'

The will proved her parentage, if necessary, but Will believed Anna even before that.

He waved a hand. 'It does not matter. We are married and we must make the best of it.'

'I know.' She sighed again. 'I just wish it were different.'

'We all wish it were different,' he said.

At that moment Anna and Ellen appeared in the doorway. Anna's face told Will she'd overheard him.

He stood. 'Come sit, Anna. We've ordered tea.'

She nodded a greeting to Will's mother who said, 'Well, you look better.'

Anna did indeed look better than the travel-weary rider she'd been. She looked beautiful.

'Thank you for the compliment, Lady Willburgh,' Anna replied.

Will directed her to the sofa and he sat beside her, briefly touching her hand as he did so. She moved her hand away.

Ellen sat facing them. 'You said you had a tale to tell about eloping. Tell it now, Will!'

He glanced at Anna, not certain if she'd wish their story told. He'd no intention of telling all of it anyway.

Not about their passion-filled nights and joyful days.

Anna's expression was impassive.

He was saved for the moment by the under-butler bringing in the tea. Without consulting Anna, his mother poured for everyone.

Will took the opportunity to directly ask Anna. 'Shall I tell of our adventure?' He tried to keep his voice light.

'As you wish,' she replied, giving away none of what she really might wish.

Still, Will went ahead and told the tale anyway, starting with how Lucius tried to stop them and how they foiled him.

'Do you mean that groom and maid that turned up here, when, honestly, we had no work for them? They pretended to be you? You let them wear your clothes?'

'They did a fine job,' Will insisted. 'It was not until Lucius saw them that he realised they were not us.'

'And you wore old clothes that were once worn by who knows who?' his mother continued sounding outraged.

Will ignored her and continued from where he left off, telling how they detoured to Langholm and how Armstrong, the innkeeper married them.

'Anna caught on right away,' Will said. 'But I confess, I was married before I even realised.'

Ellen laughed. 'So clever of you, Anna!'

His mother huffed. 'How dreadful! No proper vows at all. And in a tavern!'

'It suited us,' Will said. 'Did it not, Anna?'

Anna picked up her cup of tea for a sip. 'It was perfect,' she said. Her ring caught the light from a nearby lamp and sparkled. At least she was still wearing it.

'What is that on your finger?' his mother asked.

'My wedding ring,' Anna replied.

'You wore that ring in Scotland?' His mother sounded horrified.

'I bought it in London two days ago,' Will responded.

Ellen broke in. 'You didn't explain why you were riding today or where those funny horses came from.'

Will made a quelling gesture with his hand. 'We are just coming to that part of the story. And those are not "funny horses." Those are Highland ponies. I bought them so we could ride home.'

His mother shook her head. 'Who ever would want to ride that distance?'

Anna spoke up. 'It was my request. As was riding today.'

Will told about their riding back to London, which explained Anna's riding habit, even though his mother continued to purse her lips in disapproval. Telling of those days filled him with melancholy. It brought back the pleasure of their nights together, the joyfulness of their days, and how freeing it had been to not be a viscount. Anna's head was bowed during this part of the story. Was she remembering too? Or was she thinking that she need not have married him and that he was responsible for all of London knowing why.

He glanced at his mother, the very picture of incivility. If he wanted to assign blame for them marrying so quickly, he could give some to his mother.

But he knew the blame rested on him.

At that moment the coach carrying their trunks and Bailey and the footmen arrived. Will excused himself to be certain all was in order.

'More commotion.' Lady Willburgh sighed and turned to Anna. 'I suppose we must find a maid to attend you, although I do not know who that will be. I assumed you would hire your own person from London.'

Anna did not miss the criticism in Lady Willburgh's statement. 'There was no time,' she explained.

She was still reeling from hearing Will's words—'*We all wish it were different.*' They should not have surprised Will's mother. The woman had always made it very clear she was not happy that Anna had to marry her son. Anna even wished she had not married Will, did she not?

No. What she wished was that they could again be simply Mr and Mrs Willburgh traveling from Scotland indulging their every whim.

Loving each other.

'Let her use my maid,' Ellen suggested.

Yet another sigh from Lady Willburgh. 'I suppose that will do, although it does put an extra burden on the girl.'

All Anna wanted at the moment was to be alone, unattended by anybody. 'I do understand that the unexpected nature of our arrival has created problems for you, Lady Willburgh. For that I am sorry, but I assure you, I do not need much assistance. I do not need to be moved into the lady's chamber right away. Any room will do.'

Lady Willburgh waved a dismissive hand. 'It is too late for that. Mrs Greaves already has the servants tearing my room apart.'

'At your son's direction,' Anna clarified. 'Not mine.'

Ellen passed the plate of biscuits to Anna who selected one.

'What was Scotland like?' Ellen asked. 'Did you meet Highlanders and Jacobites?'

'She has been reading novels,' Lady Willburgh explained in an exasperated tone.

Anna set her biscuit on her saucer. 'I do not know if we met any Highlanders. We were only in the Lowlands. We might have met a Jacobite or two.' Those, like Armstrong who disdained the English. 'But they did not say that they were. They seemed indistinguishable from the sort of people you would see in a tavern in England, except they spoke like Scotsmen.'

'I certainly hope *my* daughter does not see *anyone* in a tavern!' huffed the girl's mother.

Anna regarded Lady Willburgh over her cup of tea. Would she not say one favourable thing?

The woman was still a beauty, even as she must approach fifty years. Her full head of hair still had more blond in it than grey, and the only lines on her face were at the corners of her eyes. Her daughter had the same dark hair as her brother, but had inherited her mother's flawless skin and delicate features.

In contrast, Anna had always been told her own looks were 'passable'—this by Lady Dorman and Violet, primarily. Indeed, her hair could only be called brown and her features were too big for her face. And she was taller than was fashionable and lacked sufficient curves.

For this alone she could understand Lady Willburgh's disappointment in her. At least, though, she knew precisely where she stood with the woman. She surely could never be duped into thinking Lady Willburgh cared about her.

Unable to think of a polite way to escape, Anna asked Ellen what books she had read. Anna had read many of them and Ellen delighted in discussing all aspects of her favourite novels, which seemed to include those of the author of *Waverley*. No wonder she asked about Highlanders and Jacobites.

'Wait until you see our library,' Ellen exclaimed. 'There is none like it in all of England!'

'I should like to see it,' Anna responded.

Ellen turned to her mother. 'Mama, may I show Anna the library now?'

Lady Willburgh waved her hand. 'Do. I need some solitude for my nerves.'

Chattering all the way, Ellen led Anna up the oak stairway to a drawing room that was panelled with the same sort of wood that was on the staircase. Once in the room Ellen stopped.

Anna looked for another doorway. 'Where is the library?'

'Here!' Ellen swept her arms to encompass the whole room. She laughed at Anna's confusion and rushed around the room somehow opening the panelling to reveal bookshelf after bookshelf.

Anna smiled. 'What a surprise!'

Ellen twirled around. 'It is my favourite room.'

Anna thought it might become her favourite room, as well. She was reasonably certain that Lady Willburgh did not spend much time here. The room also seemed to be absent a desk—unless it, too, was hidden behind panelling—so Will probably did not spend much time here either. And if Ellen was her only company?

At least she did not convey disappointment or disapproval.

# *Chapter Fifteen*

$\sim\!\!\!\sim\!\!\!\sim\!\!\!\sim$

Will's valet could be trusted to unpack for him, but he thought he ought to make certain Anna's trunk would be taken care of. He doubted his mother would do it. He'd hardly said more than two words to the housekeeper about it before his estate manager sent word that he needed to speak to Will urgently.

The manager's office was in an outbuilding. Will took the back stairs and went out one of the doors leading to the garden. He crossed the lawn to the building. The door was open and he saw the manager seated at a desk, looking at a paper.

'Parker?' Will entered the office. 'You need to speak to me?'

Parker, a robust man with thinning hair and a restless energy, was only a few years older than Will. His father had been estate manager when Will's father was alive and his son learned the job at his side.

He rose and strode over to Will, extending his hand to shake. 'Good to see you, Will. I hear you've managed to scandalise all of London and get married. My best wishes to you and your wife.'

Will accepted his hand, the informality normal between them. They'd grown up together as boys and Parker had always looked out for the younger Will.

Parker went on, 'My apologies for asking for you when

you've hardly set foot in the place, but there are a few things that best not wait.'

They sat while Parker detailed several problems and they discussed the solutions and made the needed decisions. That done, Will rose to leave and Parker walked with him to the doorway.

'One more thing,' Parker said. 'I thought I'd give you warning. Jones and Keen have complained to me that they do not know what to do with now two new grooms, since you brought another one today.'

Jones was the stable master; Keen, the head groom.

Why was this so difficult? 'Surely there is enough work to keep two more men busy. There are three new horses to tend, after all.'

'Seems that one of the men heard that Adams and his wife came from Lord Dorman's London house to cause trouble here.' Parker explained.

Will pressed his hand on his forehead. 'That is nonsense. Who would say such a thing?'

'I wouldn't be surprised if it was one of the Dorman servants who told him that,' Parker said. 'They've heard all the London gossip just as we have.'

Will shook his head. 'It could not be further from the truth. John, Adams, and Lottie prevented Lucius Dorman from thwarting the elopement.'

Although if Lucius had succeeded, then Anna would have been able to inherit her fortune.

'Walk with me to the stables,' Will asked. 'I'll speak to Jones and Keen.'

They walked the distance to the stables where there was plenty of activity since the carriages and horses had arrived. Will noticed right away that the Highland ponies were unnecessarily tucked away in the farthest stalls. He could just glimpse John and Adams tending to them. Toby was sitting nearby.

Will strode through the stable to purposely greet the two brothers, Parker in tow. Will did not bother to ask how they were settling in, because he knew the answer. Instead he asked Adams if the accommodations for him and his wife were adequate.

'They'll do, sir,' the young man said unenthusiastically.

'They were given a room above the stables,' John said. 'It's separate from the other men, but only by a wall.'

Will turned to Parker and frowned. 'That was the best you could do?'

'I left it to Keen, sir,' the manager said.

'Well, we must do better,' Will insisted. 'Find them a little cottage. I know we have some vacant.'

'Yes, sir,' Parker said.

'Thank you, sir,' Adams said.

Keen, apparently having heard that the Viscount was in the stables came bustling through. 'Welcome back, sir,' the man said.

Will did not mince words. 'I do not like what I see here, Keen, nor what I've heard. I expect these two men and Adams's wife to be treated in a fair manner. They are not spies from the Dorman estate. Quite the reverse.' Will inclined his head towards Toby. 'Toby can tell you all that they have done for me and for my wife. I expect you to make certain every man knows the truth.' Will did not usually show his anger so plainly. 'If in the future there are any rumours about the Dormans or about my workers, I want to be informed immediately.'

Before he walked out, he made certain to shake Adams's hand and to clap John on the back. He knew every worker in

the stables was watching him and he wanted them to know
these two men were in his favour.

Will and Parker went on to the carriage house and im-
parted the same information to Jones, the stable master.
When Will finally returned to the house it was time for
dinner. He didn't feel like changing clothes for dinner, but
did not want to risk coming to the table smelling like horse.

His valet helped him make quick work of dressing for
dinner. Afterwards he knocked on the door connecting his
room to the lady's chamber, hoping to find Anna. When there
was no answer, he opened the door and entered the room.

It appeared that all his mother's things had been removed,
but Anna's trunk still sat in the middle of the room. Had it
even been unpacked? Will did not want to snoop that far.

Instead he went to the drawing room where his mother
typically waited for dinner to be announced. Anna was there.
And his mother.

He greeted them all and walked over to the carafe of claret.
He noticed Anna did not have a glass.

'Would you like some claret, Anna?' he asked.

'I would,' she responded.

He poured and handed the glass to her.

He turned to his mother. 'Mother?'

'I have some.' She lifted her glass.

He frowned as he poured his own claret. Had his mother
not offered any to Anna?

He went to sit by her. 'I was called away,' he said. 'How
has it been for you?'

He hoped to hear that his mother had graciously shown
her around or had made certain her room was readied for her.

Instead Anna said, 'Your sister was kind enough to show
me your library. Very unusual.' Her tone was polite. Dis-
guising much.

He was dismayed. 'Yes. It is unique. You must feel free to treat it as your own.' He wanted her to feel welcome. She was bound to him. He had spoiled her chances to determine her own fate, had she become an heiress. It was his duty to do right by her.

He hated being so formal with her. They'd not been formal at all on their ride back from Scotland. He wanted to tell her what was on his mind—how John and Adams and Adams's wife were treated for one thing—but it felt like a wall between them, one made of molasses perhaps because he felt like he could slog through it with time and effort.

At least he hoped so.

Ellen came rushing in. 'Am I late? I was afraid I would be late.'

She and Will did a pantomime of her asking for claret and him pouring her only a short glass.

Their mother took a sip of her wine. 'Had Betty been delayed in helping you?'

Ellen looked puzzled. 'No. Why would she be?'

'I thought—' She inclined her head towards Anna. 'I thought she might have been busy.'

'Oh,' Ellen exclaimed. 'Anna said she did not need Betty.'

Their mother lifted a brow. 'Indeed?'

Anna smiled graciously. 'As you can see, I did not change clothes so I needed no maid.'

Their mother formed a stiffer smile. 'I did notice.'

Bailey appeared at the door. 'Dinner is served in the dining room.'

'The dining room?' Will was baffled. 'For only the four of us?'

His mother stood. 'I thought you would desire a formal dinner for your first...' Her voice trailed off so he didn't know to what *first* she was referring.

He offered Anna his arm and she accepted it. If his mother wished to be formal than he would lead the party to the dining room with Anna on his arm. His mother and sister would need to follow.

In the dining room the long table was set oddly, with Will and Anna at each end and his mother and Ellen on each side at the table's centre. At least it seemed odd to Will, because conversation was more difficult, nearly impossible between Anna and him. So the dinner was a stress to him and he worried that it was even worse for Anna. If not for Ellen's conversation, it would have been unbearable.

After dinner Will hung back while Anna, his mother, and Ellen retired to the drawing room for tea.

He stayed only to speak with Bailey. 'The table setting was not comfortable. It put us all at a distance from each other.'

'It was as your mother requested,' Bailey explained.

'I realise that,' Will said. 'But we do not need the long table.'

'I offered to remove some of the leaves, but your mother—'

Will put up his hand. 'Say no more. I understand. But do remove the leaves for tomorrow's dinner. We do not need them unless we have guests.'

'It will be done, sir.' Bailey bowed.

Will left to join the others in the drawing room, but only his mother and Ellen were there.

'Where is Anna?' he asked.

Ellen answered him. 'She begged off, saying she was fatigued from the journey.'

He was losing patience with his mother's unwelcoming treatment of Anna. 'I hope you sent Betty to attend her.'

'She said she did not need Betty tonight,' his mother responded.

He sat facing his mother. 'You need to be more cordial to Anna, Mother. No matter what you wish, I am married to her and she is my wife. This will not change.'

'I am very cordial to her,' his mother protested.

'No, you are not,' he countered. 'I expect you to do better.'

His mother pursed her lips and did not respond.

'I'll do my best,' Ellen added.

He had not been faulting her. He smiled at her. 'I know, Lambkin. I can count on you.'

He stood and excused himself.

His valet was surprised that he had come to the room so early. Will told him he wished to retire. When the man finally left, Will went to the door connecting his room with Anna's. He opened it a crack.

The room was dark and it was clear she was in bed.

He closed the door again and returned to his room.

The next morning Anna woke early and, having no confidence that a maid would come to assist her, dressed herself. She made her way down to where she supposed the breakfast room would be, somewhere near that small sitting room she'd seen when first arriving.

A footman with a dour expression pointed to the proper room. She entered and was the only one there.

After a couple of minutes the footman reappeared. 'Breakfast is still being prepared, ma'am. We are not accustomed to serving so early.'

Goodness. Did she hear disapproval in the footman's voice? 'I am well able to wait,' she responded, her tone sharper than usual. 'I will learn these things in time, but this is my first morning here.'

Which ought to have been obvious to the young man.

He did not respond directly to the statement but asked, 'Would you like tea or coffee?'

'Tea, please.'

She expected him to ask what she preferred for breakfast, but he bowed and left.

It seemed like she waited a lot longer for tea than she had even at the Dormans' when it was only her making the request. She was considering going on a search of the kitchen when the door opened and Will entered.

He looked surprised to see her. 'Good morning.'

'You've been riding.' She could tell. He carried the scent of the out of doors on him.

'I have,' he admitted. 'I usually ride in the morning when here. Take a look at the land.'

He might have asked her to ride as well, knowing how much she loved it. She averted her gaze, not wanting to reveal her disappointment.

He glanced around the room and frowned. 'Has no one seen to your breakfast?'

'One of the footmen is seeing to it.' She did not tell him that she'd been waiting nearly half an hour.

One moment later the door opened and in came footmen carrying warming dishes of red herring, baked eggs, and sausages, bowls of porridge, and plates of bread and cheese. One footman brought a pot of coffee, cream, and sugar and poured for Will. Last came Anna's tea. The under-butler asked Will what he wished to be put on his plate.

'Serve Lady Willburgh first,' Will told him.

The man dutifully asked Anna.

'Bread and cheese and an egg, please,' she responded.

When they both were served, the servants left and they were alone.

Will leaned towards her. 'How was your night, Anna?'

Lonely, she wanted to say.

But if she revealed how much she yearned for him next to her in bed, he might do so out of duty. She had no wish to be bedded out of obligation.

'I slept well enough,' she answered perfunctorily.

'You retired early,' he went on. 'I feared you might be ill.'

She felt many things—lonely, estranged, unwelcome. Angry—but not ill. 'No,' she told him. 'I am not ill.'

They ate in silence until Will said, 'You know if there is anything you need, you have merely to ask?'

Ask who? she wondered. The servants? His mother? Him? At least if she asked him, he would see to it. It would be his duty.

Very well. She would ask. 'I would like a tour of the house and grounds. So I know my way about.' And she would not have to wander around to find where she was supposed to go. 'Who should I ask to show it to me?'

He didn't answer right away. 'I will give you the tour.'

She'd expected him to assign Bailey to the task, not himself. She did not know what to say.

'We can begin after breakfast,' he went on. 'If that suits you.'

Heaven help her, she could not resist his company even if he offered it out of duty. Even if he was *disappointed* she was here at all.

When they were finished eating, Will stood and extended his hand to help her up. 'Where would you like to start?'

His tone turned stiff and formal, but the warmth of his hand in hers seeped through her whole body. She was disturbed by this visceral reaction.

'You know the house,' she managed.

'We'll start on this floor, then.'

He walked her through the sitting room where they'd first gathered with Lady Willburgh and Ellen, to another sitting room, to the dining room where he told her about the ancestors whose portraits were on the wall. He pointed out that the huge painting of fruits and nuts, oysters, and a lobster was by a Flemish artist and had been in the family for over a hundred years.

On the other side of the hall was a drawing room that led to another room filled with classical statues and a bust of Pitt and other important men. Beyond the sculpture room was Will's office.

'My duties require me to spend a great deal of time here,' he said.

The room was dominated by a large desk stacked with papers and ledgers. Behind the desk were shelves of books and other ledgers. It was saved from looking dismal by the large windows opening onto the beautiful garden outside and two comfortable chairs facing the fireplace. Above the fireplace was a portrait of a young man with powdered hair and a blue velvet coat with a red collar. She stared at it. It resembled Will.

'My father,' Will muttered, turning away from it.

She wished she hadn't stared at it. The mood grew sombre instead of merely stilted.

'Shall we tour the first floor?' Will strode to the doorway.

Anna hurried after him.

He explained who the portraits were on the stairway. There were four. His grandparents. His mother—dazzlingly beautiful as a young woman—and another of his father, older this time. Would Will look as stern as this, in ten or twenty years?

She'd seen the drawing room before, of course, but Will pointed out some special family items there. A Pembroke table and some ribbon-back chairs, both by Chippendale and acquired by his grandparents. This most formal room had the plasterwork and pale colours of years ago when Robert Adam's neoclassical style was popular. The Dormans had preferred the more modern furnishings, brighter colours on the walls and fabrics, tables and cabinets of ebonised wood or embellished with gold paint or Egyptian details.

They toured the library. She thought Will almost looked pleased that it captivated her. There was also a lovely music room brightened by the windows with a pianoforte, a harp, and a chest she presumed held sheets of music.

'Do you play?' he asked.

'A little.' She'd learned along with Violet, but never had as much time to practice as she wished.

'Use it whenever you like.'

He showed her his room, but he said little about its adornments or furniture. For some reason, Anna felt the spectre of his father strongly there. She wondered if he'd moved into the room without changing what his father had left.

They walked through the connecting doorway to her room.

He glanced at the bare walls. 'There were paintings I wanted to tell you about, but my mother has had everything taken out of the room.' He frowned. 'I'll have some more paintings brought in to be hung. There are several in the attic.'

'May I select them?' Anna asked.

He looked surprised she'd asked. 'Of course.' He then noticed her trunk, still in the middle of the room where the footman had left it.

'What is your trunk doing here? Did you not call for a footman to take it away?'

'It is not unpacked yet,' she responded.

He countered in a chiding tone. 'You must ask the maids who attend you to unpack for you and see the trunk stored away.'

'No maid attended me,' she replied.

'Why not?' He sounded disapproving.

'Betty was assigned the task, but I did not want her to do it,' she told him.

'Why?'

'It was clear she found it a burden.'

'*She* found it a burden?' He turned to face her. 'You are the Viscountess, Anna. They are employed to meet your needs.'

'Really, Will,' she shot back, annoyed now. 'My first days here I should order the servants about?'

'Unpacking your trunk was hardly an unreasonable demand,' he responded.

Should she tell him that the servants already displayed a reluctance to help her, if not animosity towards her? Following his mother's lead, no doubt.

'I prefer to tread carefully,' she said instead.

He shrugged but added. 'You need a lady's maid to attend you.' He still sounded as if he was admonishing her.

She agreed. 'I do, but I should very much want a lady's maid to want to serve me.'

They left this room to go up to the second floor. Muffled voices came from one bed chamber.

Will inclined his head towards that door. 'My mother.' There was an edge to his voice. 'That is the room she selected. It used to be mine.'

The door to a different room opened and the maid, Betty, appeared. She sent a guilty glance towards Anna and Will before disappearing around the corner.

'The servants' stairs are back there,' Will explained.

Ellen walked out of the room Betty had left and stopped

abruptly upon encountering them. 'Good morning! What are you doing?'

Will gave her a playful, endearing hug, making Anna's heart ache. Towards his sister, he acted like her old Will. 'I'm showing Anna the house, Lambkin.'

Anna smiled. 'The grand tour.'

'Oh.' The girl's brow creased. 'I am famished or I'd come with you.'

'Join us later,' Anna told her. Ellen was the only person in the household with whom Anna felt welcomed.

'I will!' Ellen hurried to the stairs.

Will smiled as he watched her disappear, then his expression sobered. 'Shall we continue?'

Was showing her the house merely another chore for him? He seemed to be taking little pleasure in it. Or was it her company he disliked?

Perhaps he could not get over the disappointment of marrying her when he had not really needed to.

They toured the children's wing and some guest bedrooms. He pointed to the door leading to the servants' rooms at the top of the house.

'That is about everything.' He headed back to the stairway.

All? 'What about below stairs? The kitchen and the rooms around it?'

His brows rose. 'You want to see that? My mother never goes down there.'

Lady Dorman never went down to the kitchen either. 'I would like to see it.' Anna wanted to know what the servants' areas were like.

'Let us use the servants' stairway, then.'

# Chapter Sixteen

They reached the lower level of the house where the servants' hall, the kitchen, scullery, still room, housekeeper's room, butler's pantry, and such were located.

Will greeted each servant they encountered by name and presented them to Anna. Anna was certain each one of them greeted her suspiciously and with disfavour.

Mrs Greaves, the housckeeper, appeared and stuck to them like a plaster to a wound. She was deferential and cordial to Will, but cool and curt with Anna, and her demeanour was mirrored in all the others they encountered.

Did Will notice? She was not sure he had.

When they toured the laundry, which was in a wing off the kitchen, Anna found Adams's wife there. 'Lottie! I am surprised to see you in the laundry. I thought you worked in the house.'

Lottie curtsied. 'Mrs Greaves moves me around, ma'am.'

Will's brows furrowed. 'Is this the best place for you? What work did you do in the inn?'

'Tended the rooms, mostly, sir,' she responded. 'I helped serve in the tavern some, as well.'

'But not the laundry?' he asked.

'No, sir. Not the kitchen either.'

He touched her arm in a reassuring manner. 'I am certain

the house needs you more than the laundry. We will speak to Mrs Greaves.'

'Thank you, sir.' She curtsied again.

He nodded in acknowledgment. 'Did your husband tell you we are locating a cottage for you?'

'We are grateful, sir.'

'What was that about a cottage?' Anna asked him when they left the laundry.

'I was not satisfied with the rooms they were given over at the stable,' was all he said.

They walked up the stairs and back to the hall.

Will gestured towards the door. 'I must meet with Parker, my estate manager, who is in one of the outer buildings. He is expecting me.'

'Do those buildings include the stables?' she asked. 'I would like to know how to find the stables.'

He hesitated. 'You can accompany me, then.'

'Thank you,' she replied. 'I will just get my hat and shawl?'

'I'll wait here.'

Anna dashed up the stairs and retrieved her shawl, still packed in the trunk in her room. She put on her hat and was out the door again, approaching the stairs.

Voices sounded from the floor above. Anna stepped out of sight.

It was Lady Willburgh. 'Remember, she is a Dorman and can be up to no good for us here.'

'Do not fear, my lady,' Mrs Greaves responded. 'We will take our direction from you.'

Anna's stomach dropped. She had suspected Lady Willburgh wanted to make her feel unwelcome. To what end? What choice did any of them have that she was here? Certainly Anna had none.

A wave of loneliness washed over her. She was the outsider here just as she'd been the outsider at the Dormans'.

Ellen seemed happy enough to have her here, but Anna would not ever put that sweet child in the middle of this muddle. The only others she knew—John, his brother, and wife—possessed even less power than she. Anna would not risk them being damaged, not after they'd helped so.

No, she was alone, as alone as she had ever been.

She listened to be sure Mrs Greaves and Lady Willburgh had retreated and, squaring her shoulders, strode back down the stairs.

Will paced the hall waiting for Anna.

Why had he volunteered to show her the house? He had mounds of work to do and he was already late to see Parker.

He simply could not resist the chance to spend time with her. He was proud of his house, his heritage and it did not want to cede the pleasure of showing it off to her to anyone else. But they were so distant from each other, as if a wall had been erected between them that was too high and too thick to breach.

That news about her lost trust sounded a death knell on their marriage.

He should tell himself it was good they were distant. He could get his work done then.

But watching her descend the stairs with that special grace of hers took his breath away. She was strong, not delicate and did not pretend to be otherwise. Her lovemaking had been strong, as well. It aroused him to think of it and he thought of it far too often.

Like right now.

'I'm ready,' she said as she reached the bottom step and wrapped the shawl around her.

He offered his arm, knowing he'd be affected by her touch. 'We can leave by the garden door. It is quicker.'

When they stepped out into the fresh country air, Will was proud anew at the beauty his grandfather and father created in the gardens and grounds. A great expanse of green lawn, a formal garden behind the house, and pathways leading to the picturesque gardens beyond.

'What do you think, Anna?' he asked.

'About the gardens?' She took in the view. 'Lovely.'

'Perhaps tomorrow I'll give you a proper tour of them.' Could they find in that cultivated wilderness a respite from what separated them? Could he get over himself? He feared he was the wall between them.

The outer buildings were beyond the gardens and the stables, past them.

She'd been quiet through most of the walk, but suddenly spoke. 'You told Lottie that *we* will speak to Mrs Greaves on her behalf. I hope you meant you would do it.'

That was what was on her mind? 'I will, if that is what you wish.'

'Good. Mrs Greaves will have to listen to you.'

Will had chided Anna about not seeking the servants' assistance, but when they toured below stairs, he noticed how the house servants reacted to Anna. If they believed Anna was a Dorman spy like they'd thought of the Adamses, he'd have to set them straight.

Anna went on. 'I want to look for a lady's maid for myself from outside the household. Perhaps from some agency in London.'

He thought that was best, too. 'Whatever makes you happy.'

She averted her face but not before he spied a cynical smile on her lips.

'Will! Anna!' Ellen ran to catch up to them. 'Did you finish the tour of the house?'

'We did,' Will said. 'I'm on my way to meet Parker.'

Ellen turned to Anna. 'Would you like me to show you the garden? I'll wager I can show you places Will doesn't even know about.'

'I'll wager you can't,' Will quipped.

'Will was going to introduce me to the estate manager and show me the stables,' Anna said.

'Oh, you can meet Parker any time.' She pulled on Anna's arm. 'Let me show you the garden, then we can go to the stables.'

Anna had the grace to turn to Will raising her brows in question.

'Go with Ellen,' Will said, disappointed to lose her, even though he ought to be relieved. He could get back to work. 'I'll see you both at dinner.'


That evening dinner was a bit more comfortable for Anna. For one thing, the table had been made smaller so she was not banished to the far end.

When Lady Willburgh saw the room, though, she'd exclaimed. 'Who did this? The room is unbalanced with the table that way!' She shot a scathing look towards Anna.

But Will answered, 'I ordered it, Mother. As long as it is only the four of us dining, it stays this way.'

His mother had pursed her lips, but she said no more. Ellen, who was becoming more dear to Anna, carried the conversation again, chattering about her and Anna's tour of the garden and asking Anna all kinds of questions about her impression of the house.

Lady Willburgh asked Will about Lottie and if it was his place to involve himself in the running of the house. Obviously she'd heard from Mrs Greaves of his request that Lottie be used in the house. Will answered that as long as he was Viscount he could involve himself wherever he wished.

Lady Willburgh said little after that and was quiet even when they'd finished dinner and had retired to the sitting room for tea.

'Play cards with me, Anna,' Ellen begged.

After some hesitation, Anna replied, 'Oh, very well. What do you want to play?'

Ellen opened a baize-covered card table. 'Piquet?'

'Piquet.' Anna pulled up a chair. 'Although I warn you I am not very good at it.

It did not help that Will watched them while he sipped his brandy. It made her heart beat faster and she lost attention to the cards.

After losing the second game to Ellen, Anna declared a desire to go to bed. 'Before I lose another,' she said, smiling.

Will stood. 'I'll go with you.'

Her heart skittered even faster.

As they walked up the stairs, he asked, 'Do you want a maid to attend you?'

'It isn't necessary,' she responded. Actually she'd rather he helped her, like he'd done in those first days of their marriage.

'I promise we'll find a lady's maid for you,' he went on. 'I'll write to an agency tomorrow.'

She thought she would be the one writing.

He opened her door but stopped her from going in right away.

'May I come to you later?' he asked softly.

She searched his face. His eyes looked sincere and a bit wary.

'If you wish,' she replied, wary as well.

They made love that night, but in a sad way, it seemed to Anna. As if they both mourned the loss of joy they'd once shared together. Their pleasure came, though, but to Anna it seemed melancholy. Still, she wanted him in her bed. Perhaps with time they could regain some of what they'd lost.

The next morning Anna woke when the first light of dawn was peeking over the horizon. Will was gone.

Her spirits plummeted. Once again she'd let herself believe he cared about her, but once again she was alone. Was he using her like a bandalore, reeling her in, then rolling her away, over and over?

She rose from the bed and donned her riding habit. She plaited her hair and tucked it into the old hat she'd worn on the travels. The footman attending the hall was dozing. She did not wake him but walked past him and through Will's office to the doors to the garden.

A milky mist carpeted the lawn and swirled at her feet as she hurried to the stables, hoping at least one of the grooms was awake. When Ellen showed her the stables she merely pointed to them; they never walked close to them.

The doors to the stable were open and, to her relief, several grooms were at work. She spied John and hurried over to him.

'Could you saddle Seraphina for me?' she asked.

The other grooms eyed her curiously—or perhaps suspiciously. When Seraphina was saddled and ready, John helped Anna mount her. Anna leaned over and hugged the pony's neck.

'I am so glad to be riding you,' she whispered.

As she rode out, Will walked in.

'Anna!' He looked surprised.

She took in a breath. He was at his most handsome,

in comfortable riding clothes and boots, almost like he'd dressed on their travels. And the sight of him brought back the night before, the lovemaking she'd so desperately missed.

She blinked, unable to meet his eye. 'Good morning, Will.'

He paused before responding. 'Wait. I'll ride with you.'

Every morning the next week Anna rose early to ride. Sometimes Will rode with her. She never waited for him, but, more often than not, he left the house when she did and they walked together to the stables. They rode together, then, too, rarely talking more than necessary. For Anna, though, it increased the pain. Riding together had once been her delight, but now a reminder of what must have been an illusion.

It was clear to her he rode with her out of obligation, what was expected of him.

He no longer joined her at night, which only intensified the pain.

His days were busy otherwise and she rarely saw him after breakfast until dinner. Lady Willburgh and Mrs Greaves continued to run the household without involving her and any time Anna tried to broach the subject with her mother-in-law, she was put off. Lady Willburgh often kept Ellen busy at her side, as well.

So during the day, Anna was very much alone. She occupied herself by reading or walking in the garden. Or tidying her room, because she did not have a lady's maid and had not yet received a response from the agency she'd written to.

Anna was accustomed to taking care of herself, so this was not a huge hardship. Requesting the service of a maid when she needed one continued to be difficult. Her requests were never promptly filled unless Lottie was available, but

Lottie could do little more than clean her room and take her clothes to the laundry and bring them back.

A trunk carrying her new clothing from London had arrived the day before. Anna had not fully unpacked her first trunk and she debated whether she should make a fuss to be given some help in unpacking this new one. This one included her new riding habit. Discovering it made her rather sad.

She was laying the riding habit across her bed when Will stuck his head in the doorway. 'I have an errand in the village. Is there anything I might do for you there?'

She closed the trunk's lid. 'I would like to come along.'

He paused as he always did when she asked for something from him. 'Very well. I am leaving within half an hour.'

Anna made certain she was ready on time and soon they were on the road in the curricle, with Toby riding on the back. Anna had not visited the village since the scandal and elopement. She supposed the villagers knew all about it. They certainly knew more about the generational feud between the Willburghs and the Dormans than did members of the *ton* in London.

She sighed at the thought of facing them.

Will noticed. 'What is it, Anna?'

She regretted revealing that much to him. 'Nothing of consequence. The villagers know me and will have knowledge of all the gossip.'

He glanced at her. 'Perhaps they will simply wish us well.' He turned his eyes back to the road. 'They will also want the Viscountess to spend money in their shops.'

Oh, yes. She carried a title now. One would not know it by how it was for her at Willburgh House.

The village was about five miles from Willburgh House and it took them less than an hour to reach the familiar streets and buildings that she had not seen since accompanying the Dormans to London months ago. Will stopped the curricle in front of the mercantile shop. Toby hopped down and held the horses. Will helped Anna climb down. She left him to his errands and entered the mercantile shop.

The shopkeeper there knew her from when she lived with the Dormans. He was welcoming and eager to assist her. Other customers in the shop nodded politely and did not leer or whisper behind her back as they had in London. But then, she was the Viscountess Willburgh, the highest-ranking woman in the area.

After making her purchases in the mercantile shop, Anna walked towards the milliner. She needed a hat with a wide brim to shield her face from the sun when she took her walks. The village milliner always had such hats for sale.

Before she reached the shop, she spied a familiar figure seated on a bench, her head in her hands.

'Mary?' Mary was Violet Dorman's lady's maid, the maid who'd been so helpful in packing her things that awful day.

The young woman looked up. 'Oh, Miss Anna!' She dissolved into tears.

Anna sat down next to her. 'What troubles you? Tell me.'

If Mary was in the village, then the Dormans were back in the country. Anna was not happy about that. It also meant that Violet was near.

The maid leaned against Anna as she wept. Passers-by were noticing and looked concerned, but Anna could not worry about that now.

Finally Mary spoke with shuddering breaths. 'Miss Dorman gave me such a scold! She pushed me out of the shop and told me to stay out of her way!'

Anna had seen many of Violet's outbursts. It used to be her task to calm Violet down.

'I—I tripped and knocked against her,' Mary said. 'I did not mean to!'

'Of course you did not,' Anna responded soothingly. 'She should not have lost her temper with you.'

'She is losing her temper all the time now!' cried Mary. 'They all are! I wish you were back, Miss Anna. It was better when you were there. Now all they do is yell at each other! I hate it there! I don't want to go back!'

Mary was distraught or she would never be saying such things to anyone, especially Anna—Anna who was now in the enemy camp. Mary never talked about the family. Anna was fond of her. She was young but sweet-tempered and talented at her job. She loved clothes and hairstyles and all of it.

'I wish you were still there, Miss Anna.' The maid whimpered.

Anna put an arm around her. 'It is Lady Willburgh now, you know.'

Mary straightened. 'I beg your pardon, miss—I mean—ma'am.'

An idea was forming in Anna's mind, one that grew stronger by the moment.

She faced Mary. 'What if—? What if you came to Willburgh House? I am in need of a lady's maid. You could work for me.'

The young woman's jaw dropped. 'Me? Work for the Willburghs?'

Anna knew what she meant. They'd all been trained to consider the Willburghs the enemy.

'It might be difficult at first,' Anna admitted. 'The servants will see you as a Dorman. They will not be welcoming, but there is one young woman there who is also new and she will look out for you. As will I.'

Mary gaped at her. 'Do you think I could?'

'I would like you to work for me.' That was the truth. It would be like having an ally there.

Mary's eyes grew wide. 'Will it not cause trouble?'

Anna laughed. 'A great deal of trouble in both households, but you know I will not scold you or push you and I will not let the others in the house mistreat you. Lord Willburgh will deal with any fuss the Dormans make. They cannot force you to stay.'

The young woman glanced away and back again. This time her expression appeared resolved. 'I'll sneak away and walk to Willburgh House. Do you not think that a good plan?'

'We will have to follow up with a letter, but that will work well enough.' Anna hoped anyway. 'Come whenever you can.' Anna stood. 'Now I am off to the milliner.'

Mary's expression turned grave. 'Miss Dorman is in there.'

Anna patted her hand. 'All the better.'

Anna did encounter Violet in the hat shop. The shop girls took notice.

Anna decided to be cordial. 'Good day, Violet. I hope you are well.'

Violet's eyes flashed before she turned away without a word.

The cut direct. Anna expected no less from Violet, who no longer outranked her. If that did not put Violet in a rage then certainly stealing her lady's maid would.

Yes, Violet would be in a rage.

# *Chapter Seventeen*

Will finished his errands and waited with the curricle. He, of course, had been treated well by the villagers. He could only hope that Anna experienced the same.

His senses flared when he saw her approach, laden with packages, her face glowing with excitement, wearing something he'd not seen much of lately. A smile.

Her smile fled when she saw him. 'Am I late?'

He reached for her packages. 'Not at all.' He stowed the packages beneath the seat and a hatbox behind it. 'You had some success shopping I see.'

'I purchased what I needed.'

The stiffness between them returned.

He helped her onto the curricle and climbed in beside her. Toby let go of the horses and hopped on the back.

'I have something to tell you.' Her voice sounded different.

He lifted his brows.

She settled herself in the seat. 'When we are out of the village.'

Will drove through the busy village streets until the traffic cleared and the village buildings receded behind them.

He did not want to wait longer. 'What do you need to tell me?'

'Well.' She sounded cautious. 'As I left the mercantile

shop I saw Mary sitting on the bench. Mary, Violet's lady's maid. She helped me pack my trunk that day in London.'

'Wait. *Violet's* lady's maid.' He shot her a glance. 'The Dormans have returned from Town?'

'Yes. Apparently they are not very happy. Mary said they are arguing all the time.'

Will frowned. 'They usually do not leave Town until later in the summer. I wonder what brought them back?'

'She did not tell me the reason.' Anna shifted in her seat.

Will's mind whirled. Had the Dormans come to cause trouble for them? He had enough to contend with without that.

She continued. 'Apparently Violet had a fit of temper and pushed Mary away. Mary wished she did not have to go back with Violet—'

Or had Dorman left too many debts in London? Will had heard rumours about gambling losses.

'So I offered her the position of lady's maid. For me.'

Will almost pulled on the reins and halted the horses. 'You did what?'

'I hired her to be my lady's maid.' She spoke as if it were the most normal thing in the world.

'No!' His voice rose. 'I'll not have a Dorman servant in my house. That is like putting the fox in with the hens. No.'

'Will.' She spoke very deliberately. 'I hired her. I am not going to tell her no. She is going to come to Willburgh House and I am not sending her away.'

Was she mad? 'I absolutely forbid it.'

'You *forbid* it?' Her voice was raised now. 'You forbid it? You told me I could hire my own lady's maid. I choose to hire Mary.'

'I said you could select from an agency. Not from the Dorman household.' The two sets of servants were as hostile to each other as the families were.

'I do not recall that conversation.' Her voice was clipped.

'Hear me now,' he said. 'You are not hiring a Dorman servant as your lady's maid.'

'Hear *me* now,' she countered. 'You may be *disappointed* in marrying me, but recall that I had as little choice in the matter as you did.'

Disappointed in marrying her? He'd never said that to her!

Then he remembered she'd overheard him say something like that to his mother.

She pointed to his hands. 'You hold all the reins.' She held up her reticule. 'You possess all the money. I am completely at your mercy. If I had refused to marry you, you would have gone on much as you do now. Perhaps your sister would have suffered, because she is a woman, too, but not you. So if you refuse to allow me this one request, I have no power to change the decision. Does that seem fair to you? I was as innocent of any indiscretion as you were, but this time it is not society who turns its back on me, it is you.'

That arrow hit its mark. 'You do not understand what is at issue here.'

'I do not understand?' Her eyes shot daggers. 'I know all about the silly feud over land. And you forget that I loved my—my stepfather. So do not tell me I do not understand. It is you who do not understand. I lost everything. I even lost a fortune I never knew I had. You lost the opportunity to select your own wife. I am asking for one thing for myself. To help Mary. I know her. She has no family. She has few choices as do I. If she becomes my maid, she has something. She has me to watch out for her. If she does indeed leave the Dormans' house, as she plans to do, and you refuse her, she cannot go back.'

Arrows. Daggers. He was full of pain. He did not want to hurt her or the poor maid, but this was an unreasonable request. Was it not? She should have asked him before she made the offer.

They spoke no more during the rest of the trip. When he pulled up to the door of Willburgh House, she did not wait for assistance. She climbed down from the curricle herself and hurried inside just as the footman was opening the door. Toby jumped down and took the horses in hand.

Will was frozen for a moment. Then he directed the footman to gather Anna's packages and to deliver them to her bed chamber. He did not go inside but turned to walk away from the house.

That evening Anna sent word she had a headache and would not be at dinner. Will knew better what was troubling her. When he retired for the night, he peeked into her room to try to talk some sense into her. She was in bed and still. He had to assume she was asleep or that she wished he'd go to the devil.

She simply did not understand the rift between the Dormans and the Willburghs. Could a servant from the other house ever be trusted? Or would they betray the family to their rivals?

He ought to have told her more about what happened to Adams, John, and Lottie simply because of a rumour that they were Dorman spies. Perhaps then she would have realised why they could not hire a Dorman servant as her lady's maid. *Especially* as *her* lady's maid. Of all the servants, the lady's maid and the valet were most likely to become privy to the private affairs of their employers. What could happen if that servant told all to the enemy?

No. He must stay resolved. She must accept that he knew best in this matter.

Will did not have a very restful night's sleep, though,

tossing and turning and continuing to see Anna's outraged expression and hearing her tell how wrong he was.

But he wasn't wrong.

He dared to knock on her door and enter her room early the next day, thinking to catch her before she rose to ride. Maybe they could talk about this in a more civilised manner on horseback. Today, though, her curtains were drawn and she sat in the dark staring into the fireplace.

'Are you not riding today, Anna?' He tried to sound like yesterday's angry words had never happened.

'I am not riding.' She did not even look at him.

He opened his mouth to tell her how ridiculously she was behaving, but he closed it again. He could sense her despondency as if it were an open, bleeding wound and he had no wish to hurt her further. Instead he turned around and made his way out of the house and over to the stables.

John had the white Highland pony saddled and ready for Anna.

'Lady Willburgh is not riding today,' Will told him.

'She is not?' John was surprised. 'I do hope she is not ill.'

'Not ill.' But sick at heart, he feared.

Will started across the field feeling aimless, but soon realised he was riding to the disputed patch of land where his property bordered the Dormans'. Sheep were grazing in his field, their bleats sounding like conversations between them.

Anna would have laughed at them, he thought.

In the distance he saw something moving. As he rode closer he could see it was not a sheep but a small, thin young woman carting a very large sack, so large that she was almost dragging it.

He knew instantly who it was and rode to her. 'Mary, is it?'

She dropped the sack and gave him a wary, frightened look as if he might be the devil himself. 'My lord.' She curtsied.

She looked very young and vulnerable standing below him, reaching for the sack again and clutching it like it contained all her worldly belongings.

Which it probably did.

How much courage must it have taken for her to make this trip, to sneak away in the dark and know she could never return? How much faith in Anna, as well.

'You are headed to Willburgh House?' Where else might she be going?

'To Lady Willburgh,' she responded. 'I—I am to be her lady's maid.' She caught herself and lowered her head. 'If it please Your Lordship, that is.'

He dismounted. 'We've been expecting you,' he heard himself saying. 'Let me relieve you of your burden.'

Had he gone daft now?

Tossing the bag onto his horse, he gestured for her to proceed on her way and fell in step with her. She was shy and frightened and very determined and nothing like a Dorman spy might appear.

'I—I am grateful to you, m'lord,' she stammered. 'Miss Anna—Lady Willburgh, I mean—was always very kind to me. It will be an honour to be of service to her.'

He asked her about her family. Her parents when they had been alive had worked for the Dormans so she worked for them, too, but, she told him, she'd always liked Anna the best. And now the family did nothing but argue and Miss Dorman had become very prone to scolds and slaps across the face.

'M'lord,' she asked as the house came into view. 'Will you ask your servants not to hate me?'

That was a shaft to his heart indeed. 'I will. But you must come tell me if any of them treat you badly.'

'Oh, no!' she exclaimed. 'I could never do that. I would never tell on them. It just isn't done!'

The young maid might do very well here after all, Will thought.

Anna sat at her dressing table combing out her hair, although why she bothered she could not say. She had no intention of leaving this room all day.

Desolation threatened to engulf her. It was one thing for Will to distance himself from her, but it was quite another for him to think he ruled her.

Although what was marriage but a woman ruled by a man? By common law a husband and wife were one person, although that never meant they were equal. A woman's property and fortune became her husband's upon marriage, and any children born to them belonged to the husband. So Will could rule her and she had no recourse.

It was just that their early days and fleeting moments afterwards had convinced her that Will was different, that he wanted to respect her, wanted her to have some say in what happened to her. It was shattering what he said to her about hiring Mary. '*I absolutely forbid it.*' How could she ever again trust his kindness when he could be so cruel?

But then, how could she trust anyone really? They all betrayed her eventually.

As she tugged at a knot with the comb, she remembered the pleasure of Will brushing her hair. And the pleasure of his lovemaking. Tears stung her eyes and she blinked them away.

She'd thought he loved her. He did not love her any more than the Dormans did. Or, perhaps, any more than her stepfather had. Will's mother loathed her and the servants loathed her. She was surrounded by people who despised her.

She put down the comb and lifted her chin.

Well, she could not care that they all despised her. She had done nothing wrong, nothing to deserve their ire. She'd hold her head up and go toe-to-toe with any of them.

The door opened and Will stuck his head in. 'Anna?'

She did not want to see him! She turned away.

'I've brought you a maid.' He made it sound like this would be welcome news. 'To help you—'

How dare he!

She swung around. 'I told you I did not want a—'

Mary had entered her room. 'G'morning, Miss Anna—I mean, Lady Willburgh.'

Anna jumped from her chair and rushed over to the young woman. She wrapped the maid in a hug. Not how a lady treated her lady's maid, but Anna did not care. She was so happy to see her.

Her gaze caught Will's. He stood in the doorway smiling and her heart swelled at the sight of him. He had brought Mary to her! He had given her something that she wanted, simply because she wanted it, even though he'd been thoroughly against it.

He took a step back. 'If you will pardon me, I must speak to a few people about our new lady's maid.' He addressed himself to Mary in the kindest voice possible. 'We'll get you settled.'

Anna wanted to pull him back to embrace him, to tell him how grateful she was, but he left too quickly.

Mary stared at where he'd disappeared. 'My goodness, Miss Anna—I mean, m'lady—I don't know why Miss Dorman and Mr Lucius said he was such a villain. Lord Willburgh was ever so kind to me.'

'He is a very kind man.' Anna blinked back tears of happiness. She took Mary's hand in hers and squeezed it. 'I am so glad you are here, Mary.'

The maid looked around the room with its two trunks in the middle of the floor and complete lack of embellishments. 'It is a pretty room, but not fancy at all, is it?'

'You can help me decorate it,' Anna said, her spirits brightening considerably.

'Perhaps I might unpack your trunks for you first.'

Will did not relish the task of telling the household about the new lady's maid. He expected them to react as he had; his mother, worse. He would tell her first.

He climbed the stairs to his old room, her new bed chamber.

Ellen caught him in the hallway. 'Good morning, Will.' She frowned. 'What is it? Has something happened?'

His expression must have given away his trepidation. 'Oh, Lambkin. I am about to cause an uproar.' He explained it all to her—except for the angry discord he'd made Anna endure.

'Violet's lady's maid?' Ellen shook her head. 'The uproar is going to be at the Dormans', I should think.'

'I'm afraid our servants will not be happy to have her,' he confessed.

She seemed to consider that. 'Probably not, but think how nice it is for Anna to have someone familiar to her as her lady's maid.'

He gave his sister a hug. 'Thank you for saying that.'

'I'll encourage Betty to be kind to her,' she said.

'That would be very good.' He took a bracing breath. 'Wish me luck. I am going to tell Mother.'

Her eyes widened. 'Good luck.'

He knocked on his mother's door and heard her tell him to come in.

He opened the door. 'Good morning, Mother.'

Luckily she was alone, seated by her window, sipping

a cup of chocolate. 'You never visit me in my room.' She glanced around. 'Such as it is. What is it now?'

He told her.

Her expression turned thunderous and she gripped the cup handle so hard he feared it would break.

'No, Will.' She spoke through gritted teeth. 'This is unacceptable. Willburghs never hire Dorman servants. You know that.'

'Anna chose her, Mother,' he said.

'Well, she might have considered my nerves.' She put her cup down and fussed with the collar of her morning dress. 'You know how distressing it is for me to have anything to do with the Dormans. They killed your father, remember!'

His anger flared. 'If you wish to add Father's death to the discussion, do not forget to include the part you played in it.'

'Oh, that is too cruel!' she wailed. 'It is unfair of you to say this to me. You know how completely I was taken in! That is why I despise the Dormans so. Look how ill they treated me.'

Oddly he hadn't specifically thought of his father's death when he'd forbidden Anna to have this servant as her lady's maid. He'd reacted to the generations-long feud, the conviction that Willburghs and Dormans did not mix. He hadn't been reliving the duel every time he looked at Anna, as he'd feared.

But he thought of his father dying in his arms now and sadness engulfed him. Sadness. Not anger.

He hardened his voice to his mother. 'This little maid did not kill my father. Neither she nor Anna had any part in that. Anna wants her to be her lady's maid. She knows her and feels comfortable with her. Anna has the right to choose her own lady's maid, after all.'

'We could find one she might like from an agency,' his mother pleaded. 'Anyone but a Dorman servant. Tell her she may have anyone she chooses from an agency. You can insist upon it.'

Obviously he would not insist. Could not insist. Nor had he been able to turn away that young maid. It had made him hate himself that he thought to even try.

He answered his mother. 'I will not insist Anna do something against her wishes. It would be cruel to her and to that maid for me to insist. Anna has made her choice and I will support it.' He raised his voice and spoke even more firmly. 'I will also expect the servants to accept this young maid. I will not brook anyone treating her ill. That includes you, Mother.'

'I will have nothing to do with her!' his mother cried. 'This is all your fault. If you hadn't compromised a Dorman we would not be in this fix! You have ruined everything!'

'Perhaps I have, Mother,' Will countered. 'But remember these decisions are mine to make, not yours, not anyone else's.' Such was the burden of being viscount.

'Mark my words, Will. That maid will do nothing but report all our business back to the Dormans. You've let a spy into our household.'

Will simply left the room.

Ellen waited in the hallway. 'I heard that.'

He blew out a breath. 'I wish you had not.'

Her expression was all sympathy, though. 'Would you like me to come with you when you tell the servants?'

'Yes.' As Viscount this was his problem alone. But he had an idea of what he would face and really felt the need of support. 'I'd be grateful if you would,' he told Ellen and straightened his spine. 'Let us do that now.'

# *Chapter Eighteen*

Lucius Dorman was lounging in the drawing room while his mother and Violet sat whispering together on the sofa. Violet was in a snit because no one could find her maid and she was threatening to send the girl packing. Lucius could not care less about the maid. He was fuming about Willburgh and Anna. He'd heard rumours in the village that they were getting along very well. Humph! The very least Willburgh could do after thwarting all of Lucius's plans was to be miserable. There must be some way to make the man suffer. Apparently the loss of Anna's fortune meant nothing to Willburgh. Or maybe to Anna

The loss of Anna's fortune meant a lot to Lucius. It would have paid his debts and his father's debts and set them up rather nicely.

He and his family had botched things rather thoroughly, Lucius had to admit, but he'd been so furious to find Anna with Willburgh that all rational thought went out of his head. Not that he held a *tendre* for her, exactly, but she was supposed to be his family's ticket to the lap of luxury and Willburgh had foiled that plan.

The thing was, what to do now? How to get revenge on Willburgh and Anna and restore the family fortune?

Lucius was still musing over this problem when his father stormed into the room waving a piece of paper.

'This was just delivered. From Willburgh House!' He flung the letter at Lucius. 'Read it!'

Lucius read aloud.

'Dear Lord Dorman,
I write to you this day to inform you that I have hired the maid Mary Jones to be Viscountess Willburgh's lady's maid—'

Lucius looked up. 'Well, that solves the mystery of where Violet's maid disappeared to.'

He read on:

'I assure you, Dorman, that I will assume the payment of any wages you owe Miss Jones, so there will be no need for you to correspond with her or to concern yourselves with any of her affairs.

Lady Willburgh and I realise this loss in your household is very sudden and we regret any inconvenience it may cause you. I am confident that you realise what an improvement in status this is for Miss Jones and that you will forgive her need to leave without notice.
Yours, etc.
Willburgh'

'Improvement in status.' Lucius threw the letter down in disgust. 'That is just like Willburgh to lord it over us.'

Violet nearly vaulted out of her seat. 'Anna has stolen Mary from me! She cannot do that! Mary is *my* lady's maid.'

'What a dirty trick!' their mother cried. 'Anna goes too far. She's completely crossed over to the enemy.'

'Papa,' Violet begged. 'You must do something! Get her back!'

Their father shook his head. 'I can do nothing! The maid was free to leave her employment at any time. She had better not ask us for a letter of reference, however. I'd make certain no one would hire her.'

Lucius vowed he'd get back at Willburgh and Anna somehow. He'd make them regret ever trifling with the Dormans.

After Mary helped Anna dress and unpacked her trunks, Anna left the maid in the hands of Ellen's lady's maid, who seemed cordial enough, and went in search of Will. To thank him.

She hurried down the stairs, through the hall and the sculpture room to Will's office.

She walked in without knocking.

He was not there.

His desk was still stacked with papers and ledgers and now two chairs also had papers on them. Poor Will! He intended to tackle this all himself? Even Lord Dorman employed a secretary. Mr Bisley. A thin, intense man who seemed delighted to spend his days with papers and ledgers much like these.

She smiled to herself. Perhaps Will could hire Mr Bisley away from Lord Dorman.

She made her way back to the hall and asked the footman there, 'Do you know where Lord Willburgh has gone?'

'To see Mr Parker, the estate manager, ma'am,' the footman told her with only a hint of the usual antipathy.

'Thank you so much,' she replied, climbing the stairs again. She'd have to wait until Will returned.

As she reached the landing, a voice from above her demanded, 'I would speak with you, Anna.'

It was Will's mother. Calling her by name? It must be the first time.

Anna made no reply until she reached the floor. 'Yes, Lady Willburgh?'

Will's change of heart had filled Anna with renewed strength. She'd stood up to him! And he'd done right by her. At that moment Anna felt she could do anything.

Even face her mother-in-law.

The older woman's eyes flashed. 'My son tells me you have manipulated him into hiring a maid—a lady's maid, no less—from the Dormans. I will not have it.'

Anna should have expected this. '*You* will not have it?' she retorted.

'I insist you send the girl packing. This very instant!' She stomped her foot for emphasis.

Anna burned with anger which she could barely keep in check. 'I will not do that.'

'You will do that!' Lady's Willburgh's face flushed. 'Our family cannot have a Dorman servant in our household. She'll be privy to all our affairs!'

Somehow Anna knew Lady Willburgh did not include her when she said *our family*. 'This is my household, too, and, as Will's wife, I am family. I have every right to select what servants I wish. Mary Jones stays.'

'You wretch!' the older woman cried. 'I knew you were a Dorman. Manipulative! Selfish! Like the lot of them. I wish that Will had never married you! You have disrupted all our lives.'

Anna could hold her temper no longer. 'I may be a *disappointment* to you, Lady Willburgh. I may be a disruption, but I am not a Dorman! What I am is Will's wife, whether you like it or not. I am the Viscountess. I have allowed you to run the house, because I did not wish to take everything away from you. Your room. Your title. I thought you would be generous enough to teach me how to manage the house and gradually pass the responsibilities on to me, but instead you accuse me of being manipulative and selfish when you know I did not choose any of this! I *am* a part of this family now, however. In fact, I am second only to Will, and you must accept this.'

Lady Willburgh's lips thinned and her chest heaved.

Anna went on. 'From now on Mrs Greaves will take instructions from me, not you. I will plan the menus. I will instruct the servants. Me. Not you. You are the dowager. I am Lady Willburgh. If I make mistakes, then it will be because you decided to oppose me rather than help me.'

Will's mother seemed to collect herself. Her eyes flashed. 'You are nobody in my eyes! A clever maneuverer, I would say. You tricked my son into marrying you—'

Anna shot back. 'You know that is not true. You were the one who said we should marry. You are no better than the Dormans. Creating your own version of how you prefer to see things rather than the way they are.'

The older woman's face turned red. 'Do not compare me to the Dormans! I am nothing like them! My son will not allow you to speak to me that way! You might have tricked him into marrying you, but I will not give over the running of this house until he tells me to and Mrs Greaves will not listen to you. My son will not hear of you usurping my authority.'

'We will see about that!' Anna whirled around and strode down two flights of stairs, through the hall and out the door. Her anger propelled her along, to the outbuildings and Parker's office.

She walked in without knocking.

Both Will and Parker looked up, stunned by her entrance.

She was panting. 'I need to talk to you right now, Will.' She walked out the door again.

He followed, looking alarmed. 'What is it, Anna?'

She paced in front of him, still so angry she could not stand still. 'Your mother!'

Will released an exasperated breath. 'What has she done now?'

'She has insisted I get rid of Mary!' Anna cried.

'Wait. What?' He pressed his fingers to his temple. 'I spoke to my mother about this. And to the servants, as well.'

Anna went on. 'She said I had no right to hire her and that I manipulated you and that *she* will not have it—' He glanced away and Anna was not certain he was listening. 'She also accused me of being selfish and a disruption!'

Will nodded, rather absently, Anna thought. 'Let's walk back to the house.'

She wrested her temper under control as they neared the house. 'I never wanted a feud with your mother. I know I am nothing she would choose for you to marry, but I will not be accused of it being my fault.'

He blew out a breath as he opened the door off the garden. 'Why does this have to be so difficult?'

Anna flared again. 'I am not being difficult! I have tried to deal fairly with your mother! I know this is a hard change for her!'

They entered his office.

She swept her arm across the room. 'And this, Will. Really. All this paper!' She could not stop herself now.

'What has my work to do with it?' he snapped.

'Nothing at all,' she shot back. 'It is just that—I came looking for you, to thank you properly for hiring Mary. When I came in here—well—I never see you asking anyone for help. Any other gentleman of means would simply hire a secretary!'

He halted and looked like he was seeing the piles of paper for the first time.

He shook his head. 'One thing at a time. I'll speak with my mother.'

But she was not sure what he would say to his mother. He might take her side, for all Anna knew.

Or he might support her, like he did in hiring Mary.

'I should tell you,' she added in a calmer tone. 'I lost my temper with your mother. I told her I was taking over all her duties.'

'Taking over her duties,' he repeated absently. He straightened. 'I will speak with her now.'

'Thank you, Will,' Anna said.

She truly hoped this would be something for which she'd be thankful.


Will found his mother in a sitting room on the other side of the house. Mrs Greaves stood near her chair. The two had obviously been talking.

'Will, thank goodness you are here,' his mother said, reaching up from her chair to clasp his hands. 'Has *she* spoken to you? Did she tell you she threatened me? She threatened to turn me out of my home!'

Will pulled his hands away. 'Cut line, Mother.' He glanced at Mrs Greaves who suddenly was examining the Aubusson carpet. 'I have had enough of this.'

His mother blinked.

Will towered over her. 'Heed me now, Mother, because you will not be given a second chance. You will treat Anna respectfully. She is the Viscountess now, not you. She has every right to take over your duties and to hire whatever servants she wishes.'

His mother turned away.

'Look at me, Mother,' Will demanded. 'A kind thing would have been if you'd taken Anna under your wing and taught her how you've run the house, but you and Mrs Greaves have shown yourselves to be unkind. That will stop now. You will respect Anna's wishes even if they disagree with yours. You will not interfere or obstruct. If she asks for your help, you will help her. Or—'

'Or what?' she asked defiantly.

'Or you will live in the dower-house.' He turned to Mrs Greaves. 'You, Mrs Greaves, will work cooperatively with Lady Willburgh and her lady's maid and you will instruct all the servants to do the same. If I hear of any of them disrespecting my wife or her maid or causing any sort of trouble, they will be terminated and you with them.'

'But—but I cannot control—' the housekeeper stammered.

'If you cannot control your servants, then perhaps you are in the wrong job.' He glared from one to the other. 'You two have made difficulties where none needed to exist. You will stop doing so right now.'

'It's that Dorman maid she hired,' his mother protested. 'She's causing the difficulties!'

Will gave a dry laugh. 'Come now, Mother. The girl has not been here even a full day.'

'The Dormans sent her to spy on us,' cried his mother. 'It is the Dormans' fault.'

'That excuse will no longer work.' He glared at her. 'Your choice, Mother. Be decent or be gone.'


Anna was not privy to what Will said to his mother, She did not see either of them until dinner. Lady Willburgh was much subdued and avoided any direct looks at either Anna or Will. When she did speak, Anna had the sense of a great deal of anger repressed, but she did not toss any of the barbs towards Anna that had been her custom.

Something had changed. Even the servants she encountered cast their eyes down at her approach and spoke carefully to her. What had Will said to them?

He spoke little, though. If it had not been for Ellen the dinner would have resembled a wake. The girl's happy mood and cheerful conversation lifted the pall over the rest of them.

After dinner Anna excused herself early without offering any excuse.

Mary came to her after finishing her meal with the other servants. 'Do you want me to help you get ready for bed?'

'I do not need much help,' Anna replied, but let the girl untie the ribbons of her dress and slip her out of it.

Anna washed herself and donned her nightdress before sitting at the dressing table and taking the pins from her hair. Mary skipped over to help her.

'How have things been for you today?' Anna asked.

Mary smiled. 'Betty has been such a help to me and she even fixed it so we can share a bedroom. Was that not nice?'

'What of the others?' Anna was not worried about how Betty would treat her.

Mary turned pensive. 'I am not sure. Mr Bailey was nice. Nobody else said much to me at the meal, but they were not mean to me.'

'And Mrs Greaves?' Greaves's treatment was perhaps the most important.

'I admit she scares me a little.' That Anna could well understand. 'She just told me what to do and things like that.'

No one had chided her for being a Dorman servant? That must have been Will's doing.

Mary put away her dress and bid Anna goodnight, but Anna did not retire. Instead she sat up listening for Will to come up the stairs and open his door. She heard his mother and Ellen come up before she heard Will's door open. She hurried to the connecting door and opened it a crack. It was Will's valet.

She left the door open a crack and waited some more until finally Will's footsteps sounded on the stairs and in the hallway. She could tell it was Will, because the footsteps sounded burdened and weary.

She'd been so angry at him that morning—until he brought her Mary—and now she felt such sympathy. He'd obviously faced his mother and that could not have been pleasant.

A wave of guilt washed over her. The Willburgh household had probably been running smoothly and comfortably until she came to disrupt everyone.

She'd planned to go to Will that night, to crawl into bed with him, tell him how grateful she was to him. Make love with him.

She quietly closed the connecting door and walked back to her bed. Alone.

The next morning Anna rose as early as usual. She was halfway dressed when Mary came in the room.

'Miss Anna—m'lady, I mean! I did not think you would be up so early. I am so sorry I was not here.'

'Mary, I did not think to tell you,' Anna responded apologetically. 'I am so used to rising on my own, but, now you are here, you can help me put on my new riding habit.'

With Mary's help she dressed quickly and was out the door and on her way to the stables. She hoped she was in time to catch Will.

From a distance, she spied him entering the stable door and she quickened her step.

The grooms were used to both of them riding at this hour and had the horses ready. Will typically rode his thorough-bred and Anna always rode Seraphina. By the time Anna entered the stable, Will was already mounted.

He nodded a greeting.

She looked up at him. 'May I ride with you a little, Will?'

'I'll wait for you outside,' he said.

Her heart beat faster as she mounted Seraphina quickly and rode out the door.

They headed in the direction of the farm fields.

'I want to check on the planting,' he explained.

Why had she not realised before? Will did not only ride in the morning for pleasure. He rode to oversee the work on his land.

They went awhile without talking. Finally Anna said, 'I gather by the mood at dinner last night and the behaviour of the servants, that you supported my keeping Mary?'

He shrugged. 'It was the right thing to do. You ought to select the servants you want.'

'That is what you told your mother?' She wanted to keep him talking.

'That and more.' He did not look at her, but kept his eyes straight ahead, on the road. 'I also addressed the managing of the household. I apologise for being remiss. I thought my mother would take care of that. Show you how to run the household. Help you. I thought she would know her place.'

'She is very strong-willed,' Anna said.

He laughed. 'Indeed.'

'What did you say to her?' she asked.

Still looking straight ahead, he answered, 'I told her she'd better stop this foolishness or I'd send her to the dower-house.'

'You didn't.' Goodness! Anna truly had caused a disruption. 'Your poor mother! First I boot her out of her bed chambers and next out of her own home.'

'Not you,' he said. 'Me. Anyway, she can stay if she behaves herself.'

Now her mother-in-law would be required to stand on pins and needles because of Anna.

They reached some of the fields where farm workers were already at work.

'Good,' Will spoke more to himself than to Anna. 'We are catching up.'

When they returned to the house, they entered by the garden door.

'I had an idea,' Anna said, as they walked through his office. 'I thought perhaps I could help you with your piles of papers. Perhaps organise them for you or put things in ledgers.'

He paused contemplating the array of work before him.

'Until you hire a secretary, that is,' she added. 'You really should use some of your money that way.'

His brow furrowed. 'My father did not have a secretary.'

'That does not mean you couldn't have one.' She swept her hand over his desk. 'In any event, I would like to help.'

He paused again, then answered, 'Come to me after breakfast.'

# *Chapter Nineteen*

The next few days were at least productive for Will, even though he felt far from composed.

Anna turned out to be very efficient and organised and quicker than he at performing some of the more tedious tasks, like putting all the receipts and bills in order and recording the expenditures in the ledger. He hated to admit it, but she rather proved a secretary would be useful.

For certain some eager younger son would not be as distracting. Will had the greatest difficulty concentrating when Anna was present. He was distracted by the way the sunlight from the windows illuminated her face and put streaks of gold in her hair. When she moved to shelve a ledger, or bent over to pick up papers that fell, or simply stretched the kinks from her neck, he was thrown into memories of stroking her skin or moving inside her.

He took to using the time she worked to meet with Parker and the other men who helped run his estate, especially his dairy manager. Their dairy cows were older and producing less milk each day. His manager found a farmer, not too far away, who had two young dairy cows for sale. The farmer agreed on Will's offer to buy them. They fixed on the morrow to make the purchase.

Will hoped his absence would not cause any difficulty.

He mostly hoped his mother would continue behaving herself. She could cause a good deal of trouble even though he'd only be gone a day. He knew that Anna had asked his mother to be present in her meetings with Mrs Greaves. He did not know how that was going. In any event, he hoped his mother knew he was serious about sending her to the dower-house if she caused any more trouble.

Having Anna's new lady's maid was turning out better than Will expected. Mrs Greaves must have reinforced what Will had told the other servants himself so they'd been civil to her.

At least he did not have to worry about Ellen. She was always so refreshingly happy.

Will walked back from Parker's office and entered his office, knowing Anna would still be there. She sat at a table near his desk writing figures in a ledger. She looked up and smiled, which always reached right into his very essence.

He sat in a chair near her. 'I will be accompanying Parker and the dairy manager to that farmer I told you about, the one selling the cows.'

'Oh?' She turned to face him. 'When?'

'Tomorrow.'

'How long will you be gone?' She looked disappointed.

'Only a day.' He tried not to get distracted by how lovely she looked in her dress, even though she wore an apron over it to protect it from the ink. 'But we'll leave very early and are likely not to make it back before dinner.'

'Is there anything you would like of me in your absence?' she asked.

Will feared that if he indulged in what he'd like of her, he might forget all about cows and ledgers, and everything but her. And then what would happen?

He glanced around the room, more orderly now that Anna

had helped him, but still stacks of papers, things to attend to. All would tumble like a house of cards.

He pretended he'd been thinking of her question. 'I believe you know enough what to do.'

Anna did not ride the next morning, but rose even earlier, wanting to see Will off. She'd arranged an early breakfast for him and insisted he eat something before he left. She also had Cook pack them some bread and cheese for later in the day.

He was dressed for riding, the attire that reminded her of their travels, even though this coat and breeches were impeccably tailored and of the finest quality cloth. Merely seeing him dressed this way always filled her with longing for what they so briefly shared. Things were more comfortable with him than they had been before their altercation about Mary, but she still feared he treated her well out of duty.

'You did not have to rise so early, Anna,' he said to her, still cool and distant.

'I wanted to.' Even if he did not want her to.

When he'd hired Mary against his own wishes, Anna had hoped it would bring them closer. It seemed like such a loving thing he'd done, just because she wished it. Then he'd allowed her to help him in his office. Should that not have brought them closer?

He simply spent most of the time out of the room, claiming other tasks and all the time her heart ached to be with him.

She'd forged a sort of truce with Lady Willburgh, but she had no illusions that the woman had any less dislike for her. Mrs Greaves and the other servants were overtly more solicitous of her, but she hated that fear of losing their employment made them that way. Even Ellen, who she thought might become a friend, seemed to prefer her solitary pursuits to spending time with Anna.

She was as alone as she'd ever been—except for Mary. Mary was the one ray of sunshine that made the rest tolerable.

And it had been Will who'd brought Mary to her. It simply made her love for him grow to even more painful proportions.

She watched him while she sipped her tea, her handsome Will, her champion, the husband who must still regret marrying her.

Anna asked him a couple of questions about his paperwork merely to dispel the silence between them. When he finished breakfast she walked with him to the hall. Outside the front door a groom waited with his horse.

When Parker and the dairy manager rode up, Will turned to her and she hoped for some sign he might miss her, at least a little. For a moment she thought she saw some softness in his eyes, but he merely put on his hat.

'I will be late returning. After dinner,' was all he said.

She knew that already. 'Safe travels, Will,' she told him.

He nodded and went out the door.

Anna climbed the steps to the drawing room which looked over the road to the house. She watched him ride away until she could see him no more.

'Safe travels, my dearest Will,' she whispered.

That afternoon Anna felt too restless to sit and write figures in ledgers. She missed Will, even though he was probably happy enough to be absent from her. She put away her pen and ink and called for Mary to help her change into her riding habit.

Riding Seraphina would calm her down. The pony always did.

It was a lovely day with blue skies and white clouds like

cotton wool. The sun was high in the sky brightening the green foliage and wild flowers and warming the air. Anna rode aimlessly and found herself at the edge of Will's property, near the land that had been the source of the Willburgh feud with the Dormans. Because of the feud the families had never resolved the land's ownership, it was left uncultivated; the wooded areas, untended. Such a waste.

How like this land Anna was, caught in some unresolvable place, belonging to no one. Left to her own devices. Untended.

She rode Seraphina carefully through the wooded part of the property. The thick green foliage parted only enough to allow shafts of sunlight to pierce the ground where ferns and flowers of the underbrush bloomed white and purple against the green. The cawing of the rooks protecting their rookeries broke the silence.

Anna could almost forget her anguish in this wild, but peaceful place.

As she rode on, the rooks' cries faded into the distance, but the blackbirds, chaffinches, and robins took over the song. Then suddenly she heard human voices.

Through the trees she could see them. In a clearing. Embracing.

Ellen and Lucius.

Anna gasped.

They parted and Lucius walked Ellen to her horse. He lifted her into the saddle and pulled her down for a light kiss on the lips. She laughed and turned her horse to ride away.

Anna backed Seraphina deeper into the woods until she knew she would not be seen, then she turned and rode faster to escape the woods and intercept Ellen.

Ellen and Lucius.

At least she knew now why Ellen preferred solitary afternoon pursuits. That embrace. That kiss. No wonder Ellen seemed so incandescently happy lately. She fancied herself in love.

With Lucius.

No doubt he had manipulated her into thinking so. To toy with her? To achieve some revenge upon Will or Anna herself? Why would he do such a despicable thing?

Anna waited on the path she knew Ellen must take to return to the house until she saw her sister-in-law approaching her.

'Hello, Anna,' Ellen cried cheerfully. 'I did not know you would be riding, too. We could have ridden together.'

Anna decided not to spare words. 'I saw you with Lucius.'

The girl inadvertently tugged on the reins. Her horse faltered. 'I—I do not know what you mean.'

'I saw you with Lucius,' she repeated while Ellen regained control of the horse. 'I saw him take liberties with you. You were in the glen at the edge of the woods. I know what I saw.'

Ellen's horse was next to Anna's now. Ellen, on a taller horse, leaned over and touched her shoulder. 'Oh, Anna! Do not tell Will. Please do not tell him.'

'That you've been secretly meeting Lucius? How long has this gone on?'

'Oh…' Ellen's eyes took on a dreamy look. 'Five days. We are in love, Anna.'

In love?

Anna could believe Ellen thought so, but Anna knew Lucius better. He'd either manoeuvred to encounter her or had taken advantage of an accidental meeting. Whichever it was, Lucius was up to no good.

'Ellen, do you realise how improper this is?' Anna spoke insistently. 'You cannot be meeting a man alone like this. Think of your reputation. You will be ruined. I have already seen him behave in ways with you more compromising than what happened between Will and me. Look at what happened to us.'

'You had to get married.' Ellen sounded petulant now. 'But you were not in love, Anna! Lucius and I are in love.'

'I know Lucius.' Anna persisted. 'He is not in love with you. He is dallying with you. You are a conquest, nothing more. He is merely using his charm on you.'

Anna knew Lucius to be very capable of trifling with a woman's feelings or even of seducing her, but he usually confined himself to opera dancers and actresses, not respectable young ladies who'd not yet been presented. Not the sister of his biggest rival.

Ellen pursed her lips together and lifted her chin.

'You must heed me,' Anna insisted. 'This puts you in great peril. You must not see him again. He is not a man of good character. He will ruin your reputation and walk away from you.'

'He would never do that!' Ellen cried. 'I told you. He loves me. He told me all about the other women, but he has never met anyone like me. He said I make him want to be a better man.'

Lucius knew what to say to get what he wanted. Ellen had fallen for his nonsense and was being primed for—what? Complete ruin?

She needed to be protected from him.

'What if I do tell Will?' Anna asked.

'You can't tell Will!' Ellen pleaded. 'He will become angry with me and pack me off to some school somewhere! You do not know how angry he can become.'

Did she not?

'Then will you agree to stop meeting Lucius?'

The house was coming into view. They did not have much farther to ride before reaching home.

'That is my bargain,' Anna stressed. 'You stop meeting Lucius or I tell Will exactly what I saw.'

Ellen glanced away.

Anna pressed her. 'Ellen, you must agree. Believe me, I will do what I say. I'll even encourage Will to send you away if that is what it takes to save you from Lucius.'

Ellen rode a little ahead of Anna and did not answer for what seemed like several minutes. When she finally slowed enough to allow Anna to catch up to her, she said, 'Very well. I'll stop seeing him.'

Was she telling the truth? Anna hoped so. In any event she would keep a close eye on her sister-in-law.

Anna did not find sleep easy that night. Half of her was listening for Will to safely return; the other half wrestling with her promise not to tell Will about Ellen meeting with Lucius.

She regretted making that agreement. Will really ought to know. He'd want to protect his sister. Anna had no doubt Will would do anything for his sister.

He'd married Anna because of Ellen, had he not? To save her from a scandal that could ruin her chances to make a good match. What Lucius was up to could be so much more ruinous to Ellen's reputation.

She resolved to tell Will, no matter her promise to Ellen. It might make Anna one more enemy in the household, but it seemed the only decision that let her settle down to sleep.

Just as she was drifting off, Will returned, making more of a clatter than she'd heard him make before. She rose from her bed intending to tell him about Ellen right away when she thought better of it. Let him rest. Tomorrow would be time enough.

\* \* \*

The next morning Anna thought she would catch Will when he went on his morning ride, but he'd told the grooms he wasn't riding today. It was disappointing. Talking while on horseback always seemed to go better between the two of them, but he was probably tired and needed the rest.

On her solitary ride she returned to where she'd seen Ellen and Lucius the previous day. Not that she expected to find them, but more to reassure herself that she indeed must tell Will. She would catch him at breakfast.

But when she came back in to the house through the garden, he stood waiting at the office door.

'I would speak with you, Anna.' He looked thunderous.

She was taken aback. 'Now?' Before she changed her clothes?

'Now.' He stepped aside to let her in the room.

She'd been proud of how she'd left his office the day before. Only two piles of papers needing correspondence on his desk. The ledgers neatly set in order on the bookshelf and the unrecorded receipts hidden in his bottom desk drawer. Had he noticed?

His angry glare made her doubt it.

And it roused her anger, as well. Why this change in him again?

She turned to face him. 'What is it, Will? What is so pressing that I cannot change out of my riding habit and into clean clothes?'

'The devil with clean clothes,' he shot back. 'I will tell you what is pressing. Our trip to purchase the dairy cows—the ones we needed so much—was wasted because someone outbid us.'

Anna was puzzled. 'That is unfortunate, but…'

'But nothing!' He glared at her. 'Do you know who outbid us? The bid we offered privately?' He didn't leave her a chance to answer. 'Lucius Dorman.'

'Lucius?' This made no sense. 'Lucius never bothered with tasks like that.' Something made even less sense. 'Why yell at me for something Lucius did?'

His eyes flashed. 'Because the farmer said Lucius knew of our bid, knew to offer more.'

'But how did Lucius know—?'

Will raised his voice. 'I will tell you how Lucius knew! *Your maid* told him.'

'Mary? No.' Impossible. 'Mary could not have told him! When would she have done so?'

He started pacing in front of her. 'She obviously slipped away.'

'I refuse to believe it!' Mary would never have done such a thing.

'One of the grooms saw her. With Lucius,' Will insisted.

'It couldn't have been!' Anna countered. 'It must have been somebody else.'

Will clenched his fists. 'He said it looked like Mary Jones. Who else could it have been? She came to spy on us. Just as I feared.'

'Mary is no spy!' She could not be. If Mary was a spy, then it meant even sweet, timid Mary had betrayed her.

'She goes, Anna,' Will glared into her eyes. 'I cannot have a Dorman spy in this house. She goes today!'

'No!' Anna straightened her spine and met his gaze with a blazing one of her own. 'I do not believe for one minute that Mary acted as a Dorman spy. You are judging her unfairly.'

'This is precisely why I did not want to hire her,' he said, leaving the rest unspoken—that Anna had insisted.

She ignored that. 'Think about it, Will. How would a lady's maid even know about the purchase of dairy cows?'

'You must have talked to her about it.' His glare turned accusing.

She gave a sarcastic laugh. 'I did not talk about dairy cows with my maid.'

'Then she found the letters in the office,' he asserted.

That was possible, Anna supposed, but very unlikely. 'Why would she go in your office?'

His voice grew louder. 'To find out our business so she could tell the Dormans.'

'No. Not Mary. It could not have been her!' Anna shot back.

He raised his brows indignantly. 'Are you are accusing one of my grooms, who has been in my employ for years, of lying?'

'Not of lying.' He was twisting her words. 'Of being mistaken.' She turned towards the door. 'Come with me back to the stables. Let's ask this groom. I want to hear for myself.'

# *Chapter Twenty*

Will strode out of the room with her and they walked briskly to the stables.

He wasn't sure why the poaching of dairy cows angered him so. He knew they would find others eventually. It was because it was Lucius who had done it.

In a way he blamed himself. He knew it was not a good idea to hire a Dorman servant. He knew what would happen. The servant would talk and the Dormans would know all their private affairs and would interfere whenever they could. Will wanted the Dormans out of their lives. He wanted rid of the foolish rivalry that was a credit to neither of them.

Instead, he all but invited a Dorman into the most private parts of his home. All because he could not convince Anna he knew best in this matter and, as a result, he could not refuse her.

Well, this time he intended to stand by what he knew was right. The Dorman maid had to go.

He would not be heartless, though. He'd give the girl a good reference and plenty of money for a new start. But she would never be able to spy on him and his family for the Dormans again.

When they reached the stable Will asked for the groom who'd told him about seeing the maid with Lucius. The man was out in the field and it took several minutes for him to be brought back to the stables. While they waited, Anna stood apart from Will. She stood with her arms crossed and refused to look at him.

The groom finally hurried over to him. 'You asked for me, m'lord?'

Anna joined them, then.

'Yes,' Will responded. 'Would you please tell Lady Willburgh about seeing the maid with Mr Dorman?'

The groom turned to her. 'I saw them. You see, one of the horses got spooked and ran off and I tracked him into that part of the woods. And I saw them through the trees.'

'Are you certain it was Mary Jones, my new lady's maid?' Anna asked.

'Well, yes,' the groom replied. 'I think so anyway.'

'Did you see her face?' Anna persisted.

'Well, no, ma'am.' He looked sheepish. 'She wore a red cloak, but it looked like your maid, ma'am. She was with the young Dorman.'

'Thank you,' Anna said.

She walked out.

Will caught up with her.

'That was not proof it was Mary.' She spoke firmly.

Will had to admit, the groom was less convincing this time. 'Who else would it have been?'

'Not a maid who's only been here a few days and has been busy learning her tasks.' She quickened her pace.

Will stopped her outside the garden door. 'It does not matter, Anna. I can never trust her now. I cannot have the worry that whatever I do or say might become known to the Dormans and be fodder for their mischief.'

'But she's done nothing wrong!' Anna cried.

Will needed to hold fast to his position. 'I never wanted

a Dorman servant here in the first place. She's an outsider. She needs to go.'

'An outsider?' Anna sounded outraged. 'Like me, do you mean?'

'A Dorman outsider,' he clarified.

'Oh?' Her brow lifted. 'You mean someone who spent years in the Dorman household because she had nowhere else to go?'

He caught her point, but needed to stay firm. That was one thing his father did teach him. To be firm. 'This sort of betrayal never happened before your maid came. I simply cannot have her here. She must go.'

'No!' She pleaded now. 'She will have no place to go. I will not let you be so unkind to her. I will not let you!'

Will felt her pain and regretted being the cause. 'I've no intention of being unkind, Anna.' He lowered his voice and spoke kindly. 'I'll pay her generously and provide her with good references. I will also give her time to make arrangements, whatever time you see fit. Will that do?'

Her eyes narrowed. 'It will not do. But you will not listen to reason.'

'I'm not debating it, Anna.' He was getting impatient now. 'I am serious. And I will not change my mind. So leave now. I'm done talking.'

Leave, because he was not feeling very good about the decision, but could not waver.

Anna opened the garden door and rushed in, so angry at him she could not see straight. She hurried up to her room. Mary was there, putting her clean laundry in drawers.

The maid's eyes grew wide. 'Miss Anna—ma'am—what is wrong? You look upset!'

'Oh, Mary!' Anna turned to her, her only ally in this

house, but she needed to know for herself. She looked directly into Mary's eyes. 'I need to ask you something. And I want you to be very honest with me.'

'Of course I will, m'lady.' She looked earnest. And wary.

'I need to know if you have met with anyone from the Dorman house and if you told them anything about us. About Willburgh family business. Anything, even something small.'

Mary looked as if Anna had struck her. 'I would never, Miss Anna. Never. Why would I do such a thing? When you've been so kind?' Her eyes filled with tears. 'Who said I did?'

Anna could not bear to tell her it was Will. 'That does not matter. Is there any way someone might have seen you with someone and thought it was a Dorman or a Dorman servant?'

A tear rolled down Mary's cheek. 'Do you mean here in the house? I haven't been anywhere else, except maybe in the yard. I don't want to talk to anyone from there!'

That was what Anna thought, but she had been fooled so many times before and Mary could have slipped away when Anna was helping Will in his office.

'I don't talk about what I hear, not to anybody,' Mary went on, her lip quivering. 'Am I being sacked?'

Anna enfolded the girl in her arms. 'What will become of me?' Mary wailed.

Anna knew that pain, that panic. She'd felt it many times before.

'Do not fear,' she reassured the girl. 'I will not allow anything bad to happen to you.'

But Will had been adamant and Anna had no power at all. She never did.

Anna was shocked at Will's unreasonableness and his sudden anger. He was completely unwilling to consider any other explanation of the events. He'd made up his mind it was Mary, merely because Mary had been a Dorman servant. An outsider. Well, Anna was an outsider, too. How could she trust that he would not be unreasonable with her as well? And how was she to predict when he'd erupt in these irrational outbursts?

Mary helped her change out of her riding habit. After Anna had washed off the dirt of the road and donned a day dress, she calmed a little. Only then did it strike her that she'd not told him about Ellen. Well, she certainly was not going to tell him now, not when he was in this unreasonable mood.

She felt the blood drain from her face. Anna knew who had told Lucius about the sale of the cows! It had been Ellen. It was Ellen the groom saw and mistook for Mary. They were about the same height and figure and who would ever believe a Willburgh would secretly meet with a Dorman?

Could she tell Will? He'd been so angry at her when he suspected Mary; how angry would he be if he knew it was his own sister who spilled family business to the enemy? And how much angrier still to discover she fancied herself in love with that enemy?

But she had to tell him. Ellen's future was at stake. When, though?

Will expected Anna to isolate herself in her room and avoid him and the rest of the family. That was her typical behaviour when upset. Instead she seemed to spend a lot of time with Ellen who had somehow contracted a spell of the blue devils. Anna's company did not seem to help Ellen's mood, though.

Will knew what troubled Anna, but Ellen's Gordian knots were a mystery. Just the other day she'd been full of cheer. Now she acted like she'd lost her best friend. And it was clear her best friend was not Anna. Ellen seemed as peeved at Anna as Will was.

From his office, he overheard an exchange between Ellen and Anna in the hall.

'I'm not going riding,' Ellen said petulantly. 'I'm going for a walk.'

'I'll go with you,' Anna responded.

'I do not want you to go with me,' Ellen cried. 'I'm just walking to the road and back.'

'To the road and back. Alone.' Anna sounded sceptical, but why would she care?

'Very well, not alone,' retorted Ellen. 'I'll take Betty with me. You can watch from the front of the house if you like.'

'I will,' Anna said.

Will checked and that is what they did. Ellen walked with Betty and Anna watched them closely.

The whole incident did not make sense to him. What did Anna care if Ellen took a walk alone? Ellen was used to walking and riding alone. He refused to ask Anna, though. He'd only spark another argument.

That night's dinner was tortuous. Anna spoke little and avoided talking to him, and Ellen was sullen. Only his mother seemed pleased, possibly because it was clear something had happened between him and Anna.

Anna excused herself after the meal was done. In the drawing room afterwards Will was alone with his mother and Ellen.

Will decided to ask Ellen about the walk.

'I overheard you and Anna arguing about you going for a walk,' he began. 'What was that all about?'

His mother perked up in interest, presumably because this was about Anna.

Ellen looked distressed for a moment, but quickly composed herself. 'I do not know why she all of a sudden does not think I should walk alone. I've walked or ridden alone a lot since she's been here. I refuse to heed what she thinks. She has no authority over me.'

'Indeed she does not,' their mother readily—and somewhat happily—agreed. 'She is behaving very oddly, I must say.' She turned to Will. 'Are we to expect this always?'

'I do not know,' he responded.

His mother leaned towards him. 'You know how much I hate to pry—' Oh, yes, his mother *never* interfered, *never* pried. 'But what did happen between you and Anna to make her behave so oddly?'

He supposed he owed her an explanation. He picked the easiest one. 'We had a disagreement about her lady's maid.'

His mother looked smug. 'I told you that girl would be trouble. What did she do?'

Will took a sip of brandy. 'Remember I told you we were out bid for the dairy cows?'

She nodded.

'It was Lucius Dorman who outbid us.'

Ellen's head perked up.

'Lucius Dorman!' his mother cried.

'Someone tipped him off,' Will went on. 'I believe it was Anna's lady's maid and Anna insists it was not. But who else would have done it?'

'Indeed,' his mother agreed. 'I am certain you are correct. I told you that maid would spy on us. You might have listened to me.'

Ellen broke in. 'The cows were that important?'

'Not the cows,' Will explained. 'It was that our personal family information was told to a Dorman. We cannot have that. We cannot trust them.'

'Indeed we cannot,' his mother expounded. 'So Anna takes the maid's side against us? That is disloyal!'

'This is because of the feud,' Ellen said with derision. 'The feud that you think is so important.'

'It is important.' His mother shook a finger at Ellen. 'Remember that feud led to your father's death.'

Ellen sobered. 'No one ever told me how.'

*Remind Ellen of Father's death, Mother*, thought Will. *That will cheer her up.*

Her mother eagerly explained, 'Because of the feud, your father and Bertram Dorman, Baron Dorman's younger brother—Anna's father—fought a duel and they killed each other.'

'Anna's stepfather,' Will corrected.

'Stepfather, then,' sniffed his mother.

'How come they fought a duel over the feud?' Ellen persisted.

Will broke in. 'Because they were foolish.'

Ellen did not need to know of her mother's fling with Bertram Dorman. That certainly would not cheer her up. He could at least count on his mother not to tell her that.

'And the feud was about that land?' she asked.

'Yes. The disputed land.' That was all she needed to know.

'Well.' Ellen stood. 'I think it is all very silly!' She walked out.

At the moment Will agreed with her. How much havoc over generations had this feud created? Was he perpetuating the havoc?

Had the feud not existed would Bertram Dorman have bothered to seduce his mother? Would his father have fought a duel with anyone but a Dorman? Would the Dormans have acted so outraged when Will was caught in the rain with Anna? Nothing good ever came from the damned feud.

A few days ago he would have hoped that marrying Anna

would turn into the one good thing that came from the feud, but look how that hope was dashed.

That night Will could not sleep.

His head told him he'd been right when he'd refused to hire the Dorman maid. So now he was right to let her go, was he not? He'd expected trouble and trouble came. Was that not right?

Anna's arguments on behalf of the maid were compelling, though. They nagged at him.

Who else could it have been? No one else made sense. He wanted Anna to see his way, though she seemed determined not to.

Everything seemed wrong. What tortured Will the most was he feared he was wrong. Was he the one who made a mess of everything?

He heard the door connecting his room to Anna's open and he turned to face it.

She was framed in the doorway. 'Will? Are you awake?'

'I am awake,' he responded.

'I would speak with you,' she said. Not *may* she speak. She was not asking for permission but making a command.

He rose from the bed as she walked towards him, the flame of the candle in her hand illuminating her face, her curls loose around her head like an aura, her nightdress flowing as she walked, giving him glimpses of her womanly shape beneath. He was naked save his drawers and he yearned to pull off her nightdress and feel her warm, smooth skin against his.

Suddenly it seemed like there was no air for him to breathe, only this otherworldly spectre coming closer and his desire growing stronger. Was she his weakness?

He managed to answer her. 'Then speak, Anna.'

She stopped a mere three feet away. 'I have a plan that will remove Mary in mere days and will avoid further *disruption* to the family.' She emphasised the word *disruption* and sounded sad, but resigned.

It had been a word he'd used, he realised. 'What is the plan?'

She took a breath. 'Mary will leave here, but I will leave with her.'

'What?' Will was shocked.

She held up a hand. 'Hear me out.' She placed the candle on a nearby table and faced him again. 'Before we decided to marry, we'd contemplated you simply supporting me, giving me enough money to live on.'

That had been what she'd wanted, and if they'd done that, she'd have wound up wealthy. His fault she wasn't.

She went on. 'It was what we should have done all along. Set me up with some sort of settlement or stipend or something—nothing extravagant—and I will take Mary as my maid. We can live very simply, except I should like to afford to keep Seraphina.'

No! He wanted to protest. She would leave him? Wanted her horse, but not him? No!

'Where would you go?' he asked, keeping the emotion out of his voice.

She shrugged. 'Oh, I don't know. Perhaps a village near Reading. Reading sounds like a nice town.'

Reading? With its iron works and a ruined abbey? What could appeal there?

'Reading,' he repeated. 'You want to leave and take the maid and go to Reading.'

'And Seraphina,' she added. 'It solves everything, do you see? Think on it.' She picked up the candle again and turned to walk away, but paused and spoke over her shoulder. 'Except I've not given you an heir. I do regret that.'

The mention of an heir sent his mind back to tangled sheets and passion and pleasure unlike he'd ever experienced before. That was what he wanted back. That and the easy camaraderie they'd once shared.

She walked back to the door, a silhouette now, even more spectre-like. As she walked away his spirits plummeted even deeper than before. He was left feeling a dislike of himself that rational thought disdained.

And beyond that, emptiness.

The next day Anna avoided Will.

It was too painful to be near him, not because of his temper, but because she loved him so. He was a good man on the whole, trying to do the right thing by everyone. Everyone but her.

When he brought Mary to her, Anna thought it the most loving act, even though she could not say he loved her. It bitterly disappointed Anna, though, that Will could so cruelly take Mary away, with such baseless accusations. He might wrap her banishment in gold ribbons, but it was the fact of being unwanted that was so deeply wounding. How could Will do that? How could he not see that Anna needed to make Mary know that she was wanted, that she belonged somewhere and that someone cared for her? Could Will not see that Anna needed him to tell her she belonged with him, that he wanted her, cared for her?

Anna might be a disappointment to him, but, in this, Anna was disappointed in Will. It was best she and Mary leave.

At the moment, though, Anna had Ellen to worry about. She stayed close to Ellen the whole day and still agonised over whether she should tell Will about her and Lucius. Even though Ellen had given Anna her word that she would not see Lucius again, every instinct told Anna she could not trust Ellen not to slip away and run to him.

So when Ellen went to the library to select a book, Anna selected a book. When Ellen settled in one of the sunniest parlours to read, Anna sat in the same room with her own book.

Anna had selected one volume of *England's Gazetteer* to read of the places she and Mary might settle. She'd not set on Reading for certain, but mentioned it to Will so he'd know she was serious about leaving. Reading was as good a place as any.

The more she read of other villages and towns, the more her spirits dipped. Living in this area since her childhood made it familiar to her. She was used to the village, the church, the people. Even more, Anna had come to love this house. Even in the short time she'd lived in Willburgh House, it felt more like home than Dorman Hall. At Dorman Hall she'd been treated as if she were Violet's lady's companion instead of a member of the family. As if she did not truly belong.

She glanced over at Ellen who was gazing out the window instead of reading her book. Those first days here Anna had hoped she and Ellen could be friends. Now Ellen despised her.

Ellen glanced over at her. 'You do not have to watch me every second, Anna. I gave you my word I would not see Lucius. Do you not trust me?'

'I would like to trust you,' Anna answered.

Was it useless to keep such a close eye on Ellen? When Anna left, Ellen could continue her secret trysts.

That was why Anna must tell Will. So Anna's word could not be trusted either, could it?

Lucius would lose interest eventually, of course, but it was the harm he could do to Ellen beforehand that Anna worried about. No, Anna would have to tell Will and tell him soon.

But not today.

In the meantime Anna could try to convince Ellen that Lucius was not of good character.

'Let me tell you a little more about Lucius,' she said to Ellen. 'About the kind of person he is.'

She told Ellen about Lucius abandoning her at Vauxhall and leaving her to the mercy of his friend, Millman, and exactly what Millman tried to do to her.

Ellen listened with a defiant expression. 'You cannot convince me that he knew Millman would try to molest you.'

Actually Anna did not believe that of Lucius. 'No, but he remained friends with him after he knew what happened.'

'Are you sure?' Ellen countered. 'You were not with him after Scotland.'

'True, but I would wager any amount of money that Lucius would care more about his friendship than about what the man tried to do to me.'

'By then he was probably very angry at you,' Ellen said. 'You ran off and married Will. That was like a betrayal to him. That silly feud, you know.'

Anna did not know what to say in response.

Ellen rose and faced her. 'I cannot bear to be inside this stuffy old house for another moment. I am going for a walk.'

Anna opened her mouth to say she would walk with her.

Ellen waved her hand dismissively. 'I do not want your company. I will take Betty. We will walk to the road and back and you can watch from the front of the house like you did before.'

'I will be watching,' Anna said.

# Chapter Twenty-One

After another tension-filled dinner that evening Anna retired to her room and had Mary help her get ready for bed. She'd hardly slept the past two nights. She hadn't told Mary about needing to leave. Why upset the girl until Anna had all the details set? Mary was happy here at Willburgh House, Anna could tell. Betty had become her friend and the two could be found together at every spare moment. Let Mary have her friendship for as long as possible.

When Mary left her, Anna crawled into bed and burrowed beneath the covers, but, instead of sleep, Anna's emotions spilled over and she wept. She'd held back tears long enough, and now the dam had broken. Her grief at all she'd lost—especially Will—flooded her. When she finally slept, though, her sleep was peaceful and deep.

Until she was jarred awake by someone shaking her, telling her to wake. 'M'lady! M'lady! Wake up!'

She opened her eyes.

Betty and Mary stood over her.

'You must wake up, m'lady!' Betty cried.

Anna sat up. 'What? What has happened?'

Mary held the candle while Betty shook her shoulder, a breach of proper servant behaviour, but Betty was distraught.

'She's gone, m'lady!' Betty cried. 'Not long ago. Maybe half an hour? Less.'

Anna brushed the hair out of her eyes. 'Who is gone?'

'Miss Willburgh!' Betty cried.

'Ellen?' Anna straightened, wide awake now.

'She's run away!' Betty stifled a sob. 'She took some clothes! What shall we do?'

Anna bounded out of bed. 'We must go after her!' She turned to Mary. 'Quick. My old riding habit!'

Mary shoved the candle into Betty's hand.

Anna ran to the connecting door to Will's room, burst in his room and in the dim light, found his bed.

'Will! Wake up!' She shook him like Betty had shaken her.

He shot up so quickly she jumped back.

'What is it?' He seemed even more awake than she was.

'Ellen has eloped!' she said. 'I'll explain later. We must go after her! Right now.'

He got out of bed, wearing only his drawers. Betty had followed her and lit a candle in his room.

'Get dressed now!' Anna cried. 'Hurry!' She ran back to her room.

While Mary helped her dress, Betty explained. 'She told me not to tell, but on those walks, she left a letter for someone in a knot in a tree that was on the road. Then yesterday she found a letter there for her.' Betty shook her head. 'That's all I know. Do you think that has something to do with her running away?'

'I'm sure it has,' Anna responded.

Betty went on. 'I thought something was up so Mary and I got up early. The clock struck four. She was in bed then, but something seemed strange so we went back and she was gone. We could not have been more than a quarter hour. Or a half hour.'

Perhaps she'd been dressed and ready to leave but pretending to sleep. But with the letters, there was no doubt that she planned this.

Will came into her room as she was putting on her boots. She gave quick embraces to both Betty and Mary and rushed out with him.

Their clatter on the stairs roused the footman monitoring the hall. He was barely awake when Will called to him. 'Tell no one we've gone!'

Then they were out the door hurrying to the stables. By this time the first rays of dawn had appeared on the horizon, enough to light their way.

'She's been meeting Lucius in secret,' Anna explained. 'And Lucius has convinced her she is in love with him. I thought I stopped it, but they were passing letters on those walks. I think he is planning a terrible revenge. I think he is eloping with her!'

'Lucius!' Will growled. 'I'll kill him.'

Will's anger alarmed her. 'We just need to stop them in time.'

When they reached the stable door and opened it, Will's voice boomed. 'Grooms! Now! To saddle horses!'

He'd already picked up the saddles and brought them to the horses when John and Toby appeared, hastily.

'Saddle Anna's pony and my thoroughbred,' he ordered and turned to Anna. 'My thoroughbred is the fastest.'

The two grooms asked no questions, but made quick work of it. Will and Anna were soon mounted and ready to ride.

'Be ready if I need you,' Will shouted to John and Toby. 'I do not know how long it will be.'

Will galloped off and Anna followed him. He had the gate open for her by the time she reached it and he was standing in the middle of the road, looking down.

He looked over at her and pointed. 'They went that way.' He remounted.

'Ride ahead, Will,' she told him. 'I'll come as fast as I can.'

Will needed to keep his wits about him.

He needed to conserve his horse's strength. How long before he could catch up to them? He didn't want his horse blown.

Will was reasonably sure Lucius and Ellen were headed to Aylesbury to a coaching inn. The tracks looked like Lucius drove his curricle. Lucius was not likely to take his curricle all the way to Scotland.

If Scotland was where he intended to go.

Will would not let himself think of the alternative—to merely ruin her thoroughly. Just in case, Will kept his eye on the road to make sure their trail did not turn off this main road.

As Will rode, the puzzle pieces fell into place. While he and Anna were working together on his papers and ledgers, Ellen was happily riding or taking walks alone. Meeting Lucius. It was Ellen, not the poor maid, who'd told Lucius about the sale of the cows, probably innocently, but still... Had it not occurred to her that Lucius would take advantage of the information? Why had she allowed the maid to take the blame?

Anna discovered this and was making certain Ellen did not meet him again. That was why Ellen turned sullen and why she turned against Anna.

Everything fit.

What a fool Will had been. He'd been as much a prisoner of the feud as Lucius was, as their ancestors were. Would he have been so unfair to Anna, if not for the feud? Would he have been so harsh on poor Mary Jones? Would Lucius have bothered to trifle with a respectable sixteen-year-old?

He must have ridden at a good pace for at least an hour. They'd started out in near darkness and now the new day had dawned. Sheep appeared on the hillsides, birds sounded in the bushes and took to flight when he rode by. He saw farm workers making their way to the fields. The road was still empty of traffic, though. He was not too far from Aylesbury. Another hour, perhaps. He wanted to overtake them before they reached the town. It would be the very devil to find the coaching inn at which they would stop.

Will finally spied a vehicle in the distance, but it was coming towards him. As it got closer, he could see it was a farm wagon carrying hay and pulled by a sturdy farm horse. A grizzled man drove the wagon and a young boy sat next to him on the wagon's bench.

When Will came close enough, he asked them, 'Did you pass a gentleman and lady in a curricle, by any chance?'

'I did, sir.' The man answered in a very unhurried manner. 'Thought it odd they were up so early, but you can never tell.'

Will could barely contain himself. 'How long ago did you see them? Are they far? Are they still on this road?'

'Oh, they were on this road all right. Not too many side roads worth bothering with around here.'

'How far?' Will pressed.

'Not too far.' The farmer turned around in his seat and gestured to the road behind him. 'I passed them just over this hill here. Not too many minutes before seeing you. You can't see over the hill but if you could, you'd see it is not too far.'

'What is your name, my good man?' Will intended to send him a reward for his help.

'Name's Begum,' the farmer replied.

'Thank you, Begum.' Will rode on increasing his speed.

He did not see them over the hill but galloped over the next hill.

And he saw them!

He gave his horse its head and he closed the distance between them.

Lucius turned at the sound of Will's approaching horse. 'Blast it! It's your brother.'

He drove his horses faster, but Will caught up and brought his horse next to one of the curricle's horses. He took hold of the reins. Lucius stood up and thrashed Will with his whip, but Will kept hold, slowing his horse and the curricle.

Ellen pulled on Lucius's coat, yelling, 'Stop! Stop!'

There was a tiger riding on the back, a youth barely breeched who looked terrified.

With the curricle stopped, Will seized the whip and pulled it. Lucius kept his grip, but lost his balance and tumbled out of the seat onto the road.

Ellen shrieked, 'Lucius!'

The tiger had the presence of mind to hop off and run around to hold the horses. Will dismounted and was striding towards Lucius as he was getting to his feet. As soon as Lucius stood, Will pulled his arm back and punched him in the face. Lucius spun around and fell again.

'Will, no!' Will was close enough to the curricle that Ellen pounded him with her fists. 'Don't hurt him.'

Lucius got to his feet again, rubbing his chin. 'Always the brute, Willburgh,' he snarled.

'That's what you deserve and more,' Will shot back. 'Good God, man. My sister is only sixteen years old!'

'I'm old enough to know my own mind!' cried Ellen. 'We are to be married! Just like you and Anna.'

'That's it, isn't it, Lucius?' Will approached him again, fists clenched. 'The perfect revenge. I married Anna and your family could no longer steal her fortune, so you take my sister. Did you not realise that I could prevent you from having her dowry?'

Lucius raised his own fists but backed away. 'You wouldn't do that, though, would you, Willburgh? You'd never deny your sister. I'll bet her dowry rivals Anna's wealth.'

It didn't, but Ellen was worth a sizable amount.

'Stop this talk of money!' Ellen cried. 'Let us be on our way!'

'He's not taking you to Scotland,' Will told her. 'You are coming home.'

'No!' She closed her arms over her chest. 'We love each other and we will be married.'

'No you won't!' Will advanced on Lucius and threw another punch.

This one Lucius dodged. He was clearly trying to avoid Will.

'You will let me marry your sister,' Lucius said. 'Unless you want a scandal that goes beyond all scandals. A scandal so terrible your sister will be ruined.'

'By God if you've violated her!' Will charged him and seized the front of his coat, lifting him off the ground and thrusting him away.

Lucius fell again but laughed. 'Not *violated* because she was willing. Very willing and there are consequences for being willing.'

'I was willing!' Ellen insisted. 'Very willing.'

Will's anger surged so high his vision turned red. 'You've got her with child!'

'Do not insult me, Will!' Ellen cried. 'Of course he did not get me with child.'

Lucius laughed again. 'No, I am not that depraved, but you know the truth matters little to a London gossip rag.'

Ellen looked perplexed. 'What are you talking about, Lucius?'

Will took a step towards Lucius again. 'I swear I would gladly kill you!'

Lucius walked to the other side of the curricle, with Ellen in between Will and him now. 'You would not kill me, Willburgh,' he said. 'Not unless you could do so with honour. Would you like to kill me with honour?'

Will was so angry he could not think. He raged, not only about Lucius Dorman running off with his sister, but about all the Dormans had done to Anna, what they'd done to his father. And even his mother. Will was engulfed in his emotions. Reason had fled.

Lucius reached under the seat of the curricle and took out a box. 'Here is how you can get your revenge with honour.' He lifted up the box. 'These are my duelling pistols. I challenge you to a duel for the honour of your sister.'

'I accept,' Will said.

Anna knew she was near to catching up with Will. And with Ellen and Lucius. The farmer in the wagon told her. Already she felt relieved. Will would stop them. He would save Ellen from making a terrible mistake.

She rode Seraphina a little faster.

When she came over the crest of the hill she saw the curricle and horses stopped in the road. She glanced to the right and gasped.

In the field, two men stood back to back and began to pace away from each other.

Will and Lucius.

A duel.

'No, no, no, no, no,' she cried.

She urged her horse into a gallop, sailed over the hedgerow on the side of the road and, right when both men turned to fire, rode straight in between them.

The sound of the shots exploded in her ears. Seraphina squealed and toppled to the ground, throwing Anna off. She landed hard in a heap.

She could see the field. Saw Lucius run over to Ellen, seize her by the waist and run towards the curricle. They were getting away! Will ran towards her, calling her name. Seraphina writhed on the ground near to her and incongruously a youth in livery stood stunned a few feet away.

Will reached her just as she regained her breath. He slid to the ground. 'Anna!'

'I'm—I'm not hurt,' she managed, hoping it was true. She sat up. 'Go after them, Will.'

Lucius and Ellen were in the curricle, driving off.

'I'll come back for you.' He ran to his horse.

Anna crawled to her pony. 'Poor Seraphina.' She stroked the pony's neck.

To her surprise, Seraphina rose to her feet. She'd been certain the pony had been shot. Anna gripped her mane to help her stand, as well. She checked the pony all over, felt its legs for breaks, but found none. There was a gash on the horse's shoulder, not very deep, not even bleeding much.

'Poor Seraphina!' Anna laughed in relief. 'The shot just startled you.' She turned to the liveried servant, recognising him as Lucius's tiger. 'Nick, is it? Come help me mount.'

The poor lad roused himself enough to come to her side and help her into the saddle. She rode away leaving him befuddled and alone. They'd come back for him, but she didn't have time to reassure him.

# Chapter Twenty-Two

Will rode as fast as he dared. Lucius was driving his horses at a dangerous pace. Ellen looked like she was hanging on for dear life.

If anything happened to her, how could Will forgive himself? He'd managed everyone and everything into complete disaster. He could not have possibly made more mistakes.

The road was rough in some places where rain and wagon wheels had dug ruts. The curricle bounced and shimmied over the surface and Will feared it would simply come apart.

When the road made an abrupt turn to the left, Will held his breath.

The curricle horses scrambled to keep their footing. The curricle tipped onto one wheel which hit a rock in the road. It flew in the air and Ellen's screams filled Will's ears. The curricle crashed onto its side tossing Lucius onto the road. Ellen hung on while the horses dragged the curricle several feet. Will caught up and brought the horses under control.

He helped a shaking Ellen to the side of the road, seating her there, and ran back to Lucius's still body.

Had Will succeeded in killing him? God, he prayed. Please. No.

'Is he dead?' Ellen wailed. She rocked back and forth.

Will felt for a heartbeat.

And found it.

'He's alive.'

But Lucius was unconscious. He'd hit his head when he fell. What's more, his shoulder looked broken. Will eased him onto his back and held him up, hoping to ease his breathing. Lucius moaned when Will moved him.

'Ellen!' Will called. 'Find something in the curricle to elevate his back.'

She simply rocked back and forth.

'Ellen!'

But she was insensible. What was he to do?

At that moment, though, Will saw Anna riding towards them. Intrepid Anna. He should have known he could count on her.

Before she could ask, he said, 'He's alive. Unconscious, but alive. Can you find something to put behind his back?'

She rode over to the curricle and dismounted. First she went over to Ellen and spoke quietly to her, putting a comforting hand on her shoulder. Then she dashed to the curricle and ran back to Will carrying a blanket and Ellen's portmanteau which had fallen out.

Will propped Lucius up and, after making certain he was as comfortable as possible, got to his feet and embraced Anna.

'I am sorry for it all, Anna.' His voice cracked. 'All my fault. All my fault.'

'Nonsense,' she murmured. 'You are not responsible, but we need to figure out what to do.'

He released her. 'Yes. Yes. Help me turn the curricle.'

Anna held the horses, while Will tried to set the curricle on its wheels, which seemed intact. Lucius had purchased a high-quality vehicle so that made sense. It would roll if Will could only set it to rights.

But he could not do it, not after several tries. He sat down near Lucius to catch his breath.

'Maybe tie one of the horses to it and have them pull?' Anna suggested.

Will nodded. It was a good idea.

He tied his thoroughbred to the curricle and led him away, but they still could not set the curricle back on its wheels.

'Should I ride for help?' Anna asked.

'We're about halfway between Aylesbury and home,' Will said. 'I do not know which way you should go.'

Anna looked towards Ellen. 'I'm worried about her, too.'

Ellen had curled herself into a ball and was shaking. Lucius moaned and tried to stand up.

Will went over to him. 'Stay down, Lucius. You are injured. Best not to move.'

Lucius shoved off Will's attempt to help him. 'Guh 'way,' he slurred. 'Hate you. Always did.'

He went down on his knees and vomited, clutching his injured shoulder as he did so.

Will eased him back against the blanket and he moaned in pain.

What was best to do? They could wait for the ordinary traffic to come down the road, but Will was afraid they needed help sooner. He was reluctant to let Anna go for help, though. She'd suffered a fall, too. She said she was not injured, but he was not sure. The horses were getting restless. Lucius's horses were already spooked. Who knew what might set them off again?

'Someone's coming!' Anna cried.

Two men on horses approached from the direction in which they'd come. One of the men had Lucius's tiger riding behind him.

Will stood. 'It is Toby and John!'

They rode up to him.

'We thought it best to come after you, m'lord,' Toby said. 'In case you needed help.'

With Toby and John's help, they soon righted the curricle and sorted out the horses' harnesses. They put Lucius and Ellen in the curricle with John driving. The tiger rode John's horse.

'Let's take them back home,' Will said.

He rode next to Anna. 'Are you certain you are not injured?'

She smiled at him. 'I will probably ache tomorrow, but, no—nothing broken.'

They rode a while in silence.

Will spoke, needing to tell her and to hear himself speak aloud. 'I was angry enough to kill him. Angry enough to agree to the duel.'

'Stealing Ellen away was reprehensible,' she said.

She did not reproach him for it? Will could not believe it. 'When I turned to fire—in that instant I saw my father's duel—I could not do it, Anna. I could not fire at him. I deloped.'

She looked over at him but he could not read his expression. Was it understanding? Admiration? He could not believe either one.

'Maybe that's the only thing I got right,' he murmured.

John called back to him. 'The gentleman's delirious!'

Will rode up to the curricle.


Anna watched him.

Will ordered Ellen to hold on to Lucius. When she did not respond, he rode closer so she could not fail to see him. 'Buck up, Ellen!' he demanded. 'He needs you. Hold on to him!'

She did as she was told.

Anna was filled with emotion.

Will was doubting himself, blaming himself, and yet he was handling all of this. Her heart burst with pride for him, but also ached with his suffering. She wished she belonged with him, because she loved him. If anyone was at fault for all that happened it was Anna. Her presence had caused him and his family all this trouble.

The ride back was fraught with tension and seemed endless, but finally they neared the gates of Willburgh House.

Will sprang into action again. 'Toby, ride to the village. Get the surgeon. Bring him here. We will take Dorman to the house.'

Toby nodded and galloped off.

To Lucius's tiger Will said, 'Ride to Lord Dorman. Tell them their son is injured and they must come.'

The youth cried, 'Yes, m'lord!'

The household must have been watching for them, because the door opened before they pulled up. Lady Willburgh took charge, immediately having Lucius carried to a guest room, and taking Ellen under her wing while listening to Will's explanation of what happened.

Anna was not surprised that she went unnoticed. She did not need anything, after all. She went to her room with Mary who helped her to quickly wash and dress in clean clothes.

It was Anna who was there to greet Lord and Lady Dorman and Violet, to fill them in on what happened. She took them up to Lucius's room.

The surgeon arrived and examined Lucius thoroughly. He was most concerned about the injury to Lucius's head. It was bad enough for Lucius to go in and out of consciousness. If Lucius survived the night, the surgeon said, his chance of recovery was good, but the next twenty-four hours would be crucial.

Lady Willburgh and Will told the Dormans they were welcome to stay. They could use the drawing room to rest when not with Lucius. Or they could sleep in the guest bedrooms. Lady Willburgh said refreshments would be provided for them.

The Dormans said they would stay in the drawing room for the whole day and night. Anna went to the kitchen herself to make certain Cook would be prepared for the extra guests. Mrs Greaves was there.

'Lady Willburgh gave those directions already, ma'am,' Mrs Greaves said.

For once Anna did not resent being usurped by her mother-in-law. 'She thought of everything,' Anna said with true admiration.

'Yes, m'lady,' Mrs Greaves agreed.

Would Anna ever be able to do even half as well as Lady Willburgh, if she stayed? Anna wondered.

Anna walked back upstairs and decided to check in the drawing room in case she might be useful there. When she approached the door, she heard Will's voice.

'I know this is not the time, Dorman,' he said. 'But I want you to know that I believe it is time to settle the land dispute. If you want the land, I can deed it to you. If you would prefer funds, we can negotiate a sale of sorts. Do not tell me now, but think on it when Lucius's health improves.'

Lord Dorman's voice quavered, 'Do you think he will improve?'

Anna peeked in the room to see Will put a comforting hand on Lord Dorman's shoulder. 'I think Lucius is strong. And he certainly is determined. He'll get better.'

Violet came down the stairs. She had a handkerchief in her hand and dabbed at her eyes.

She stopped when she saw Anna.

'How is he?' Anna asked.

Violet blinked before answering. 'The surgeon said he dislocated his shoulder. He put it back in place, but it must have hurt.'

'Must have been hard to witness, as well.' Anna gestured for her to come in the room. 'I'll pour you a cup of tea.'

When Violet saw her father, though, she ran into his arms and wept into his chest.

Will walked over to Anna. 'Come. Let us leave them alone.'

She walked out with him. 'You haven't changed your clothes, Will.'

He was still in the clothes he'd hastily put on before dawn. His face was shadowed with a growth of beard, making him look like a drawing of a pirate she once saw in a book.

He looked down at himself. 'I suppose I should change. That must be why Carter is hovering. Waiting for me.'

She walked with him to the door of his bed chamber. 'I overheard you talking to Lord Dorman about the disputed land.'

He looked surprised, then nodded. 'I want to be rid of it. The dispute, that is. By any means.' He smiled down at her. 'You did well today, Anna. Except for charging into the middle of a duel—'

She interrupted. 'I wanted to stop it.'

He nodded. 'I know.' He lightly touched her cheek. 'You might have saved my life. And I know you saved Ellen's.' He glanced towards the stairway. 'Maybe even Lucius's.'

Lucius's life was saved. By the next day the surgeon declared him out of the woods, but warned that he must stay put. He would need rest and quiet to completely recuperate. So his stay at Willburgh House stretched to a fortnight.

Anna did not press to leave while Lucius was there. That

was enough of a disruption in the family. Her leaving would merely be another one.

It was a very odd two weeks. A member of the Dorman family—or all of them—visited almost every day. Having endured this crisis together, the animosity between the families seemed to dissipate. Will had been true to his word and ended the dispute over the land. He paid Lord Dorman an exorbitant sum for a clear deed to half of the land. Anna suspected it was the sum that would cover Lord Dorman's debts. Certainly that must have eased a great deal of stress in the Dorman house.

Anna was extremely impressed with Lady Willburgh's cordiality to the Dormans. She was especially kind to Lucius who, after all, had tried to elope with her sixteen-year-old daughter. The maids told Anna that Lucius had apologised to Lady Willburgh and to Will for his behaviour. He especially apologised to Ellen, confessed that he'd manipulated her out of a desire for revenge upon her brother, and that she was indeed too young to contemplate marriage with anyone.

Anna avoided Lucius as much as possible, but when she was in his company he seemed changed. He was courteous. Subdued. Completely lacking in sarcasm.

Ellen had changed as well, but in a way that made Anna sad. Her youthful joy and exuberance disappeared and it seemed like she spent as much time alone as Anna did.

Even though the venom that had permeated Anna's relationships with her mother-in-law, sister-in-law, and Will was eased with the more pressing issue of having to attend to the Dormans, Anna felt separate from them all. As if she'd already left. Even though Will was unfailingly polite and kind to her, he also seemed to treat her as if she'd already left.

Except for that one brief moment when she'd reached the

site of the curricle accident, the intimacy they'd so briefly shared was not repeated.

They'd still not told anyone else that Anna was leaving, but when Lucius was almost ready to move back to Dorman Hall, and summer was nearing its end, Anna decided it was time for her to leave. Soon harvest would make more work for Will and she wanted to make this least burdensome to him.

That afternoon Will answered a knock on his office door. It was Anna.

She never came to the office, not since he'd accused her maid of spying for the Dormans. His desk was rapidly returning to the chaos it had been before she'd briefly become the secretary he had yet to hire to help him deal with it.

'Anna!' Will stood. 'What may I do for you?'

She glanced down at his paper-strewn desk, but quickly lifted her gaze back to him. 'I wish to talk with you, is all, Will. For a moment, if you do not mind.'

'Not at all.' He hurried from behind the desk. 'Sit. Shall I call for tea?'

'No. I shouldn't be so long.' She let him lead her to the sofa and chairs.

She sat on the sofa. He chose a chair facing her and felt a cloud of doom engulf him.

She arranged her skirts before speaking. 'I thought this might be the proper time to plan my—my departure.'

Will lowered his head, knowing she'd be able to read his expression. 'There is no hurry, Anna,' he murmured.

'This seems like a good time, though,' she said.

Will's chest began to ache, making it hard to breathe. 'What were you thinking?'

She took a breath. 'I think Mary may want to stay here. Will you be able to keep her on?'

'Of course she may stay.' He dared to reach over and clasp one of her hands in his. 'You don't have to leave either, Anna. You may both stay. Everything is different. I have changed.' He glanced away. 'Or I hope I have. I strive to do better.'

She regarded him with a look of tenderness on her face. 'Oh, Will. Do not take this on as your fault. I've been the disruption. We both know so.'

He knew no such thing. One could just as easily say she was the solution to all the family problems.

She went on. 'We were never meant to be together. Neither of us chose it, remember?'

He may not have chosen it then, but he did now. He wanted to be with her. 'We could keep trying.' He swallowed. 'I want to keep trying. I want you to stay.'

Anna's eyes filled with tears.

'It is no use. I want to leave,' she said.

The first part was true enough; the second a lie. She wanted to stay more than anything, but she was convinced she would only cause more unhappiness. Things were better, because, in so many ways, she was already gone.

He released her hand and spoke sadly. 'If that is what you truly want.'

He was sad now, she thought, but he would be happier without her. She was sorry she did not give him an heir, but how dangerous it would be to make love with him again. She could never leave if they joined together again, flesh to flesh, climbing to that incomparable peak of pleasure.

He cleared his throat. 'But I insist you travel to where you want to live to see if you truly like it. You may wish to live elsewhere.'

He was not arguing with her. Did that make her happy or despondent? She did not know.

'Very well,' she responded. 'I will make a trip to Reading first before arranging to move there.'

'I must accompany you,' he added. 'Since I am paying, I must be certain it is worth the money.'

That made sense. Besides, it would give her more time with him. 'I—I have another request,' she said. 'A silly one, I am sure you will think,' she said.

'What is it?' He seemed to brace himself.

'Might we ride to Reading?' she asked uncertainly. 'On the Highland ponies? Like we did leaving Scotland?'

Like those happy days, did she mean? The ache in his chest grew stronger. 'We can do that.'

# Chapter Twenty-Three

They left in two days, telling everyone Will had business in Reading and Anna was accompanying him. They were simply wished safe travel; no one seemed to think anything more about it. Will's estate manager questioned it, but Will told him the business was personal and Parker accepted that. If anyone thought it odd that they rode Highland ponies to Reading, no one said so to them.

They left without fanfare, mounting the ponies and starting on their way. John accompanied them, but after a while, he rode ahead to arrange accommodations for them. Anna and Will rode side by side.

They did not have the beautiful weather that had graced them on their long ride from Scotland. The sky was overcast and the day was one of the warmest of the summer. Reading was a good day's ride and Anna told herself to savour the trip, no matter the weather. It was time with Will and she'd soon be saying goodbye to him for ever.

Will was not pushing the pace, which suited Anna. Mid-morning they stopped at an inn to rest the horses and have some refreshment, but the weather was not improved when they started on their way again. They did not talk much, reminding Anna of those first days when they travelled to Scotland.

Her mind kept wandering to the glorious days and nights she shared with Will on the trip back from Scotland. Especially the glorious nights when everything seemed full of promise. Anna would be alone again. Alone, because she would not be with Will.

The grief of it overwhelmed her. Tears rolled down her cheeks. She slowed enough to ride a little behind him so he could not see. She swallowed the sobs, not wanting him to hear her weeping.

She'd doomed herself with this foolish notion of moving away. At least if she'd stayed at Willburgh House she could see him every day. All she wanted to do was turn around and gallop with him all the way back…home.

She felt a drop on her cheek that was not a tear. Soon more drops fell.

Will turned in his saddle. 'It is about to pour! Look for shelter.'

They rode faster as the raindrops increased.

Finally he pointed. There in a nearby field was a shelter. They left the road and crossed the field to a wooden structure, open on one side, probably meant for exactly this use—shelter from a sudden rainstorm. There was room for the two ponies and them. They dismounted and dried off the horses as best they could and took off their hats and gloves. There was some hay to keep the horses entertained including a bale that they used as a bench.

Anna was acutely aware of the nearness of him. She had not been so close to him since the day of the curricle accident when he embraced her.

He laughed softly.

'What makes you laugh?' she asked.

'The irony of it,' he responded. 'Our first meeting was in a rainstorm and now…' His voice trailed off.

She gazed through the rain across the field. 'This is unlike Vauxhall, though, is it not?'

'And it seems a long time ago,' he said.

'Not even three months.' She turned to him. 'Do you know what else is amusing?'

'What?' he asked without any humour at all.

'Today is my birthday.'

He frowned. 'I should have known that.'

She shrugged. 'I never told you the day. It lacks any importance now.'

'Because I lost you your fortune,' he said.

Impulsively, she grasped his hand. 'Do not think that way, Will,' she pleaded. 'We did not know. Before the Dormans became such *nice people*—' she said this with sarcasm '—they did a very bad thing. A series of bad things.'

He leaned back against the wood of the wall. 'I cannot conjure up the same level of rage as before, but I doubt I will ever trust any of them.'

She sighed. 'They make it easy to blame everything on them. But I made so many mistakes that I regret.'

He sat up straight again. 'You? No. What mistakes did you make?'

She averted her face. She could not speak the biggest mistake. Insisting on leaving. Not accepting Will, his mother, his sister, as the people they were, and staying with them.

He leaned back again and closed his eyes. 'It was me, Anna,' he murmured. 'I let my hatred for the Dormans colour everything. Be my excuse for everything. The truth is I've never forgiven my father for dying in that duel and leaving me to deal with all his duties when I didn't know how. I still don't know how. But then I fought a duel, as well. Was there anyone so foolish?'

She gathered up the skirt of her new riding habit and

turned her whole body to face him. 'But you didn't fire at Lucius.'

'I almost did,' he countered. 'I might have killed you.'

'You chose to delope,' she reminded him. 'You made that choice before you turned, didn't you?'

She moved next to him and put her head on his shoulder. 'The duel was my fault, to be honest. I should have told you about Ellen and Lucius right after I caught them.'

He scoffed. 'And might I have done worse then?'

She threaded her arm through his and laced her fingers with his. 'I wish I could do everything all over again.'

He clasped her fingers in his. 'Do you?'

Will savoured this closeness they fell into, like a habit they'd acquired on the road from Scotland. He liked feeling her hand in his again, liked the easy conversation, the feeling that they were alone in the world, just the two of them. They had everything but the joy of those days.

He did not want to break the spell. 'I'll wager you wish you'd refused to marry me. Think on it. You'd have your fortune today.'

'No,' she said. 'That was not what I was thinking.'

He turned to face her. 'What, then?'

She pulled her hand away and sat up. 'I wish—' she began, then waved the words away.

He wanted to press her, to insist she tell him whatever it was, but, no. That might drive her away. He wanted to bring her closer.

She rose and stood at the open side of the shelter. 'The rain is slowing. Nobody to stop us here like at Vauxhall. We should be able to resume the trip soon.'

'I do not want to,' Will muttered under his breath.

She spun around. 'What did you say?'

'Nothing.' He waved a hand as if to erase his words.

She stepped towards him. 'No. I heard you say something. What was it?' Her voice was turning sharp.

The last thing Will wanted to do on this trip was argue with her. He tried to sound flippant. 'I said I did not want to.'

'Did not want to, what?' she asked.

'Resume the trip.'

She searched his face as if trying to figure it out. 'I did not mean to leave the shelter now.'

'Neither did I.' He inhaled, getting courage. 'I meant I do not want to resume the trip. I do not want to take you to Reading.' He rose and held her by the shoulders. 'I do not want you to live elsewhere. I want you to come home. I love you, Anna. I've been too foolish to always show it, but I've loved you since Scotland.'

She looked up at him, not speaking, until he thought he'd made another terrible blunder. He must release her. Must let her go.

He could not read the expression on her face, but he'd guess it was tenderness.

'Oh, Will!' she exclaimed. 'I have loved you just as long. I want only to stay with you always.'

It took a moment for her words to register. Then he smiled. He whooped with joy, picked her up and spun her around.

And kissed her.

'Then let's go home,' he said.

'I have a better idea,' she said. 'Let's go on to Reading. Meet John as planned. Let's spend the night there, like we did on the way back from Scotland. We can ride home tomorrow.'

He grinned. 'You called it *home*, Anna. Yes, my love. Tomorrow we go home.'

# Epilogue

*Buckinghamshire,*
*July 1819*

They were all finally home to Willburgh House after a long Season in London—Anna, Will, his mother, and Ellen who'd made her come-out now that she was eighteen. No riding back from London this year for Anna. She was expecting their second child in November. Their darling son, Will's heir, named Henry after Will's father, was a healthy fourteen-month-old who'd accompanied them to London because neither Will nor Anna wished to be parted from him. It made the entourage to London and back more complicated, but they refused to consider leaving the child in the country with only his nurse. They travelled in three carriages. Anna, the nurse, and Mary in one; Lady Willburgh and Ellen in another because Anna's mother-in-law's nerves could not tolerate a crying, fussy toddler filled with energy. The third carriage held the other servants—and Will's secretary. Will rode, the lucky man.

Lucius rode with him. He just happened to be riding back to Dorman Hall at the same time and met them on the road. He kept Will company, although Anna suspected it was Ellen's company he most desired when they stopped for the horses and took refreshment.

Ellen had plenty of suitors for her first Season, many invitations, many social outings, but no offers she wanted to accept. Lucius was not one of the suitors, but he often found time to speak with Ellen when they happened to be at the same entertainments. His attentions could be described as brotherly, if you could imagine Lucius as behaving brotherly. The accident did seem to alter him, though.

Lucius continued on his way when they finally arrived at Willburgh House. Little Henry was wailing and flailing his arms and legs as they all piled out of the carriages. Nurse ran him into the house.

'Good gracious! What a racket!' Lady Willburgh huffed as she entered the hall and handed her hat, shawl, and gloves to the under-butler.

'He has good lungs,' Will told her.

Ellen laughed.

She'd not quite returned to the girl she was at sixteen, but some of her *joie de vivre* had returned. Anna thought she was wise not to feel compelled to marry at eighteen. Look at what happened to Violet, who'd married Raskin, the poorest choice of a husband Anna could imagine.

Not so her Will. Anna wrapped her arm through his and he responded with a hug. Will was the best of husbands.

He kissed her. 'How was the last part of your trip?'

Anna savoured the warmth and scent of him. 'I think you heard. Your son indeed has good lungs and great stamina. He is tired and hungry, I expect.'

'Poor you and Nurse,' he responded. 'But how are you?'

They started up the stairway together.

She touched her swelling belly. 'The baby kicked whenever the road was too bumpy.'

When they got to the doorways of their rooms Will pulled her inside his and kissed her properly and thoroughly and made her wish it was time to retire rather than time to dress for dinner.

'I missed you,' Will murmured.

'You could have shared our carriage,' she replied. 'There was room.'

He laughed. 'I believe I'll content myself with spending more time with you now we are home.'

She leaned against him and felt the beating of his heart beneath her ear. 'Yes.' She smiled. 'The whole family is home.'

* * * * *

*If you enjoyed this story,
why not check out one of Diane Gaston's
other great reads?
'The Major's Christmas Return' in*
Regency Reunions at Christmas

*And why not read her
A Family of Scandals miniseries?*

The Lady Behind the Masquerade
Secretly Bound to the Marquess